PREMEDITATED

PREMEDITATED

josin l. mcquein

delacorte press

Text copyright © 2013 by Josin L. McQuein
Jacket art copyright © 2013 by Luis Valadares

Visit us on the Web! randomhouse.com/teens

Educators and librarians, for a variety of teaching tools, visit us at
RHTeachersLibrarians.com

Library of Congress Cataloging-in-Publication Data
McQuein, Josin L.
Premeditated / Josin L. McQuein. — 1st ed.
p. cm.
Summary: "A contemporary thriller about the lengths one girl will go in order to get revenge on the boy who ruined her cousin's life"—Provided by publisher.
ISBN 978-0-385-74329-7 (hc : alk. paper) — ISBN 978-0-375-99105-9 (glb : alk. paper) — ISBN 978-0-307-98316-9 (ebook)
[1. Revenge—Fiction. 2. Cousins—Fiction. 3. High schools—Fiction. 4. Schools—Fiction.] I. Title.
PZ7.M478829Pr 2013
[Fic]—dc23
2012020287

The text of this book is set in 12-point Adobe Garamond Pro.

Book design by Stephanie Moss

Printed in the United States of America

10 9 8 7 6 5 4 3 2 1

First Edition

To my father, Stephen Hatton

ACKNOWLEDGMENTS

There's great irony in a novel. Writing is a solitary occupation, but no book is solely the work of one person by the time all is said and done. So thank you to those who I've been blessed to come into contact with, and to those who have offered their hands to help pull me a little farther along:

My mother, who is nothing like Dinah's, and who taught me to love books before I could read them on my own.

My father, who was the embodiment of the word *tenacity*, and who managed to turn "six months to live" into more than twenty years. I wish he could have seen this day.

My family, who probably still think I'm the odd one of the bunch, and who are probably right.

My teachers, first for telling me that the rules should never be so rigid as to beat the story out of a novel, and then for reminding me that they should be just rigid enough to give it a backbone.

The sharkly Janet Reid, who gave me the push to finish a novel I was debating scrapping and who steered me toward my first agent. Hopefully my efforts are sufficient to ward off the minions she threatened to send my way if she didn't get to read this book.

Suzie Townsend, who took a chance on me, found the flaws I couldn't see, and helped me sew up the holes I hadn't realized I left in the story. She managed to keep her feet firmly on the ground, despite my best efforts to drive her up the nearest wall.

Krista Vitola, who took sandpaper to the story and found a way to grind down the rough edges so there'd be nothing left to trip a reader up.

And God. This whole endeavor has been miraculous from start to finish, and I thank God for that.

In a Wonderland they lie,
Dreaming as the days go by,
Dreaming as the summers die.

—Lewis Carroll, "A Boat Beneath a Sunny Sky"

1

Killing someone's easier than you think. All it takes is decision, aim, and follow-through. Like basketball, only you shouldn't expect people to leap to their feet and cheer if you hit the free throw.

The whole thing's a done deal in a matter of seconds.

Revenge, on the other hand, and I mean real, calculated, make-him-sorry-he-was-ever-born vengeance, takes time and planning and patience. You have to smile when you want to scream. You have to look your target in the eye when you'd rather claw his eyes out. And you have to ignore the slow-spreading burn in your gut until it turns to ice and sets your resolve so completely you can't turn away without splintering.

Do it right and their blood will be on their own hands. Just another tragic teen suicide on the back of page three in the local newspaper, with a memorial page in the school yearbook. Lots of flowers, and stuffed animals, and card collages stuck to the door. Pretty words and puffy, red-rimmed eyes from people who question why but don't look hard enough to find out.

No matter how messy it gets, or how much blood's involved, suicide's a clean kill.

Though any scenario ending with Brooks Walden in a mangled heap would have worked for me.

The morning I started Lowry, I should have been wandering the halls of my generic public high school with my hair dyed that particular shade of black that screamed "back off" to anyone not invited into my space. Maybe the metal on my boots would clink because the floor wasn't as smooth as it should have been. Instead, the only metal I wore was the seat belt buckle latched tight against my left hip. Knees that hadn't seen daylight outside of PE poked out from under the hem of a blue and burgundy plaid skirt.

If I'd been at the place that passed for home, no one would have recognized me.

"You don't have to do this, you know," my dad said from the driver's seat.

He'd been working up his nerve for nearly ten minutes, gripping the steering wheel harder the closer we got to the school, and by the time he actually said it, his voice came out loud and hard, which made him stop talking to rein it in. He adjusted his Braves cap, pulling it lower in the front, then tugging it back again (most likely the habit that cost him his hair on top). The only times he ever removed his cap were for church at Christmas and Easter, or family dinners when Nonie used to come over. Serious stuff. He took it off there in the truck and Frisbeed it onto the dashboard above the steering wheel.

"I can enroll you back at Ninth Street and it'll be like you never left. You can sleep in the back of economics with Tabs, and start food fights with inedible spring rolls. Help Brucey flood a toilet or two."

"He hasn't done that since middle school, and it was an accident," I said.

"You don't have to be *here*, Dinah."

"It's fine, Dad, really. I *want* to be here."

He didn't believe me, and I didn't expect him to.

"Here" was the Eleanor Lowry School—the sort of place people call "storied" or "venerable," where one day's biology partner became the next day's business contact. The names on the rosters hardly ever changed, with the exception of a few scholarship cases, because the surest way to get in was as a legacy.

I was *not* a legacy, nor did I rate a scholarship, but I had Uncle Paul. And Uncle Paul had enough money to make both of those non-issues.

The school loomed ahead, appearing suddenly from behind the trees, despite the fact that the top spire should have been visible for miles. An old building, built with older money. Ivy covered most of the facade, letting glimpses of white stone peek through. The grounds were pristine and protected behind high gates Dad had to enter a code to get past.

Definitely not my old school, with its genuine cinder block walls and the latex paint in bright orange and gray, guaranteed to burn faster than paper and choke us all if the place ever caught fire.

Dad kept staring at me. He hadn't quite figured out why I'd done everything but get on my knees and beg to go to prep school, but he knew something was up, and he knew that it had to do with Claire. I think he was expecting a breakdown. I certainly felt like I'd have one at any moment.

Everything about Lowry screamed privilege and perfection, while everything inside me screamed terror and fury. I was fostering the latter to deal with the former, hoping they'd cancel each other out, and I flipped the visor mirror down to make sure neither showed. I couldn't help Claire if I got caught because I wore my emotions on my face.

I was ice—a plastic, perfect doll. I was a mole. I was nothing but the new girl, and the only expression I would allow myself was the kind that came with intestinal butterfly infestation.

The smell of rotten meat.

A curdled milk shake.

Whatever collected at the far end of the gutter that squished through my fingers when I cleaned it out.

Focusing on disgusting things gave me a semi-sick glaze that went well with the pallor left behind after I'd gotten rid of my usual makeup. One stubborn pinpoint on my nose still showed through where I'd taken out my nose ring; no matter how much I smudged around it, it wouldn't blend.

My head still burned from bleaching out the dye, and I couldn't stop picking at my scalp to soothe the sting. I reached up and adjusted the hateful blue band I was required to wear, letting a few more bangs fall forward until I looked more like I was planning to hide in the bathroom than plot the surgical deconstruction of the local Golden Boy.

Biting my cheek helped.

"Your hair's fine, D, but I wish you'd've let Helen help you. I keep expecting it to fall off your scalp from the roots."

Typical Dad attempt at small talk. He was usually better

than that, but considering the week we'd had, it was no surprise that he was off his game.

"I read the directions."

"Your aunt and uncle really appreciate your staying," he said, rather than argue the point.

He let the thought drop, the way everyone did when they started to mention Claire. They all choked on her name, like she was a ghost who hadn't quite caught on yet.

"Don't think you have to shoulder this, kid."

"I want to stay close in case something changes, and I don't want to go back to Ninth Street if I'm only going to be here a few weeks." That was the conservative estimate. Claire would either wake up, or they'd stop expecting her to. "I'd just have to say goodbye to everyone again when Mom makes me come home. This way, I'll only be leaving strangers, and Aunt Helen and Uncle Paul didn't waste the tuition money."

It was a lame excuse, but also the only one I could think of to counter my mother's objections. Compassion wasn't enough of a hook; money was the only thing she'd listen to.

"In a few weeks, they won't be strangers anymore," Dad said.

Our truck melded into the flow of sedans and SUVs circling a paved drive with an ornate fountain in the middle. Stone deer and bear cubs played in marble flowers while fairies poured water into a stream that emptied into the main bowl.

My old school had a flagpole and a dirt ring that, according to legend, had held daisies at some point.

"People from a place like this will always be strange to me."

"I'm proud of you, D," he said.

D, which is short for Dinah, which is short for my

great-grandmother, is my given name, and the first recorded instance of my dad protecting me from my mother. She intended to name me Diamond Rain or Rayne or Rhane—the spelling changes with each lament when she retells the story. Kind of like plain old Stacy became Stacia for the acting career that never was. Dinah and all associated nicknames were rejected as too plain for her taste; they set off her allergy to the mundane. But Dad still had a spine in those days, and filled in my birth certificate before her meds wore off.

Unfortunately, my first initial and middle name still spell "drain"—a far-too-accurate assessment of my life.

Dad's hands tightened on the wheel again as he coasted into the "arriving" area, where other kids were climbing out of other cars. They gawked like they'd never seen a no-longer-quite-cherry-red truck outside its natural habitat of the mechanic's shop before.

"Batter up, baby doll."

Sports analogies are my dad's mother tongue.

"You haven't called me that since I was—"

"A real blond?" he teased.

"Young enough to count my age on my fingers," I said.

"Same thing."

"Bye, Dad."

"It's nice to see the real Dinah again."

"The real Dinah," also known as the Dinah no one had seen since sixth grade, was how he referred to my choice of clothing before I actually had a choice. When my mother used me as her personal paper doll and paraded me down every pageant runway within a hundred-mile radius.

"Don't miss your flight." I shut the passenger-side door as he shouted a last request for photographic evidence that I'd returned from the dark side to give Mom when he got home.

Over my dead body.

Lightning was welcome to strike me down—so long as Brooks went first.

I counted the stone steps as I climbed toward the school's entrance, tucked into the surge behind the twin blazers in front of me. One blond head and one brunette, both with the same blue band pushing back stick-straight hair—just like mine.

"Welcome to Stepford," I mumbled under my breath.

Inside the Stepford Academy (Lowry definitely had an "academy" vibe) everyone looked alike, everyone moved alike, and everyone sounded alike. Apparently when perfect little rich girls grew up, their acceptable color choice darkened from pink to burgundy—the faceless drones and I were covered in it, thanks to a crested blazer with a diamond logo. Boys were stuck with blue, though it had transitioned from the baby palette of robin's-egg to navy. Everyone was clearly labeled, so there was no way for one of us to forget our place, and no chance for an outsider to sneak in.

I was having a panic attack over the idea of home ec in a place like this. There would be chocolate chip cookies and pearl necklaces and frilly lace aprons involved, I was sure. If we were lucky, maybe they'd hand out gray face paint so we could go completely fifties-mom monochrome, like those old TV shows that rerun in the middle of the night. Then I could get Brooks for a partner and give him food poisoning; my lousy cooking skills would make everything the school's fault, not mine.

Lowry was a fortress, with stones in the front wall as long as my arm. The crowd carried me along, passing through a set of double doors with lead knockers that looked like they were built to withstand a major siege. It should have been a safe place—Claire should have been protected there.

Maybe she would have been if she'd ever made it inside.

I shoved the thought out of my head and wiped the stinging tears away. Weepy eyes and blotchy skin weren't going to help me; they'd just get in the way.

"Could you tell me where to find the principal?" I asked a random girl in the hall while my fingers twirled the tiny golden bird on my necklace.

"The headmistress's office is at the end of the hall on the right: Ms. Kuykendall." The girl flashed a flawless smile that made her look like a flight attendant; all she needed was the drink cart.

"Thanks."

The direction she pointed led past a row of arched windows where any other school would have had lockers. There was no chipped paint or trash on the floor. I missed the weight of my earrings and the click of the barbell that usually speared through my tongue. Knocking it against my teeth had become a nervous habit, and losing the sound made me sure someone would hear how loud my heart was beating or how fast my breathing had become.

The office took up the whole end of the hall and was made of glass walls so visitors could see inside. A secretary in a dark green business suit sat at the desk while a student filed papers away in a cabinet taller than she was.

"Good morning," the secretary said when I opened the door.

"Good morning," I said back, because I wasn't sure what

else I was supposed to say. Something about the place made me want to be polite, almost like I was afraid they'd snap if they figured out I wasn't one of them. "I'm supposed to check in with Ms. Kuykendall, I think."

The secretary blinked at me behind her glasses.

"My uncle was supposed to call. Paul Reed." I tugged on my necklace again.

"Oh! You're Diana, of course! Come right in, dear."

No, I was Dinah, but Nameless didn't give me a chance to correct her. She waved me around the counter, leading me down another hall within the office itself.

"We were so sorry to hear about Claire. Such a horrible thing, especially for someone so young. And then to find out we'd be getting another young lady in her place . . . well, we've all been just rushing to adjust the papers and even out the classes. Not that it's your fault, dear. Of course not, I don't mean that at all. But now we've got one too few freshmen and one too many juniors, and—oh, I'm sure it'll all get sorted."

Claire had become paperwork. She was a chore.

The fist at my side got tighter, until it began to shake. I had to peel my fingers loose one at a time, and wondered that they didn't crack out loud from the pressure.

We stopped outside a wooden door with the school crest set above the nameplate. "Kuykendall" didn't look the way I expected. It sounded like there was an "r" in it, not a "y." I was betting nothing here was as it seemed.

Nameless opened the door while I waited to be summoned, tamping down memories of the time I ducked into a restaurant to use the bathroom and the manager evicted me before I even got close. I kept expecting someone to see through the pastel eye shadow and pink lip gloss I'd nabbed from Claire's room and tell me to get lost, I didn't belong there.

"Diana Reed to see you, Jane," she said.

I groaned at the double butchering of my name.

"Go right in, dear," Nameless said, holding the door until I complied.

Irrational fears aside, I'll admit that most of my assumptions of what to expect from a private school headmistress came from TV and movies. (Until I was ten, most of them came from knowing that our neighbor, Mr. Dodds, had been kicked out of his house for having a mistress. I didn't know a schoolmistress was different until I read Harry Potter.) So you can probably imagine my relief when what was on the other side didn't involve doily explosions, offers of tea, or even (and especially) torture scenarios.

The inside of the office was as dark as the halls had been bright, with plenty of burgundy and blue. Two leather chairs with those heavy brass tack things sat in front of the kind of desk that belonged in a lawyer's office.

"Diana?" asked the woman standing at a window behind it.

No tail. No horns. No hooves. Just an over-the-thirty-five-year-old-hill, ex-model of a woman whose hair made my shade look downright filthy. She pointed to one of the chairs, and I sat, careful not to let the casters squeak against the carpet when it rolled forward.

"Dinah," I corrected. "Dinah Powell. Reed's my uncle's name."

"Oh, good, I was worried someone had botched your paperwork. Mrs. Hotchkiss' hearing is terrible, but it's easier to deal with than refiling you." She pulled a slim folder from a drawer in her desk and flipped it open. "I understand you won't be with us for the entire term."

"I'm staying with my aunt and uncle for now, but I think they're hoping I'll like it and stay for good."

They'd offered, more than once. Last spring, when Mom announced her anything-but-brilliant idea to pack me and Dad up when I finished tenth grade and trek cross-country, Aunt Helen had tried to get her to let me stay. She'd tried offers of better schools, like Lowry, or concessions of letting me stay with my friends, but Mom said no. The idea that I'd choose Aunt Helen and live in the world she'd stumbled into horrified my mother more than anything.

"I don't imagine it's easy to hopscotch from school to school so frequently." Ms. Kuykendall had an accent, but I couldn't place it.

I wouldn't know. We'd only left New England in June. I'd never seen the inside of my school in Oregon.

"My parents expect me to come home once my cousin's out of the hospital."

"We were so sorry to hear about her condition. Has there been any sign of progress?"

"No, ma'am, not really." Headmistress Kuykendall definitely struck me as a ma'am. "She opens her eyes sometimes, but the doctors say it's more reflex than anything. They don't say much when I'm in the room, so I don't know a lot."

If she caught the lie, I didn't notice a change in her demeanor.

I knew plenty—more than the doctors or Aunt Helen or Uncle Paul. And I certainly knew more than the people who thought Claire's stint in the hospital was nothing more than a "condition" of some kind flaring up.

"I'm sure your aunt and uncle appreciate having someone around."

That's what people kept telling me. I really couldn't see how having someone who reminded them of Claire, practically living her life, was anything short of horror movie material. But if they were willing to let me stay, I wasn't going to question it.

"They told Uncle Paul I could get a uniform shirt here. Claire's was too big."

Despite batty Mrs. Hotchkiss' ramble about me throwing off their student-teacher ratio, most of the problem with me replacing my cousin on the school's roster seemed to stem from the difficulty of getting a new uniform so quick. Three days didn't give them enough time to order one, but Claire and I were almost the same size, except up top. Somehow the twerp had managed to steal all my hormones, which meant I was still in a training bra while she could have gotten a gig at Hooters long before she was legal.

The headmistress opened another drawer and pulled out a plastic-wrapped blouse. I slipped it over the blue tank top I'd worn that morning and put the blazer back on. At least my friend Tabs' mom had been able to alter *that* into a close imitation of tailored. Plus, it covered the wrapping wrinkles.

"Here's your handbook and paperwork." Headmistress Kuykendall handed me a burgundy folder embossed with the school's crest. "Claire Reed" was printed in gold letters at the bottom.

"Have your aunt or uncle sign the forms, and bring them back to your homeroom teacher tomorrow."

Thankfully, she'd moved on from any sort of conversation I was supposed to participate in. I was two seconds and half a breath from saying, "If the school's so hard up for cash you have to recycle a two-dollar piece of folded rag paper, I'll buy myself a folder and write my name in with a Sharpie."

I stashed another piece of Claire's life in my bag, where I could keep it safe, determined to preserve everything I could for her.

"You're a few minutes late, but Mr. Tarrelton shouldn't hold it against you, since you were here."

She walked me to the door and held it open.

"Do I need a slip or something?"

"Abigail will handle it," she said, then disappeared back behind her door without telling me who Abigail was or where I could find her.

That problem, at least, solved itself once I was back in the main office. Abigail was the girl I'd seen filing papers. As soon as I rounded the partition, she slipped her arm through mine and held on. I pegged her as the kind of person who would add "please" to a "Kick Me" sign on her own back, to be polite, so long as getting kicked meant she got to participate.

"Diana?"

"Dinah," I corrected.

"Oh! Sorry. People must butcher your name all the time."

Yes. Yes they do. And I can never find one of those monogrammed ornaments at Christmas with my name on it, either. That always annoys me. Dinah comes out of the Bible, according to Uncle Paul. Christmas ornaments should cover the Bible names; they just should.

"I'm Abigail. There's not much you can do to that, unless you want to call me Abby, which no one ever does."

Yep. Definitely overeager. Her crazy curls were as energetic as she was, defying the evil headband to hold them in place.

"I'm the office page for first period. Where's your class?"

"Um . . ." I fidgeted, jostling notebooks and pamphlets. "Looks like trig, with Tarrelton, in . . ."

"Two seventeen," Abigail-not-Abby finished for me. "I have him next period. He's fine, except he takes forever to explain things that really aren't that hard to understand."

Smart and overeager. Oh, joy. This was not improving my first impression of Abigail-not-Abby, who went on my list of people to avoid, not because of her personality, but because she had found a way to keep her knee socks from falling down without having to half hop as she walked to hoist them back in place.

"Tarrelton's close to my English lit class. Do you have Greystone?"

"No, it looks like I have—"

She snatched the paper slip out of my hand.

"Looks like you have Tripp for English lit when I have trig. You're lucky. I have Greystone the Gargoyle—she's a total troll."

I smiled and nodded, pretending I didn't want to staple her mouth shut.

"Mr. Tripp's pretty cool. And he won't make you do the new-kid-introduction speech, either."

I tried to mimic Abigail-not-Abby's perma-grin, but the muscles in my face revolted after twenty seconds. If the whole school was this happy, I was in trouble.

Abigail-not-Abby led me through the school's main floor, our matched heels clicking and clacking in time as she pointing out key features like the cafeteria and the library. With all the doors closed, and all the students behind them, we could have been walking through a white marble tomb, or some old museum where you're afraid to touch anything because it'll set off alarms if you breathe too hard. Maybe I could use this for a sociology project when I got shipped back West: *Private School, the Total Immersion Experience,* or *My Life in the Hive.*

"You probably figured this out already, but the two hundreds are on the second floor," she said as we started to climb an actual staircase with carpet and rails, not the cement incline with a retaining wall we had at Ninth Street. "The ones are downstairs, and the threes are in the annex outside. If you have drama or tech theater, then you go out the main doors and take the left walkway all the way to the end. Gym's down the right walkway, but it's faster to cut through the building and go in the back."

I absorbed her words more than I listened to them, too caught up with the possibility that I was about to put a face to the sucking chest wound that had formed in the last week. All I knew about Brooks Walden was that he had dark hair and brown eyes, like about sixty percent of the people I'd seen that morning, and that he was a junior, like me, which meant we could be in the same trig class.

At least, it had seemed possible in the beginning, when I was still thinking of Lowry as "not that big" compared to public school. In reality, the place was huge, and the idea of having to locate rather than bump into him was taking over my mind.

"Here you go, two seventeen." Abigail-not-Abby knocked,

then opened the door before anyone could so much as say "Come in." "New student, Mr. Tarrelton. Dinah Powell."

I hung back and took a quick survey of the room.

More windows, which was going to take some getting used to after years of class-in-a-box. None of the faces stood out as particularly evil. There were more guys than girls, and only two of them *didn't* have dark hair, which made things difficult. I couldn't get a good look at their eyes without staring, and I wasn't about to get myself tagged as the Creepy New Girl Who Stares at People.

One of them glanced up and caught my eye, so I diverted my attention to the board to see if there was any clue to the day's lesson.

Great. Forget creepy, I was going to be the Stupid New Girl Who Does Math on Her Fingers and Toes.

I'd never been a bad student; most of my teachers considered me smart, even. But apparently public-school smart and Lowry smart didn't carry the same definition. The writing on the board might as well have been Greek. In fact, some of it *was* Greek. Sigma or phi or epsilon or one of those other letters I thought wouldn't enter my vocabulary before freshman rush at college.

It was the first week of a new term. How were they so far ahead?

"Class, this is Miss Powell," Mr. Tarrelton started. I was beginning to think he'd forgotten me standing there by his desk like an idiot. "She's just moved here from . . ."

"Oregon," I said. "But I didn't really move. My aunt and uncle enrolled me here while I'm staying with them. Their daughter's in the hospital, and they don't know how long she'll be there."

My answers sounded robotic, and not at all the way I wanted. I certainly hadn't intended to say that much.

"Oh. I'm sorry to hear that, Miss Powell," Mr. Tarrelton said awkwardly. He was so flustered that he didn't make me finish orientation by way of public humiliation. "If you'll take your seat, we can get back to class."

He pointed to the only seat not occupied (second row, by the wall), and I did my best not to dive for it to get out from under the weight of every eye in the room. Mr. Tarrelton fell straight back into the roll.

"Courtney D'Avignon," he called. I was surprised to see one of the dark-haired boys who wasn't Brooks Walden raise his hand. The only Courtney I'd ever met was a girl.

"You're lucky," the guy behind me leaned up and whispered.

"Huh?"

"You missed one of Tarrelton's famous pop quizzes. Two minutes earlier and you'd have been trapped with the rest of us."

Pop quizzes in week one—if I hadn't hated private school already, I would have hated private school.

"I'm Dex."

When Mr. Tarrelton called out "Jackson Dexter," he raised his hand.

It was actually a relief to find out he wasn't Brooks. He had the dark hair and brown eyes but was too friendly. And I think if I'd found out Claire's personal demon was sitting so close, I'd have blown my chance right there by attacking him with a freshly sharpened #2 Mirado Black Warrior.

"Dinah," I said back.

Hayden Leung turned out to be a not-Brooks, as did William McHenry. Daley Nifong was a dumpy blond with freckles. The guy in front of me was a not-Brooks named Marcus Norwood.

Channing Pepperidge sat forward on her chair as though it were made of upended tacks, so her weight was off her butt and her toes were overpointed, the way you see models sit in magazines. She was the only one who bothered to say "Here."

Jordan St. Croix was a paper-thin girl with short black hair that made the uniform headband disappear. That just left one possibility, assuming he was in the room at all.

"Brooks Walden."

He sat on the far side of the room, fourth row, next to the window. I turned my head, pretending to familiarize myself with names as they were called. His head was down, and he was twirling a pen between his fingers. When he heard his name, he raised his hand and flicked the pen in Mr. Tarrelton's direction.

Target locked. Game on.

By the end of trig, I'd figured out no less than twenty ways to kill Brooks Walden before he left the room. True, not all of them were practical, and half of them were gratuitously messy, but they'd have worked well enough—if I'd wanted him to get off easy.

Claire didn't get an easy out; neither would he.

I settled for the daydream, trying to keep up with the lesson, and hated Abigail-not-Abby just a little bit more for describing Mr. Tarrelton's lectures as needlessly slow. He talked like he'd been mainlining caffeine. So rather than pretend I knew what was going on, I copied everything he scrawled on the board and focused on staying awake. Not only would detention have been bad, but I was pretty sure I'd dream of maiming Brooks, and with my luck, I'd talk in my sleep.

At my old school, math had been my best subject, one I liked, but here . . . *ugh*. After thirty-one minutes of equilateral something-or-others getting mixed around with isosceles whatchamacallits, I wanted to strangle myself with a hypotenuse. (I'd fallen so far into my delirium, that joke was actually funny.)

Marcus, in front of me, gave up on note taking and drew tiny cartoons of Mr. Tarrelton being eaten alive by psychotic sigmas, and to my left, Jordan's hands under her desk made the distinct *click, click, click* of someone texting. Channing half coughed a laugh, so I was fairly certain who was on the other end of the message.

To my horror, when the bell finally rang, I glanced at my notes and couldn't even read half of them. My brain had disconnected from my hand at some point during the hour and decided that random doodles were a better way to fill my paper.

"It's not really trig."

As I shoved my papers into my book and then my book into my bag, a shadow far too tall to be my own appeared on the wall. Dex leaned on the desk that had belonged to Jordan St. Croix, so we were facing each other.

"What's not trig?" I asked.

"This class," he said.

"Then why did I just suffer through it?"

He smiled in a way real people shouldn't be able, warming the room by at least ten degrees.

"Because whatever passed for trig at your old, and I'm guessing public, school—which actually *was* trig—wasn't up to Lowry standards. They changed the curriculum a couple of years ago. The class you're in now is what most schools call precalculus."

I *really* hated private school. And Jackson Dexter wasn't too high on my list of likes, either. I mentally squished him between the building and Abigail-not-Abby. (She kicked him in the face; it was great.)

"That your subtle way of telling me you know I'm not part of the club here?" I asked.

"No more than I am. I went to Massey Junior High. I was slated to start Ninth Street before I got my scholarship."

"I went to Ninth Street before I moved to Oregon this summer."

"It takes a few a days to learn the rhythm, but you'll figure it out. Trust me."

Nope, sorry. Trust was a no-go.

"When'd you lose the nose ring?" he asked.

"About two hours after I figured out I'd be going here, so . . . three days ago. How could you tell?"

"I'm observant. And I'm guessing the lisp means you had one in your tongue, too?"

"Orange barbell." Sticking my tongue out was a reflex whenever anyone asked about the piercing; it was weird not seeing it.

"Would've guessed pink."

"Not my color," I said, retrieving my schedule slip to locate my next class.

It was in the annex, so I needed to go out of the main building and into the one behind it. I shifted into the flow of students on their way to the staircase. Dex followed me.

"Where you headed?"

"English lit."

"Not Greystone." He cringed.

"Tripp."

"Perfect." He reached for my bag, adding it to his shoulder, then grabbed my arm the same way Abigail-not-Abby had in the office. "You'd never have survived the Gargoyle. She loves fresh meat."

"Um . . . what are you doing?"

"Being charming and walking you to class. New girl gets a guide, I'm fairly certain it's in the school charter."

"You don't have to do that." We fought over possession of

my arm until I gave up for lack of space and excess of interest from onlookers.

"You're making a scene, new girl." Dex smirked.

"Smirked" is a weird word. You see it a lot in books and think you know what it means, but it's not a feat many can pull off. Not like him.

"You really don't have to follow me," I insisted. "Really. Truly. *Preferably* . . ."

It's exceptionally difficult to map out someone's social downfall if you're dragging a five-foot-ten, hundred-and-sixty-pound stalker. I'd hoped to figure out where Brooks went after he left not-trig, but the window of opportunity on that one had shut. "I know where I'm going."

"We're side by side, which puts this firmly into escorting territory, and no you don't." He angled the shoulder with my bag on it away so I couldn't take it back.

I was sure he thought this routine was creating endearing aggravation, but all it did was tempt pre-Lowry Dinah into coming out to play for a few minutes and reminding him how different girls from Ninth Street were compared to the ones here.

"Ones downstairs, twos upstairs, threes in the annex," I said.

"And Mr. Tripp outside in the courtyard."

That wasn't on my schedule.

"It says room three twenty." I waved my slip in Dex's face as I wondered what the school charter had to say about sending the new girl on a wild-goose chase.

"Normally, yeah, but he's got some sort of special project brewing, and he told us to meet outside since the weather's been so warm."

"If you're lying, I *will* hurt you."

"If I'm lying, you'll get your chance in detention. I'm in the same class." He confiscated my schedule and looked it over before sticking it in his pocket. "I'm also in your gym class, and theater."

He took my arm again.

"So you're trying to pass off convenience as manners. I think I need to see a copy of this charter thing."

"You have one, if Headmistress Kuykendall gave you a new-student folder."

I tried to get ahead of him and slip into traffic, resigned to letting him keep my stuff for the time being, but that wasn't as easy as it should have been. Not when the person I was trying to evade was taller and had control of my arm. Dex pulled me to the right when I headed left at the bottom of the stairs to go out the back doors.

"Courtyard's this way," he said.

"This school needs GPS," I grumbled.

"You don't need it. You've got me."

I made a mental note to tone down my Claire impression in the presence of any boy but Brooks. There was no other explanation for Dex's response unless hair bleach was made from smart-ass pheromones. Random guys did not just walk up to me, take possession of my body parts, and assign themselves as my personal entourage.

"I'd rather figure things out on my own," I said.

"We'll just end up there at the same time anyway. I might as well get some brownie points out of the deal."

"You don't strike me as the Girl Scout type."

"I have a little sister," he said. "Brownie points are very important."

"Only if you earn them."

"I earn everything I get," he said. "Otherwise, I get nothing. People like us have to look out for each other. Once you pass the front doors, 'friend' becomes a multitiered arrangement, and, believe me, we're never on even ground."

Okay, so maybe Dex was climbing up the "like" list a bit.

We went out the front doors and turned down a covered walkway that led past the parking lot. I hadn't noticed much about the grounds when Dad dropped me off, other than to realize they were very green, but now that I had a chance to look around and take it in, Lowry was beautiful. Even the area not covered by an awning wasn't really open to the air. Huge oak trees grew everywhere that wasn't asphalt. Leaf-patterned shadows created a shaded patchwork on the ground and our skin. This was the sort of place they used as backdrops for our class photos in fifth grade, and the kind that showed up in travel magazines when fall turned the leaves different shades of red and gold.

"This way." Dex tugged on my arm again.

We left the walk and headed to the side of the school building, where a tall iron gate grew out of the wall stones. Beyond, a group of students milled in a courtyard, staking claim to ornamental rocks for seats. A couple of people took off their blazers and sat on them instead.

They gathered around a middle-aged man with a silver suit, silver hair, and silver-rimmed glasses, who had taken over a bench under the biggest tree I'd ever seen outside a brochure for Disney World.

"It was planted the year they laid the school's foundation,"

Dex said, pointing at the tree. "Eleanor Lowry's husband and son are buried under it."

"You made that up."

"It wasn't all that uncommon in her day. They died in some kind of epidemic; the tree's a memorial. She's buried here, too, but her grave's sealed under the foyer. There's a marker carved into the marble if you want to look for it."

I was going to school on dead people. Scratch that—my aunt and uncle were *paying a fortune* for me to go to school on dead people. The only things buried under Ninth Street were gerbils.

Rich people were weirder than I thought.

"Does it bother you?" I asked.

"The graves?"

"Being around so many people who come from a completely different place even though they live in the same zip code?"

"It's more complicated than that."

"Money uncomplicates a lot of things," I said. "I didn't have the bloodline or the grades to get in here. My uncle made one phone call and the next thing I know . . . Prep School Barbie."

"Your choice or his?" Dex asked.

"Mine. I thought it would be worth it."

"It can be. Just think of Lowry as a stepping-stone. Things aren't all that different here." He pushed the gate open and held it for me. "If you watch where you're going."

"Sure they aren't."

I glanced back at a parking lot full of Porsches and BMWs; I was sure I spied a Lamborghini near the edge.

"There but for the grace of God and a seven-figure trust fund go I," he said.

As promised, Mr. Tripp didn't make me give a speech or stand in front of the class to introduce myself. He scribbled my name in his ledger, handed me a book out of his crate on wheels, and told me to find a seat with everyone else.

Dex didn't give me a lot of choice about where that would be. After he'd dragged me up to meet Mr. Tripp, he led me back the other way to an empty spot on the ground next to a pair of girls who were too absorbed in their own giggles to notice they had company. He opted for the "make a pallet from your blazer" approach; I flopped down on the bare grass and stretched my legs out, while double-checking to make sure English lit was free of people I wanted to flay alive. I could only hope Brooks was saddled with the Gargoyle and thoroughly miserable—preferably in a room where the ceiling dripped asbestos-tainted water on his head.

"So what's in Oregon?" Dex asked.

"Sky." I picked at some of the pricklier shoots of grass and let the breeze blow them off my fingers. "Mountains. Rivers. Lots of open space."

"Sounds nice."

"Yeah, it does sound that way, doesn't it?"

"Ouch."

The sound of pain, very appropriate. Oregon was beautiful, but so are most deadly creatures. And for the few months I'd lived there, I existed in a vacuum. No air, though I was surrounded by it. I could shout and scream, and all I'd get for my trouble was my own echo mocking me.

"Is it safe to ask about your cousin," he asked, "or does that look on your face mean something's about to burst out of your thorax and kill me where I sit?"

Old movie references. He sounded like my friend Brucey.

"She's in the hospital," I said, just like I had in not-trig. I pulled my knees up under my chin so I could rest my head against them.

"Does she have cancer or something?"

"No."

There were ways to treat cancer. Claire would have fought cancer. Cancer wouldn't have left her in a bloody mess on her bathroom floor with a razor still clutched in her hand. What got Claire was subtler than cancer. It had rotted her from the inside out and left no trace of itself behind.

"An accident?" Dex guessed again.

"Not exactly."

Not at all. It was intentional, and malicious, and selfish. Evil, like the devil himself.

I mulched another handful of grass. Too much that time; it left green splotches on my hand that wouldn't wipe off.

"What happened to her?"

"Long story."

Claire met Brooks; he was evil—the end.

Dex finally took the hint that it was a subject best dropped, and moved on.

"Look, I get that you're in a bad place. You got tossed into a new school that you obviously don't like—"

"I like it fine."

"If this is fine, I'd hate to see you angry."

"You've known me all of fifty-five minutes."

"I'm good at reading people."

"Then maybe you should try another translation. I'm—"

"Fine?" he asked. "I won't argue with you, but sometimes it helps to get an outside perspective."

But what do you do when you *are* the outside perspective?

I was the intruder. I was the one who didn't fit, and apparently all my effort at remaking myself into a typical prep-girl had flamed out. Starting conversations wasn't something I did naturally. I stuck with the friends I'd had since grade school, even after I moved out of state. Tabs, Brucey, and I talked more online than I did to anyone in Oregon (despite my mother's best attempts to pair me off with every new acquaintance she deemed worth my time and hers).

Why couldn't I do this? People did this every day. Claire did this—easier than anyone I've ever seen. I just had to figure out the mechanics and apply them.

"What do you want to know?" I asked.

"Anything," he said. "Something simple. I know you don't like pink, so what else are you hiding under that blazer?"

"I refuse to be held responsible for my actions if you ask me my favorite color."

I didn't get to find out if he thought that was funny or not. The bell rang, signaling the start of class, and Mr. Tripp called for attention. At least he was interesting to watch; male teachers with ponytails certainly weren't the sort of people I assumed I'd be stuck with at Lowry.

"Tell me why you got rid of the nose ring," Dex whispered

while Mr. Tripp was busy trying to set up a large easel for his whiteboard.

"Because it's against the dress code."

"But why didn't you keep the metal and go back to Ninth Street? Wouldn't you have been happier there?"

Dex had this way of talking that made it impossible not to pay attention to him. He wasn't what I'd call handsome, but he was . . . *captivating*. Maybe that's the word. The tone of his voice was like listening to someone with perfect pitch. I know it sounds stupid to say it like that, but it's true. You couldn't sit close to him and not feel better.

Most people look at you, or past you, when you speak to them, but Dex looked me straight in the eye. We must have blinked at the same times, because I never noticed him move at all. It was unnerving, and after a while, I didn't have to pretend all those butterflies were flitting around in my stomach. I could have puked monarchs.

"What does it matter?" I asked.

"It doesn't." He shrugged and took up my habit of picking grass. "I just wondered why your parents sent you here."

"They didn't mail me—I asked to come back."

"You didn't want to move to Oregon in the first place, did you?"

"I begged them to let me stay with my aunt and uncle." If we hadn't moved away, I'd have been here when Claire needed me. I dug my heel into the ground until the dirt showed through, ruining the green perfection of the lawn. "Claire's the closest thing I have to a sister."

"Claire's your cousin?"

"Yeah."

"Pretty name. I like it." He smiled as though there were a good memory attached to his words.

"You'd like her, too." Everyone did. "When my uncle called about her being in the hospital, Dad flew me back, first thing."

"Just your dad?"

"Mom doesn't do well with hospitals."

Dex nodded idly, as though he understood, but he couldn't. The only way to understand my mother and the poison cloud that rises from her presence is to experience it firsthand. Dex didn't deserve that for being nice to me.

I obliterated a flower that had the misfortune of growing close enough for me to reach. It was a weed, so I was sure no one cared.

"Dad said I could stay here if I wanted, and my aunt and uncle had already paid Claire's tuition for the year, so I asked if I could come to Lowry instead of Ninth Street. Going to school here makes me feel closer to her."

"She was a student here?"

"This was supposed to be her first year. Uncle Paul came into some money, and she's definitely smart enough to fit in here. He thought she'd like it."

As much as people didn't fit with me, they would have clicked with Claire in an instant. She would have had thirty new numbers in her contact list by the end of the day, easy.

My thoughts turned sour, picking up the thread of all the things Claire should have been doing besides lying in a hospital bed, and I became acutely aware of the fact that I was wearing her clothes. Her itchy skirt and the stabby headband she would have found a way to love, and her white knee socks picking up grass stains. It should have been her sitting there on the ground, chatting with a guy who wasn't Brooks Walden and wouldn't send her into a tailspin because he got bored. She should have been the one getting guided tours and flirting in Eleanor Lowry's family cemetery, not me.

When Mr. Tripp finally won his battle against the whiteboard and started class, I tried to pay attention, but it was no use. It didn't even matter that the lesson was a darkly ironic reading of *Alice Through the Looking-Glass*. I couldn't get my thoughts to settle down; it took all my energy and concentration not to start crying right there in front of everyone. That would have meant looks and whispers and questions I didn't want to answer.

If Dex spoke again, I didn't hear him. He was a distraction, and I'd let him knock me off my goal too easily. I'd offered up too much information. The more specifics people knew about Claire, or me, the more likely it was that Brooks would figure out that my presence had something to do with her. I'd almost said as much to Dex. He was too easy to open up to, and I wasn't familiar enough with the phenomenon to know how to counter it.

So I went on autopilot. I set my inner alarm to ignore and coasted through class; then I drifted to gym, following Dex as he once again appointed himself my escort. I changed my clothes and lined up obediently with the rest of the girls the way Coach Blackwell told us to. I played basketball. I shot. I ran. I even scored six points.

All while wearing a burgundy T-shirt with "C. Reed" stenciled on the back.

As my body was guarding a girl named Brooke (who should be happy I didn't hit her in the face with a ball for that fact alone), my mind was back on point. I had a purpose for being at Lowry. One that didn't involve things like trying to make friends or flirting for the fun of it when someone else started the game. Forget the fact that under normal circumstances, Dex was a guy I might have actually liked to talk to, or that his personality reminded me of friends I already had. I was there for Claire, not me. And by the time I was finished, things like friends and chitchat wouldn't matter anymore.

Dex was a traitor.

Worse—he was a minion. I'd spent the better part of my morning being grilled by the devil's right-hand demon and hadn't even realized how dangerous he was. After he took me to the door of my history class (which was next to his), he spent the last five minutes of the passing period cutting up with Brooks and trying to get me to participate.

"I found a stray puppy and brought her in out of the rain," he said.

"It's not raining, idiot," Channing spat. She stood leaning close to Brooks in what I assumed was a move to mark her territory. I should have known the leech would be attached to the beauty queen.

"Hi," Brooks said with the sort of smile I'd have thought charming if I hadn't known better.

"Hi," I said back.

A one-syllable test word to prove to myself I could speak to him without any sort of crackle or rise in my voice. Thankfully, his fingers were once again occupied with his pen, so he couldn't shake hands or anything else that required skin contact. Speaking, I could force myself to handle. Touching, not so much.

"What's that?" I angled for a better look at the paper he was holding on top of his book.

"Nothing, really. Just something to fill the time when Greystone wasn't watching."

"That's an awful lot of ink for nothing."

"It's a high-rise," Channing supplied. "Brooks designs buildings, but his plans are too complex for anyone to actually build."

"They won't be someday." Brooks slid his paper into his book. "You're Diane, right?"

"Dinah," I corrected, mentally cheering that Mr. Perfect had screwed up.

"Oh . . . sorry. I'm usually better with names."

"'Sokay. You're only about the eighth person to say it wrong. *Today*." I turned to the girl beside him. "You're Channing, right?"

"Chandi," she corrected. "I'm changing it. Channing's too long for a stage name. Plus, there's a guy already using it and I don't want to end up androgynous."

Oh. My. God.

I had found my mother's real daughter.

"You're an actress?" I asked. I could chat the girlfriend up if it meant maybe getting information out of her later.

"She thinks she is," Dex said.

Chandi straightened from where she'd been leaned against Brooks' shoulder; her face hardened.

"I'd tell you to bite me, but you'd only take it as encouragement."

"Not worth the risk," Dex said. "I might catch something nasty."

If Brooks hadn't caught her, Dex would have ended up with a perfectly sculpted french tip embedded in his eye socket.

"They're always like this," Brooks said, still hanging on to Chandi. He tried to laugh but couldn't quite cover the annoyed expression on his face. Personally, I didn't find anything funny in the way his hands were dug into her skin deep enough to turn it white. "But they hardly ever draw blood. I think they're showing off for company."

I was more interested in what Brooks was showing off. We'd been so far apart in not-trig that I hadn't gotten a decent look at anything other than the side of his face nearest my seat. But when he made the grab for his girlfriend, he exposed the other half—along with the nearly healed gouges below his jaw and down his neck. Someone with long nails had taken a swipe at him and left their mark.

Too bad I knew it wasn't Claire. She hadn't fought back, because she hadn't known he was the enemy.

The warning bell rang, splitting our conversation. Chandi followed me into one room while Brooks and Dex went into the other. She snapped her teeth together as she and Dex crossed paths, and I wasn't quite sure whether it was a joke, a threat, or a near miss on an actual attempt to bite him.

History was an experience best forgotten as soon as it was over. You don't need the details other than to know I achieved a state of semiconscious lucid dreaming that should only be possible when illegal drugs are involved. I was seriously considering turning our teacher in to the DEA for testing. The only problem was, the woman (who had one of those Jones/Smith/Davis names that a billion people have) was so nondescript I couldn't even remember what she looked like when I left the room.

I made the mistake of eye contact with Abigail-not-Abby, which she took as an invitation to replace Dex as my personal valet when we reached the door. Her hair had completely subdued the evil headband, drowning it somewhere inside her curls.

"Ready for lunch?"

Food was the last thing I wanted, but I was too fried from the history of hallucinogens to protest.

The trip to the cafeteria was quick, filled with Abigail-not-Abby's voice as she bounced from subject to subject, running down people and teachers and classes like she assumed I knew everyone involved. Names rattled off like roll call at camp, so fast I barely snagged five of them.

"Which one's the food line?" I asked. If I gave her something to think about, I was sure she'd stop talking long enough for me to catch up.

"All of them," she said.

"Why are there four?"

We only had two at my old school. One for the day's official menu, and one for the people who would rather eat hamburgers.

"We have a salad bar," she said, and pointed to the first line. Chandi was picking through apples at that one while complaining to Jordan-from-homeroom. I couldn't hear her, but Chandi's face was so twisted-up furious that it was hard to believe she was the same model wannabe I'd seen all day.

Jordan started to put a hand on her arm, but Chandi jerked away, stopping to adjust her sleeve where it buttoned over her wrist.

"Line two is for people with dietary restrictions. No wheat, no dairy, no meat, no pork. That kind of stuff."

That line was vacant, except for the woman at the cash register.

Abigail-not-Abby kept prattling about food, as though there wasn't a predator close enough to use for a pitching target. I had to stifle a laugh (okay . . . a cheer) when I gave Brooks the same mental treatment I'd used on Dex earlier, only instead of Abigail-not-Abby and a swift kick, it was Chandi's ninety-five-mile-an-hour speed apple.

"Line three is fish today, because it's Friday. And line four is for people who don't want any of the other stuff. I'm going four—the pasta's pretty good."

"I think I'll have fish." I don't actually like fish, but I didn't want to wait in line with Abigail-not-Abby or Chandi, and I didn't trust the smell coming from the "restricted" line.

For that span of five minutes, it was a normal school day and nothing more. Cafeteria ladies with hairnets and blue aprons, little bowls of chopped-up peach bits, and the familiar sound track of voices blending into a soothing thrum.

If I closed my eyes, I was simply at lunch, about to sit down with my friends.

Dex spotted me and waved me over, but that would have involved sitting with Brooks. There was no sense risking health or appetite by inhaling brimstone at the devil's table. So instead, I pointed to Abigail-not-Abby and shrugged at him, mouthing "sorry" as though I'd already agreed to sit with her. He gave me a double thumbs-up and forgot I existed.

Brooks sat cattycorner, to face both sides of the table at once. He leaned his chair back a bit. (No cheap bench seats bolted to folding tables at Lowry.) Even though he had the spot at the top of the table, no one's attention was really on him. Dex had them all mesmerized.

I couldn't see him clear enough to know what he was putting in his mouth, but the instant reaction from Chandi and Jordan as they sat down said it probably wasn't food. Chandi flicked something off her arm, like he'd sprayed her, then moved her chair closer to Brooks so that any additional volley would hit him first. Jordan scowled and took her tray to the far end of the table to sit with Hayden Leung.

I pulled out my phone, hiding it under the table so no one would see, and started my list.

Brooks went into the enemy category. Chandi and Dex I put in limbo. I didn't know enough about either of them yet, but I had the feeling Chandi was going to fall in line under Brooks' name. Even if I told her about Claire, she had no reason to believe me over a guy she'd probably known and crushed on for years. Dex was inching closer to the friend category, but I wasn't ready to slide him over yet; it would depend on how wrapped up he was in Brooks' lies.

Abigail-not-Abby went on the list as a friend. She couldn't be anything else; the girl wore her whole life on her face. Jordan, Hayden, and the few others I'd seen enough times to learn their names went down as bystanders. They were possible minions, but without a reference, I couldn't list them that way.

A quick check of line number four showed Abigail-not-Abby close enough to snag a tray. That gave me a minute or two before she reached the register. I closed my list and scrolled to one of the IMs Claire had sent me over the summer. I'd saved them all to my phone so I could read through them if I needed to double-check something.

Clarity_Dawn: ding-dong

She always started conversations that way, to make sure I knew it was her, and not someone using her phone or computer.

Poison Poet: dong-ding

Just like I always answered back in the reverse for the same reason. My mom got it into her head one day that impersonating me by IM would be as simple as using my computer when I was logged in, which was stupid even for her. Claire wrote back in her best middle school French German–ish and made a string of posts about how to best prepare a poodle casserole.

Clarity_Dawn: <—haz news.
Poison Poet: I'm waiting.
Clarity_Dawn: New guy! Is YUM!
Poison Poet: What happened to Nick?
Clarity_Dawn: *growl*

I'd known Nick wasn't going to last; Claire was way out of his league. He was the sort of guy you'd expect to show up on America's Most Wanted someday, either as the person at large or the actor playing his part.

Poison Poet: Who's Mr. New?
Clarity_Dawn: Lowry guy.

And that should have been my first red flag. Claire had gone to the Wilson Peete junior high, like me. And people from

40

Lowry didn't mingle with people from our school. Even the pretty ones.

I understood it better once I was on the inside, but there was no way a kid from Wilson Peete could act like one from Eleanor Lowry. It would be like learning to speak English in some random Midwest town in America versus learning it in London. You might be able to hold a conversation, but the words wouldn't sound the same, and you wouldn't know the slang.

> Poison Poet: Meet at Lowry registration?
> Clarity_Dawn: Nope—my secret. He thinks I'm a
>   townie. And . . . he's a jr!

Even if she had told him she'd be starting Lowry this term and he'd assumed she'd moved up from a private day school, Claire must have had "new money" flashing across her forehead in giant block letters. She was a gazelle at the watering hole being stalked by a lion.

> Poison Poet: You're fourteen, girlie.
> Clarity_Dawn: Only for two more weeks.
> Poison Poet: Does he know?
> Clarity_Dawn: Doesn't care.

Claire was too trusting. She always had been.

This should have been red flag number two. Yes, there are guys who are juniors who will date freshmen because they actually like them, but a random summer hookup? The rules are different, and Claire didn't know that. I should have told her, but sometimes it was hard to remember that she wasn't as mature as she sounded in my head.

If Mom hadn't made us move, I'd have known. There was no way to look Claire in the eye and not see the innocence there. She believed everyone.

> Poison Poet: SPILL. I want a name.
> Clarity_Dawn: Brooks
> Poison Poet: 1st name, loser.
> Clarity_Dawn: B-R-O-O-K-S
> Poison Poet: Cuckoo dates grl :/
> Clarity_Dawn: BrookS <—No "e," has "s"
> Poison Poet: Cuckoo dates two girls :-D
> Clarity_Dawn: ,,!,,

In person, Claire would never flip someone off. She never cursed, and blushed if she said "butt." She might work up the nerve to use "backside" or "rear." The girl looked eighteen, wasn't even fifteen, and in many ways still acted like she was eight. Danger wasn't real to her, and she was far too easy to tease.

> Poison Poet: Details, girlie. Tell me about your girl-boy.
> Clarity_Dawn: BROOKS IS A BOY!
> Poison Poet: Give me his address.
> Clarity_Dawn: Why???
> Poison Poet: I'll kill him if he hurts my Cuckoo.

At that point, it was a joke, because I believed her when she said he was her guardian angel and not a devil in disguise.

Poison Poet: I'll make your Brooks into a Brooke?

Clarity_Dawn: >.<

Poison Poet: Can I stomp his big toe and make him limp?
      No—give me photos. I'll maim him by Photoshop!

Clarity_Dawn: *smack*

Poison Poet: Be careful, girlie.

Clarity_Dawn: I'm not stupid.

Poison Poet: No, you're Cuckoo.

Clarity_Dawn: I've got a shadow in the door.

I hated the idea of someone reading over my shoulder, but I couldn't help but think that if Uncle Paul or Aunt Helen had been close enough to read what she was saying, maybe it would have made a difference. No way would they have let their fourteen-year-old daughter date a seventeen-year-old without some serious parental interference. Just knowing someone was paying attention could have been enough to scare him off to easier prey.

Maybe . . .

What if . . .

If only . . .

My life had been nothing but questioned actions and second guesses since Claire fell. *Maybe* Brooks hadn't meant for things to go so far. . . .

What if she'd told me before things got so bad she had to take a razor to her own wrists? . . .

If only she had fallen straight to the floor, or sat down, instead of bouncing her skull. . . .

A person could go crazy with enough what-ifs; I was very nearly proof.

I cleared my screen and stared at Brooks across the cafeteria—another room full of windows. So much glass made up the building, it was a wonder it could even stand. I propped my phone up and took a quick burst of pictures, then squirreled it away back in my bag.

"Fail trig."

Abigail-not-Abby dropped her tray across from mine and took her seat.

"Huh?"

"Fail trig," she said again. "Take my word on this—you want to."

"Not that there isn't a distinct possibility of that happening, but why would I want it to?"

"Because the inhumanly gorgeous bit of eye candy you just snapped a photo of isn't merely a pretty face."

"I wasn't taking a picture of Dex."

"Dex? No." She made a face like she'd swallowed sour pickle juice. "I meant Brooks. If those pictures are of Dex, we have bigger issues to discuss than your math grades."

"Brooks is good at trig?"

"Brooks is good at everything. It really isn't fair that so much talent gets packaged in so much pretty."

"And because of this I should fail?"

"Exactly."

She stole a french fry off my tray.

"I think I'm missing a few steps in your thought process. Back up."

"It's simple. If you fail trig, then you get a tutor. Brooks has been the go-to since ninth grade."

All girls, too, I bet. Tutoring sounded like the perfect way

44

for him to find out who was and wasn't a viable target. He'd get to be alone with them for at least an hour at a time—they probably let him into their houses, assuming he didn't invite them to his to get a home field advantage.

"I'll think about it. Thanks."

"Anything to pry Channing off his arm."

"Sounds personal."

"Not really. I just hate her with every fiber of my being and feel the need to vomit whenever she's within ten feet."

Abigail-not-Abby nicked another french fry, so the nausea couldn't have been too bad.

"She didn't seem so bad to me."

"In the hall?" she asked.

"Yeah."

"Meet her in a room without Brooks. Bring a flak jacket."

I hadn't noticed it before, but Abigail-not-Abby's whole appearance was a blatant imitation of Chandi's—from her not-quite-the-right-color shoes to the drugstore knockoff of whatever makeup she wore. The same colors that worked on someone like Chandi didn't go well with Abigail's coloring.

"I skipped a grade to get here," Abigail-not-Abby said. "She treats me like a little kid, others follow her lead."

Chandi slipped over the line to "enemy" in my head.

"Why would she do that?"

"I don't know," she said. "I try to make myself look older, but when you're competing against sixteen-year-olds who can walk into a bar and not get carded, managing to look sixteen when you're fifteen doesn't count for much. No one wants to sit at the kiddie table."

I lost another french fry.

"She makes fun of you?"

"It's mellowed into more of a maintained avoidance scenario. She's progressed to pretending I don't exist, and in return, I systematically obliterate every curve on every test I can while making sure she never gets her photo in the school paper or the spotlight pages of the yearbook."

"Passive resistance?"

"Psychological warfare."

Say what you will about teenage hormones and angst, but there's no better source for data mining than the kid shuffled to the fringes who does nothing but watch everyone all day.

"And Jackson Dexter, who you will avoid, is a complete idiot. It's odd, considering he's a scholarship case and probably the smartest guy in school."

"He hides it well."

Just then, he was hiding it by engaging one of the posters on the wall in a heated (and one-sided) argument. He scolded the "healthy living" bicycle rider—loudly—for insulting Chandi's choice to wear a shirt that was two sizes too small and therefore required open buttons. She pulled her blazer tighter and hunched her shoulders when she realized most of the room was listening in.

"Complete loser, by choice," Abigail-not-Abby said. "He spends all his time trying to distract people because he's afraid they'll remember he sleeps on the couch since there's only one bedroom in his house and his mother and sister have to share it."

"Why should I avoid him?"

"Because he's weird, and he gets ideas that turn into disasters for everyone involved."

"So he's a typical teenage boy?"

"Not really," she said. "Grades or not, I doubt he'd still be here if he didn't have Brooks to hide behind."

"I sort of pictured the two of you teaming up against Chandi."

"Ah. She told you about the name change? Did she tell you that she was changing Pepperidge, too? She thinks a cookie last name makes her sound like a stripper."

"Funny, I thought it was the missing buttons on her shirt that did that," I grumbled.

Abigail-not-Abby snorted and stole another fry. She hadn't even touched her pasta.

"Brooks doesn't mind people ogling his girlfriend?"

"She's not his girlfriend. Not really. Channing thinks she is, but she also thinks no one remembers her old nose."

She reached for my tray again; I scooped the fries to her side of the table.

"She and Brooks have been friends since primary. He puts up with her because in his head, they're still friends. In hers, they're destined for each other. It's sad, really. She can hardly function without him, and he's too nice to make her try."

I was beginning to wonder if one of Mr. Wonderful's hidden talents wasn't hypnosis. Since when was issuing orders considered "nice"? If Chandi was so completely taken in that she'd transferred control of her own life to this guy, then reaching her was going to be more difficult than I thought.

I wondered if those were her scratches on his neck, which got me to thinking about the way she kept playing with her sleeve. The safe bet was that if she'd left her mark on Brooks, he'd done the same with her.

"Brooks is a light touch," Abigail-not-Abby said. "Especially considering who he hangs around. He doesn't ignore me, anyway."

"He should tell her the truth," I said, but I knew there was no chance of it happening. What guy would give up his between-hookups fallback girl?

"Why? Hoping to fill the gap?"

"Dating him is the last thing on my mind."

"Flunk trig," she said again, and downed the last french fry.

7

By last period, I'd stopped thinking of the Lowry School as Stepford and reassigned it as Wonderland. It was easier that way. No one seemed quite human if they were absurd characters in a storybook.

Channing Pepperidge was the Queen of Hearts, able to slaughter detractors with barely a look. I'd seen it firsthand in history, and in our shared chemistry class after lunch. Half the guys in the room had to have her inverse image burned onto their retinas from staring so hard.

Dex was the Mad Hatter. Pretty much everything he did made sense to him (and only him), but if he threw a party, you knew everyone would come.

Abigail-not-Abby played the White Rabbit. She was always hurrying from here to there as though she was already late before she even had a destination in mind.

The shifting chorus of extras who shared space with the group made pretty convincing Tweedledees and dums. (They could fight over who filled which role, because honestly, there wasn't enough for me to go on.)

That left Brooks to embody the Cheshire Cat.

He was the one who, no matter how hard I looked or how long I watched, I couldn't quite pin down. But I was always aware of his presence. When he entered a room, the air changed, and attention shifted in whichever direction he stood. He was everyone's friend, and someone was always repeating words he'd used or recounting something he'd done. Even when he wasn't visible, Brooks hung around like a barely-there moon in the background that followed me wherever I went.

(I blame Mr. Tripp and his free-form English lessons for the detour down the rabbit hole.)

Drama classes in Wonderland weren't all that different from those at my old school. We still sat in theater seats while the teacher—Mr. Cavanaugh—sat with his legs dangling off the edge of the stage into the pit. He was dressed nicer than Ms. Bonner, who was my teacher at Ninth Street, and there weren't any cigarette holes burned into our chairs, but the room had the same feeling to it. This was where you could be anyone you wanted to be.

"There are many kinds of acting," Mr. Cavanaugh said. "You have your dramas. You have your comedies. You have action and horror and romance." He mimed each genre with exaggerated expressions, juggling for comedies and the doing the *Psycho* stab scene for horror. "But with all of those, there are only two kinds of actors."

"Male and female?"

Abigail-not-Abby was right. Dex was an unapologetic moron when he wanted to be.

"Not even close, Dex, but thank you for the sexist viewpoint. Don't expect me to intervene when the young ladies attack."

"Wouldn't dream of it," Dex said. "Rescue spoils the fun."

There was a collective groan, followed by fewer laughs than Dex expected, if his face meant anything. He pouted while those closest to him split off and switched chairs. That left

Dex alone and put Brooks one seat forward and to the left of me.

"I'm talking about those who want to be seen and those who want to disappear."

"You mean stars and everyone else," Chandi called out.

"That's oversimplifying," Mr. Cavanaugh said. "But in general, yes. There are those who slip into a character's skin so completely, they can't be seen underneath, and those who, no matter how they try, will always be pretending. Both are important, but which of the two is the star is up for debate."

He had this weird auburn mustache that looked like it had been glued, slightly askew, to the underside of his nose. It bounced up and down as he talked.

"The star's the headliner," Chandi argued. "Everyone else is set dressing."

"Then how do you explain scene stealers?" I asked. I hadn't intended to engage her, but she was too annoying not to poke back. Someone needed to remind Miss Model-Perfect that hers wasn't the only voice in the room worth listening to.

"If the star knows what she's doing, no one will be able to steal her scenes."

"You think it's that easy?" Mr. Cavanaugh asked.

"For some of us." She glared at me, a clear indication that she didn't include me in "us."

Fine with me.

"It seems we have our two camps," Mr. Cavanaugh continued. "Those who will grab the audience's attention and hold it so long as they're onstage"—he glanced around the room, settling on Dex and Chandi—"and those who aren't playing at all. They become the person on the page."

His attention settled on my section for a beat before moving on, but the pause was enough to sear acid into the sides of my stomach.

"So the question is, do you want someone to look at you and say 'That person is a real star,' or to look *through* you and see a stranger who can be anything?"

Easy answer. You can't hunt on the predator's home turf if he can see you coming. Make him think you belong, get him so used to your presence that he misses it when it's gone, and you'll be able to look him in the eye when you deliver the killing blow.

"Which one makes more?"

Dex again.

"The headliner, loser," Chandi said, then wadded up a piece of paper and fired it at his head. Everyone (other than Dex) laughed.

"Today, we're going to test Miss Pepperidge's assertion that grabbing and keeping someone's interest is a simple matter of will and skill." Mr. Cavanaugh hopped to his feet and clapped his hands for attention. "Everyone cinch up. No spaces. If you're in the back rows, move forward to the middle two. If you're in the front, scoot back."

Up to that point, we'd been spread out wherever we happened to fall when we came in. Abigail-not-Abby had taken what she'd deemed her seat and shooed me toward the side of the room, where Brooks and Dex had settled.

I threw my bag over the seat in front of me and claimed the spot next to Brooks, as I was in the "move up" area. This was my first excuse to get near him that I hadn't had to manufacture or needed Dex to initiate, and I wasn't losing it to someone

else. Especially not Chandi "I don't want to be a cookie" Pepperidge. She'd made the choice to hold court with a group of
girls in the far right front, and I'd already climbed over the row
into my new seat by the time she figured out where Brooks was
sitting and headed his way. If she hadn't been so hateful, I probably wouldn't have grinned at her.

She flopped into the seat next to Jordan-from-homeroom
like it was the one she wanted.

"Everyone pair off," Mr. Cavanaugh said. "Mr. Coleman
with Mr. Nieves. Miss Jackson and Miss Highview. Miss Pepperidge with Mr. Grant. Dex and Miss St. Croix . . . Sorry, Jordan. Next time, watch where you're sitting. Mr. Walden and
Miss Powell. Mr. Yancy and Miss Bell. Mr. Kane and Mr. Law-
son, and Mr. Leung and Mr. Sanders. Is that everyone? Good."

Me and Brooks.

I couldn't have planned it better if I'd tried. Now I not only
had an excuse to sit close enough to get a feel for how he did
things, I had a reason to talk to him that didn't involve awkward introductions or evading his girlfriend.

Mr. Cavanaugh clapped again, letting the room's acoustics
carry the sound, and we all turned back to the stage.

"Now that everyone's settled—no, Jordan, you can't move—
your assignment. You and your partner have five minutes to
plan, then we're going to do a little experiment. People in the
back row, you're going to attempt to get the attention of those
in the front row. People in the front row, you're going to anchor
your attention elsewhere. Take out your iPhones, iPods, and all
those other iThings we teachers pretend you don't have stashed
in your pockets and bags. Until the experiment is over, the 'i'
means 'invisible' to me."

"Spot me a phone, Wally?" Dex turned around in his seat.

"Only if you swear never to call me that again." Brooks dug into his pocket and pulled out a sleek phone, then tossed it over the seat.

Dex's face lit up with the glow from the screen as he turned back around and switched on a game that sounded suspiciously like my uncle's brainchild.

"This isn't fair, Mr. Cavanaugh," one of the Tweedles whined. "How are we supposed to get someone's attention when they're busy? It's impossible."

"That's the point." Apparently Chandi had a thing for paper balls because she lobbed another one at the Tweedle's head. "No one gives you attention, you have to take it."

"Exactly right, Miss Pepperidge."

She flashed a triumphant smile, which soured into something more sinister when she glanced my way.

"Okay, everyone. Games on, earbuds in. Planning time starts . . . *now!*"

All around me, the room morphed into a combination of whispers and flashing lights from people's phones. Everywhere except for me and Brooks. Neither of us said a word.

I could understand the silence on my part—there's no ice-breaker tailored toward making small talk with your cousin's almost-murderer—but Brooks made no sense. Not only was he not speaking to me, he wasn't even looking in my direction. He was doodling on a piece of paper, adding another tower to his Skyscraper of the Future.

"Aren't we going to make a plan?" I finally asked.

"No need. I'll hit Dex in the back of the head; he'll turn around. Assignment over."

"What about Jordan?"

"She'll turn around to watch the hitting."

This was not the way things played out in my head. Brooks Walden was not supposed to be ignoring me in favor of pencil sketches and notebook paper. He was supposed to be treating me like the perfect mark. A topic shift was obviously in order.

"Abigail says you're the one to talk to if I'm failing trig," I said carefully. Damsel in distress is an act that's all about balance. You want the guy to think he's rescuing you from something, but without sounding so pathetic that it becomes a pure mercy save. It needs to be a chance to impress, not pity.

"I'm going to sew her mouth shut," he groaned.

"Was she wrong?" I asked. If Abigail-not-Abby's jabber jaw botched this, I'd hold the thread while he stitched. "I didn't ask her . . . she was sort of acting as your personal PR firm."

"She acts as *everyone's* PR firm," Brooks said. "We call it getting caught in the Gail."

Abigail-not-Abby had a nickname after all. She just didn't know it.

"So you're not a tutor?" Disappointing, but not too tragic.

"I used to be."

"Looks good on a college app, I bet." Ivy Leaguers were raised to think college application fodder from the time they were in pre-K.

"Just like baseball, soccer, piano, Junior Congress, the Red Cross, the Sixth Street Shelter, and Academic Decathlon all look good on a college app. People keep volunteering me for things. It's too much. I had to drop some of them, no matter how much my dad complains."

That last bit he grumbled in a lower voice while stabbing

holes in the paper he'd been drawing on. The Golden Boy had daddy issues—generic, predictable, but also potential ammunition. All I needed was to know whether Brooks was the type who'd knock himself out for the old man's approval or if he was one of those who'd spite his father just to watch him twist.

"No rowing? I thought you blue-blood types were all about the team pull and throw."

"Not when you fall into the Charles River on a family trip to Boston and nearly drown, then get rescued just in time for a bout of hypothermia to eat the rest of your vacation. And my blood's red, thank you very much."

"Sorry."

Cringe.

"I hate that blue-blood crap."

"I was just teasing." Better to turn it into a tease than an insult. "Where I come from, anyone who goes to school in a place like this is a blue blood."

"Prick your finger and prove it."

Double cringe.

"Hi," I said, desperately trying to salvage the situation. I held out my hand; it looked like touching him was going to be a necessity after all.

"What are you doing?"

"New girl gets a do-over. That's the rule—I checked the charter," I said, co-opting Dex's earlier line. "Hi, my name's Dinah, and I'm trying unsuccessfully to convince you to save my trig grade from self-destruction."

He laughed through his nose.

"Brooks," he said, then took my hand. When he actually faced me, my eyes were drawn straight to those scratches on the side of his neck. They couldn't have been more than a few days old. "I'm trying unsuccessfully to dodge the humiliation of being hydrophobic by snapping your head off."

"You think being afraid of water is more embarrassing than calling it hydrophobia?"

"No?"

"Pretty much anything sounds better than implied rabies."

He gave me the nose snort again.

"Fine. I'm afraid of water. I don't go on boats. I can't even use a bathtub. Rain freaks me out if it means puddles."

"Interesting bit of information," I said. "Very *specific.*"

"Blame Abigail. She can incite random moments of TMI from across the room."

"So that's why I feel compelled to blurt out that I used to wear enough metal to set off security systems and potentially die inside an MRI?"

"You are a randomness rookie. I know my height in Smoots."

"You made that up."

"You'll never know unless you Google it. . . ."

I refused to laugh because he was charming or funny. I chose to laugh because it was what he expected. He absolutely was not easy to get along with. It simply wasn't possible.

"I'll find another tutor," I said, building the perfect impression of desperation: cast-down eyes focused on my hands, where I picked at my fingernails, and a strategically chewed lip. "It's just . . . I really need the help. My old school wasn't as . . ."

"Advanced as this one?"

"Advanced. Funded. *Clean.* Take your pick." I could play the grateful, fawning sycophant if he wanted to rub it in and put the poor kid in her place. "And my mom's already betting

I'll fail within the week. I don't want to give her another excuse to gloat."

My attempted pout was interrupted by Mr. Cavanaugh and his inconvenient need to continue our class.

"Time's up," he announced. "Let's see what you've come up with."

Not much, with nothing on the side.

"I'll make you a deal," Brooks said. "Ace this, without touching him, and I'll do it."

"That's all?"

"You don't know Dex and his ability to tune out the world in favor of Empyrean Meta-Craft. He forgets to eat. You could dance naked on the stage with Cavanaugh and he wouldn't notice."

"Wanna bet?" I asked.

"I thought I just did."

This had possibilities.

"Mr. Cavanaugh, what are the rules?" I called out. The room had become a garbled mix of shouts and motion as each pair attempted to secure the attention of someone determined not to give it.

"There aren't any," he answered. "I told you, for the duration of class, I don't see anything."

Definite possibilities.

"Hold this."

I shoved my bag into Brooks' lap, then pulled off my blazer and dropped it over the seat in front of us. Dex didn't even flinch.

"Dinah, I was kidding. What are you—"

Next came the tie and the button-up shirt. Brooks sank down in his chair.

"This was not my idea, Mr. Cavanaugh!"

"Coward," I said. "I'm not naked."

As if he wasn't watching through his fingers . . .

The tie and shirt had no more effect on Dex than the blazer.

"Told you so," Brooks whispered.

"Shush, you, I'm not done." By that point, I think everyone *except* Dex was staring at us. "I still have my secret weapon."

I pulled my arms inside my shirt, unhooked my bra in the back and slipped it out through one of the armholes. Yes, it was humiliating. No, it wasn't Victoria's Secret. Mr. Cavanaugh probably would have said something to stop me before that point, but he seemed to have lost the ability to form words. His face turned as red as his hair until he hid it behind his hands. (He needed a little more help not noticing things. It wasn't like I was the only girl in the school not wearing a bra.)

I flicked my discount cotton bra with the purple hearts on it over the back of Dex's chair, and let it hang from my fingers next to his face. After a second, I bounced it up and down and was finally rewarded with a bit of movement.

Dex turned sideways, staring at the bra. Then he glanced at Jordan, who had her own head ducked into her hand, laughing. He looked down to where my discarded clothes lay in a pile on both their laps, and nearly plowed over the back of his chair as he turned around.

"We win," I said, then slipped my bra back on the same way I'd taken it off. "Boys will always notice naked. Even if it's only in their imagination."

"Yes, well . . . ," Mr. Cavanaugh started. He looked everywhere but at me and couldn't get his eyes to stop moving. "I suppose that's a part of the lesson we haven't yet covered."

"Sex sells?" Dex asked.

Brooks smacked him in the back of the head as he snatched his phone out of Dex's hands.

"Know your audience," Mr. Cavanaugh corrected. "Nicely done, Miss Powell. . . . Please never do that again."

"Yes, sir," I said over the final bell.

"I want you each to develop a short monologue to perform next week. Make the voice clear, and do your best to completely embody the character you create . . . while remaining dressed," Mr. Cavanaugh shouted over the end-of-period clamor. "Class dismissed."

"You're my new hero." Jordan bunched up my clothes and passed them over the seat as a still-scowling Chandi sidled up to Brooks and slid under an arm he didn't offer to put around her shoulders. She laced her fingers through his to hold it in place.

"Walk me to my car?" she asked him while staring straight at me.

Brooks handed me my bag back.

"So?" I asked.

"I concede victory. Text me your address."

We switched phones to add our numbers to each other's call list.

"Is Sunday okay?" he asked. "I have to be at Five Points tomorrow morning, and I'm not sure how long I'll be there."

"Thanks," I said with as much cheer as I could force into the word. As soon as I reached the door, Chandi lit into him. Too bad there was no way to stay and watch. School was officially over for the day; I had somewhere more important to be.

Just the same, it was nice to know it didn't take much to trouble the waters of Brooks' calm existence.

"Marry me." Dex fell in step with me outside the theater doors. "Marry me. Or date me. Or whatever other arrangement will get me another look at your, um . . ."

His attention dropped from my face to my chest.

"Unmentionables?"

"Yes. Pretty unmentionables, and maybe matching other unmentionables."

Dex was such a drain. And he was totally blocking all my attempts with Brooks. Their brains must have been cross-wired.

"You don't have to beg."

"Really?" His eyes lit up, and I'm not entirely sure I didn't see drool.

"Sure. Walmart. Women's underwear aisle. I usually shop off the end cap."

"You're trying to kill me, aren't you?" he asked. "It's a game, right? See how long it takes for the new girl to drive one of the rich kids completely insane."

"Ah, but you said you weren't a rich kid."

"A minor technicality. You can't disqualify me for that."

"It's no fun driving someone crazy if they're already over the line."

"She thinks I'm crazy," he lamented to a random piece of yard art. I think it was probably a rabbit at some point, but it hadn't held up as well as the fountain on the front drive. "Tell her, Cottontail. Tell her I'm perfectly sane."

"You didn't actually expect the marriage proposal to work, did you?"

"It could have. . . ."

We turned onto the main walk and headed for the front of the school. After the day's horrible, trig-contaminated start, and all the assumptions I'd had about what I'd be walking into when I entered Lowry, it was nice to find someone normal, even if he did turn out to be one of the devil's friends.

"Okay, the line sucked, but it's all I could think of. It's not my fault—all those purple hearts scrambled my brain. And what's the deal with you and Brooks?"

"You saw how lost I was this morning. He's going to help me catch up with what I missed in trig."

"I could do that."

"I don't think I'm *quite* pathetic enough to need two tutors."

"Maybe, but Brooks may not be in any shape to run numbers for a while."

Under one of the trees, Brooks stood beside the open door of a silver BMW as though he was getting in. Unfortunately, Chandi had followed him from the theater and was still going strong. Dex waved, which only ratcheted the fit up another notch.

It was one of those moments where I was happy that telepaths don't exist. No need to share the mental touchdown dance playing out in my head. Dex wasn't the only one going on an unmentionable-free streak.

"If he falls through, let me know, okay?" Dex dropped the goofy edge from his voice and ran off.

Leaving Lowry felt surreal, I guess.

I'd accomplished my one concrete goal—locating Brooks—but had no idea what to do next. I'd charged in without any real plan to speak of. . . . Maybe I thought I'd fail, so there was no point in planning. I don't know. Evil was supposed to be an abstract, yet in meeting Brooks, I'd managed to find proof of its existence.

A low rumble of commotion and whispers drew my attention to the line of waiting cars in the pickup area. It was the same as this morning, a monochromatic stretch of neutral colors but the standout this time was my ride home, sitting just outside the security guard's stand. I left through the "walk-in" gate (another ivy-covered iron monster, which locked behind me, lest someone unauthorized sneak through on foot) and approached the passenger's side.

"Hey, Tabs," I said.

Tabitha Guthrie had been my best friend since we'd conspired to dig a hole large enough to trap Kyle Smith on the playground. He was a year older and had been picking on a friend of ours during recess. We'd seen the "dig-a-pit" thing on TV with tigers and figured if it could hold one of those, it could hold Kyle. He was nowhere near as smart as your average tiger.

Of course, we got bored after about ten minutes, so instead of tossing Kyle into a tiger pit, we jumped on him and did as much damage as a couple of five-year-old girls armed with toys were able. Kyle never picked on our friend again, and maintained an irrational fear of My Little Pony well into junior high.

Even after the forced march to Oregon, Tabs was the first one I'd thought of to help with my deconstruction-of-Brooks-Walden scenario. With me on the other side of the continent, she was Claire's cousin by proxy, and had reacted to her hospitalization about as well as I had—mainly because she took Claire's condition as a personal defeat. It was a crazy idea; none of this was her fault.

Tabs had known Claire since she was little, but she couldn't read Claire like me. She was a friend, not family, and Claire wouldn't have told her about Brooks even if Tabs had known to ask. But knowing that didn't help her guilt. I had to talk her out of looking up every B. Walden in the county and chasing them down with Grimace, her purple beast of a car. My way meant he suffered longer; hers meant forensic evidence on her bumper.

"You look like a cupcake," she snarled.

"Nice to see you, too."

Tabs stood against Grimace wearing a T-shirt that declared "I'm the evil twin" in a bloody red font. Baggy black pants set low on her hips were pulled lower by the weight of steel studs on her belt. She had her arms crossed and was glaring at anyone who dared make eye contact.

Ninth Street let out at three-fifteen, which gave her just enough time to make it to Lowry and become the center of attention before I made it out the door. (Yes, I was pretending I didn't know she'd skipped last period to make it with time to spare.)

"A cupcake with frosting and extra sprinkles."

"Shut up."

"Security is *watching* me."

"They're laying bets on whether or not you'll burst into flame if the clouds break."

"They wouldn't let me in without the code. *And* they took my picture."

"You won't show up."

She flipped me off as she circled to the driver's side.

"Get in before all this sunshine fades my interior."

Tabs gunned the engine, which, considering most of the parents' cars were hybrids, actually sounded like an engine, and drew the attention of the few who weren't already looking as she spun us into the line of exiting cars.

"Subtle." Perhaps I should have picked someone more inconspicuous to be my ride home. . . .

"Oops." Tabs grinned, and the green stud below her bottom lip bobbed up. "I've got real clothes in the back if you want to shed the secret identity, Lois Lane."

"Lois Lane didn't have a secret identity," I said.

"No, but you tend to maim anyone who calls you Diana, so Wonder Woman was off the list. How'd it go?"

"Not bad."

I crawled over the seat into the back and found the paper sack of "real" clothes—jeans and a T-shirt made to look like faded lace.

The tint on Grimace's rear windows was jet black, meaning you could pretty much do anything you wanted back there and no one could see unless they wanted to press their face against the glass. And the way Tabs drives . . . no one's that suicidal.

"Not bad as in you found the guy who trashed Cuckoo, or

not bad as in you've already been brainwashed, like this place, and can get out and walk the rest of the way in your underwear?"

"The first one," I said, wriggling into the jeans. It had been so long since I'd worn a skirt, I'd forgotten how weird it felt not to have anything on my legs.

"Good. I'd hate to think I wasted the gas driving over here. Which one is he?"

We'd stopped while the line bottlenecked at a red light before allowing us to turn onto the main road from the private one that belonged to the school. Our position placed Brooks and Chandi's sparring match squarely in the rearview mirror.

"Dark hair, blue blazer," I said.

"Maybe a bit more vague would help."

"Student parking, silver Beemer, getting gnawed on by the model behaving badly."

Tabs reached up and adjusted her rearview mirror. In it, Chandi's gestures and flailing grew more erratic the longer she ranted, until Brooks grabbed her by the shoulders and shook her.

Watching Chandi fall apart, then crumble, was disgusting.

"Nice," Tabs said.

"It wasn't that hard. He's easy enough to approach, and has a girlfriend with a short temper."

"No wonder the Cuckoo bird fell for him—he's hot."

"Stop it," I ordered as I climbed back into the front seat. "There will be no lusting after evil incarnate."

"That's not fair." Tabs slipped into the most annoying mock-whine you could imagine. "You know I've had a crush on you since fifth grade."

"I'm not evil, I'm committed."

"Yes, you very well could be."

"Shut up."

"Fine. I'll keep my fantasies in my head. Brucey wanted me to ask you if he can have the uniform when you're done with it."

Not likely. I planned on giving it a Viking funeral in Uncle Paul's pool.

"You told Brucey? Are you crazy?"

When you're keeping secrets, a self-professed anarchist who believes password-protected files are the seeds of a totalitarian regime is not the guy you tell said secrets to.

"He knows the cover story. Oh—and he hates you a little for picking this place over Ninth Street. But he says he'll be fine."

"Why does he want Claire's uniform?"

"He needs another prep school costume for his film project. Apparently yours is more authentic than the ones he made himself."

The line started moving again.

"I am not using my cousin's uniform to do porn, Tabs."

"He doesn't want you, just the skirt."

"When I'm done, he's welcome to the ashes."

"When you're done, it'll be in an evidence locker as property of the state."

"I don't plan on getting caught."

"We're going to end up on one of those 'ripped from the headlines' shows, aren't we?"

"You wanted in."

"Remind me to block your cell when we get to the hospital."

Trinity didn't really look like a hospital on the bottom floor, more like a hotel lobby, with squishy couches and coffee tables covered with magazines; it even smelled like potpourri. If it weren't for the wall-mounted television that doubled as a call system for families waiting for people in surgery, it would have almost been comfortable.

The main hall was carpeted green, with flower-covered rugs every five feet or so. Paintings lined the wall on one side, with visuals for the twenty-third psalm in the spaces between.

Tabs and I paused between the multicultural group hug for "Goodness and Mercy" and the watercolor painting of a country church labeled the "The House of the Lord" and waited for the elevator. Claire was considered in serious condition but no longer ICU material, so we had to go to the fourth floor. The doctors weren't planning to move her to the psych ward on five until she was awake and lucid enough to speak to a counselor, though they told Aunt Helen and Uncle Paul to be prepared for her not remembering much. With any luck, they'd be right, and the amnesia would wipe Brooks away, too.

The elevator opened into the ninety-first psalm. I wasn't sure where the other sixty-odd psalms went, but they hadn't made an appearance anywhere in the hospital that I'd seen, and I had pretty much committed the entire floor plan to memory.

"Which way?" Tabs asked

"End of the right hall."

Technically, Claire's room was number 419. Unofficially, the staff called it the Angel Room, because instead of a window at the bend in the hall, there was a huge painting of a fiery man with wings standing guard outside her door. Uncle Paul, who knows these kinds of things, said it was a painting of St. Michael, who knocked Satan out of heaven. I took that as a good sign. Mitch, as I called him, certainly looked like he was capable of protecting a fifteen-year-old kid. If he'd already defeated the devil once, maybe he could do it again.

"Hey, Mitch." I slapped the painting's frame with my open palm on the way into the infection-fighting icebox that was Claire's room.

I hated the cold, but not the air conditioner. It doesn't matter if you're in a tiny two-room apartment, or a mansion, or a hospital on death watch, the scent coming off an air conditioner is the same; there's something comforting in the continuity of that. I leaned against the window that couldn't open in Claire's room, with the heat through the glass warming my back and the arctic air from the AC flowing down from the vent above my head, and let the smell convince me that everything was okay. That the chill that stole the last bit of natural warmth from my body was nothing but a side effect of the thermostat being set too low.

"She looks better," Tabs said in the way people do when they really mean "is she even breathing."

In that moment, I knew I'd be forever grateful to her for making me change clothes in the car. It was hard enough not to throw up in jeans and a T-shirt; if I'd walked into that room wearing Claire's uniform, the nurses would have seen the Lowry School's lunch menu firsthand.

Claire didn't look better; she looked pale. And Claire *never* looked pale. She was never inside long enough for "pale" to apply. This was a sick color, pasty—the shade reserved for someone who didn't have enough blood in her body.

Tabs drifted away to one of the chairs in the room and began the traditional search for reading material that always happens inside a hospital. (If you've never seen a teenage girl with four facial piercings, another seven in her ears, black and purple hair, and combat boots paired with spiked jewelry flipping through a DIY mag dedicated to making animal-shaped snack foods, you don't know what weird looks like.)

I took one of Claire's cold, gauze-wrapped hands and bent over her bed.

"I found him, Cuckoo," I said. "Feel free to thrash me for getting into your business, but I had to. I'll make this better."

Tabs snorted from her seat across the room; she tried to cover the sound by holding up her magazine and pointing to a picture of a chocolate cat with licorice whiskers. "They put pudding in it," she said.

"I think rich people must be obsessed with windows, because Lowry has them in every room, even the principal's office."

"Now I want pudding," Tabs announced behind me. That was her way of telling me that if I could hear her, she could hear me, and she didn't want to eavesdrop.

"Don't be mad at me for using your clothes," I told Claire. "I didn't so much as spill a soda on them or drop ketchup at lunch. I was careful. . . . Well, there may be grass splotches on your socks, but we'll just call it an even trade for all the times you stretched out my stuff with your insanely mature figure, okay?"

Though if she'd wanted to wake up right there and argue the point, I wouldn't have minded.

According to the doctors, that's what we were waiting on. The waking-up part, not the yelling. Claire hadn't done enough damage with her razor to actually kill herself. When she cut her wrists, she did it like they show on TV—a side-to-side slash over the blue line. It only took a few stitches to close, and she barely nicked the vein at all. Anyone who really wants to end it knows that won't work.

Sometimes it's tempting.

At least, it used to be. If I cut myself now, everyone would blame Claire for it. They'd say I got the idea from her, that I was so upset I didn't know what I was doing. But if anyone hadn't known what she was doing, it was Claire. Otherwise, she wouldn't have been barefoot, and she wouldn't have slipped when her blood pressure crashed. She wouldn't have bounced her head off the sink, then the tile, hard enough to crack her skull.

When Uncle Paul called and told Dad that Claire was in the hospital with a subarachnoid hemorrhage, I asked him if it was a brown recluse, because they get into the houses around here and hide in the corners. I thought she had a spider bite.

"They keep giving me your stuff at school; it's weird. All the papers and forms they gave me to get signed say 'Claire Reed' on them, like we're interchangeable or something. Don't worry, I'm not going all changeling on you. I don't want your life."

Truthfully, I wouldn't have minded a time-share on it sometimes, but I didn't want it all to myself. I wanted my Cuckoo back.

"I'm going to steal pudding. I can't plot with low blood sugar," Tabs blurted.

In her head, I'm sure that sounded better than "I'm going to escape awkwardly while you talk to the vegetable." She darted out the door before I could agree or argue or even ask her to remember that I hated chocolate.

With Tabs out of the way, I went to the table and upended my school bag.

"I brought you some cherry lip gloss. They said your lips could get all cracked being in here so long, and they don't have any good stuff." I uncapped the tube and held it close to her nose. "Smell familiar?"

There was no answer, but I kept hoping. She didn't even flinch when I ran the gloss over her lips.

"Please hang around to yell at me for doing something so stupid as trying to pull this off, Cuckoo. I'll never learn my lesson if you don't, and who knows . . . I might decide to make it a habit or something. Going around, pretending to be random people."

It was kind of nice not having to be myself, or even try to figure out what that meant, but it was frustrating, too. It had only been one day, but I thought if I made myself as close to a copy of Claire as possible, Brooks would at least give me a sign that he was interested. I should have been his type.

"He's not taking the bait as quick as I'd hoped. I thought I did everything. I changed my hair and my clothes. I'm working on the personality, I swear. I even try to smile when I think about it—"

"Mission accomplished." Tabs popped back in with a dinner-tray consisting of three pudding cups, a bowl of blue Jell-O, and two plastic-wrapped spork packets complete with salt, pepper, and sugar.

"Tell me you didn't loot the pediatric ward's dessert cart."

"I got them in the hall," Tabs said. "They were clearing lunch trays, and it looks like no one on this floor likes pudding."

"You stole used food that's been in rooms with sick people?"

"Still sealed." She flipped one upside down and shook it. "Besides, some insurance company is paying like twelve bucks for this pudding. This way, they get their money's worth."

"Do you see what happens when you leave me alone?" I asked Claire. "I have to go in search of a new Jiminy Cricket to be my conscience, and all I can find is the dessert thief."

"I found a strawberry," Tabs sang, jiggling a pink pudding cup in my direction.

"You'd better snap out of this soon, Cuckoo, or else you'll come home and find all your pretty pastels replaced with kohl and red and purple. I'm serious."

I reached for her hand again and curled her limp little finger around my own.

"There. It's been pinky sworn, and I have a witness, so no use trying to wriggle out of the deal by claiming you were unconscious and didn't know what you were agreeing to. Now I have to go eat the evidence of Tabs' culinary crime spree." I leaned over the bed rail and kissed her forehead, careful not to jostle the bandages wrapped around her head.

"What is all this stuff?" Tabs was trying to navigate the mess I'd made out of my messenger bag when I dumped it on the table.

"Lowry's new student endurance challenge."

She picked up the folder Headmistress Kuykendall had given me that morning and flipped through the pages of things I had to get signed while I shoved the books away to make us a clear space to eat on.

"Have you actually read this thing?" she asked.

"I only got it this morning, and it's the student handbook, so . . . no." No one reads those things.

"First of all, this is *not* a student handbook. It's the school's honor code." She pulled a sheet of rose-colored paper out of the folder and held it up. "It's a contract between the students and school, signed by them and their parents, and submitted as a binding obligation of enrollment. Don't look at me like that, I read it straight off the page."

Tabs coasted the blue Jell-O across the table to me.

"Put it back before you get pudding on it." I had no desire to turn in my forms on their fancy, crinkly paper covered in brown spots and reeking of hospital chocolate.

"It's part of their disciplinary code, D. They don't want to get embarrassed if anyone does something stupid, so they handle it in-house."

"And?"

"And being the idyllic little military state that it is, Lowry operates on the principal of 'spy on thy neighbor and rat him out.'"

"Meaning what?"

Tabs began reading from the contract again. "'Any allegation of wrongdoing found to be of suitable merit shall be investigated to the full extent of the power and influence granted the school and its Board of Regents.' "

"I say again—meaning what?"

"If the school gets a viable tip that a specific student or students are using, then they have the right to demand an immediate drug test. Signing the contract forfeits your right to refuse on pain of expulsion."

" 'Viable tip' as in even if it's anonymous?"

"Isn't zero tolerance wonderful? No pesky fact-checking or assumptions of innocence to deal with."

"But what good will a test do unless he's actually on something?" I asked. "It's not like we can hold him down and force-feed him ecstasy."

"Did you know my mother is an asthmatic?"

That was a random shift, even for Tabs.

"Your mother's a hypochondriac."

"This is true," Tabs said. "However, one of her current hypochondrial conditions is asthma. And since doctors learned many years ago that she was never quite so sick as she appeared, they stopped giving her prescription meds."

"Fascinating."

"It is—really. Especially the part where she decided that Western medicine had it in for her and started seeing an acupuncturist instead of a regular doctor."

"This is one of those conversations that sounded right in your head, isn't it?"

"Yes. But it will also make sense to you in about three seconds when I mention ma huang."

"Who's that? The acupuncturist?"

"It's an herb, genius, not a person. Specifically, it's the herb said acupuncturist gives my mother for her hypochondrial asthma."

"And?"

"And, she stopped taking it when her company ordered blood tests for their employees and hers spiked for amphetamines."

"It made her fail a drug test?"

"Oh yeah. She was furious—especially when she found out that the bitter orange she takes for her stomach could do the same thing. Mom went on a two-day Google binge looking up anything and everything that could create a false positive. If your body chemistry's right, even Advil can sink you."

"Somehow I can't see Brooks agreeing to down a whole bottle of Advil, either," I said.

"What has living on the other coast done to your brain cells?" Tabs opened a packet of sugar from the tray and dumped it into her pudding cup. "Herbal remedies are capsules full of powder," she said as she stirred it in. "Presto, change-o, rearrange-o. No one knows the difference, and Boy Wonder's left with a lovely black mark on his permanent record."

Then she wadded up the sugar packet and flicked it right between my eyes.

Maybe I had a plan after all.

10

Six desserts later (Tabs made another pudding run), we had the beginnings of an idea. It involved sports drinks and the hope that bitter orange tasted enough like regular orange that it wouldn't tip anyone off who happened to drink it.

Not much, but at least it was another step.

By the time Uncle Paul opened the door to Claire's room, the Lowry stuff was back in my bag, Tabs' notes were tucked away, and we had removed all evidence of criminal mischief except the pudding cups.

"Hi, Mr. Reed," Tabs said. "I stole pudding. Want one?"

"Maybe later," he said. "And I've told you that you can call me Paul."

"I've called you Mr. Reed since I was four. It sounds weird."

"Does that mean I need to start calling you Glam—"

"No!" Tabs jumped up. "It's not necessary to repeat that name in its entirety ever again." She grabbed her keys and the empty pudding containers. "I'll just go dispose of these and get out of the way so there's no chance of hearing it. Ever. Again."

Uncle Paul grinned; Aunt Helen drifted across the room and perched on the chair beside Claire's bed. This was the first time she had been away from Claire's room for longer than forty-five minutes since Claire was hospitalized. In the few days since I'd been back, she'd aged ten years.

"Bye, Tabs," I said.

"Bye, D, Mr. . . . er . . . Paul, Helen. If the Cuckoo bird comes to while I'm gone, tell her I was here, okay?"

"Sure." I nodded.

"Tomorrow?" she asked.

"At the house."

And then she was gone, leaving me, Claire, Uncle Paul, Aunt Helen, and the quiet no one knew how to break. For hours, I did my homework at the table until I couldn't stand the vacuum anymore.

"The school sent papers for you to sign," I said, but the world was stuck on pause.

Uncle Paul bobbed his head, not really agreeing or even listening. He turned his attention from Aunt Helen and Claire to some random spot out the window, as though the clouds would give him something to say.

A nurse came in. She did the things you come to think of as routine while you're in a hospital: checked Claire's vitals, copied numbers off the machines by her bed, adjusted her pillows so Claire wasn't lying in the same position anymore. This time she had a guy in a lab coat with her. He drew a tube of blood and scanned Claire's wristband to make a label for it. The shift change must have clued Uncle Paul in to how late it was.

"Helen, I'm taking Dinah back to the house," he said when they left, and I wondered if substituting "house" for "home" was intentional. Right now, it was just a building where they kept their furniture. It wouldn't be a home until Claire came back. "I'll be back in about an hour."

Aunt Helen didn't answer; she kept staring at Claire.

"D, grab your stuff. Let's go."

The drive to Uncle Paul and Aunt Helen's house was grueling, even in a Land Rover. The car itself was comfortable enough, but the atmosphere was heavy and full of half-formed sentences and things we each thought we might say but never actually voiced.

"So . . . um . . . how was school?" He reached for the burger bag he'd tossed onto the dash after our pit stop for dinner and fished out the one stamped "No Onions." That's how I knew things were worse than he was letting on. Normally, all Uncle Paul will eat on Friday is fish. I didn't say anything because I was afraid it would make him feel worse.

"Fine."

"Just like Claire. That's all she ever tells me, too." He laughed a little; the light came back into his face but faded as soon as he realized what he'd said. "I'm sorry. . . . I'm really bad at this."

"No you're not. We just need a safe topic." Maybe if we kept Claire off the table, there'd be some semblance of normalcy for both of us.

"Okay. How about . . . well, I'm not asking you about boys."

"Please don't." The less said about Brooks, Dex, and any connection between the two to my underwear, the better. I was surprised the school hadn't already ratted me out to my aunt and uncle for the striptease.

"So what's a safe topic?" he asked.

"Is it okay if someone comes to the house this weekend?" I asked, then filled my mouth with a bite of my burger.

"Tabs and Brucey are always welcome. You don't have to ask."

"What about someone from Lowry?"

"Sure." Uncle Paul was terrible at hiding the surprise in his voice. "I'm glad you're okay . . . with Lowry and all. I wasn't sure it was a good idea or not, but if you're already making friends—"

"More tutor than friend."

"Why do you need a tutor your first day?"

"Because Lowry's way ahead of . . . well, pretty much anything I've ever seen. And aside from the fact that the classes were—*mostly*—taught in English, all I heard was 'Wah-wah-wah,' like from a Peanuts cartoon."

"Do you need me to help you? High school's a bit far back, but I wasn't too bad a student."

He wasn't too bad the way Abigail-not-Abby thought our teachers were slow. Uncle Paul's a certified genius. *Certified.* With an actual certificate, and a special card in his wallet from some genius club that only like one in a million people qualify for.

"One of the guys in my class said he'd come by on Sunday, if that's okay?"

"Ah. Gotcha," Uncle Paul said. "I'm pretty sure we already covered the 'I won't ask you about boys' rule, so we'll just stop here so I can say yes to your *tutor* coming to the house. And I can go back to pretending you're still my little niece who thinks boys are icky and trips them into the mud."

"Thanks, Uncle Paul."

"My little niece has a playdate at two with her little friend who happens to be a little boy. Yep. All is right in my world."

Pretending Claire and I weren't growing up wasn't as much of an act as he made it sound. He took mention of a teen boy in his house as reason to turn the radio to the nineties station and sing along with Nirvana at the top of his lungs. I guess his genius card didn't come with a guarantee of common sense.

At the house, Uncle Paul didn't pull around front, like usual; he pulled up to the garage, where he kept the cars he didn't drive so much as tinker with and look at on occasion. Yes, *cars,* plural. When the money started flowing, Aunt Helen bought a house; he bought cars.

"I was going to mention this sooner," he said. "But your dad asked me to wait until after he was gone so he'd have plausible deniability if anyone asked."

Anyone meaning my mother, no doubt.

"Your aunt and I got you something for your birthday, but we didn't have a way to get it out to Oregon." He pulled a key fob from his pocket and hit the lock on it. Halfway down the first row a set of headlights blinked on and off with the usual horn blast.

"You got me a car?"

"We tried," he said.

Uncle Paul was nervous. I could tell by the way he kept hitting his toe against the cement floor and the way he wouldn't look at me. Hopefully, he'd get to do this with Claire in a couple of years, but if not, he was trying to salvage something normal. The car wasn't just a birthday gift; it was one last chance for us to be anything close to the way we were before.

If I rejected the gift that my mother had obviously refused to let him and Aunt Helen give me, I was turning my back on them again. Dad had already cast his vote, and given me permission to take an act of kindness in the spirit in which it was meant rather than as the act of war Mom always tried to turn things into.

"It's not pink, is it?" I asked.

The grin I got in response made me feel like I was back in the life I'd had before the move.

"Take a look," he said, tossing me the keys. "Your aunt picked out the key chain, so any retaliatory gestures can be directed her way. I take no responsibility for the matching house key, either."

Aunt Helen had gone all out and gotten the "designer" keys. Mine were black with red and gold stars covered in glitter that matched the key chain—a bird with my name written across them in gold scroll. Seeing "Dinah" engraved on something for a change was nice.

"She tried to find a dodo bird but had to settle for the dove."

"They're great," I said, jingling the keys. "My favorite colors and everything."

"Hmmm." Uncle Paul scowled. "Maybe we should have gotten a black car, then."

It occurred to me that I hadn't actually moved yet. I was still standing by the door, and my neither-pink-nor-black mystery car was waiting somewhere in the mix for me to find it.

I waded into what would have been a slice of Dad's heaven, and then I saw it. *My baby*. Gunmetal-blue without so much as a fingerprint on the finish, sitting right next to the beat-up old truck Dad loved too much to take to Oregon, where Mom would have sold it for scrap.

"I know it's not the one you and your dad have been working on, but you don't need to be tethered to us while you're here. With me and Helen going back and forth to the hospital—"

"I don't mind going to the hospital," I said.

"But it shouldn't be the *only* place you go. Whether you're here for a few days, a few weeks, or whatever else we're able to work out, you should at least have the kind of freedom that comes with blowing out all sixteen candles on your cake."

"It took two tries. Dad sabotaged me by stealing frosting."

"Then it's a good thing I wasn't there to see you lose on a technicality," he said.

None of them had been there at all. I'd gotten a card, a phone call from Aunt Helen, and a long IM rant from Claire about how angry she was when they'd canceled their trip at the last minute. She'd just gotten her Lowry uniform and wanted to show it off. She hadn't understood why they couldn't come, and honestly, neither had I, but now it made perfect sense.

"Helen had it all planned. She wanted to mail you the key so you could open it on your birthday, but you lived so far away, and—"

"And Mom said no, didn't she?"

There was no way distance had kept Uncle Paul from giving me my car; he wouldn't have bought it if he hadn't been certain he could get it to me. And there was no way my mother would have let him. Not a new car. Not *this* car. Especially not this car from him and Aunt Helen.

"I'm sure she has her reasons, Dinah."

"Don't do that. Don't make excuses for her. Everyone does, and she uses that as permission to keep doing things that need excusing."

I couldn't shake the possibility that Mom's birthday tantrum was what had put Claire over the line. Claire had been counting on seeing me, storing up all the things she didn't want to say on the phone to tell me in person. I was her safety net, and Mom's fit cut it out from under her.

My mood shift sort of put a damper on the whole new-car moment, but I indulged Uncle Paul's forced enthusiasm, sitting behind the wheel so he could take a picture to show Aunt Helen.

I'm sure he thought I'd take the Mustang out for a spin and maybe not come home until after midnight, but I was exhausted. I didn't want to go anywhere other than straight to bed, so once I'd waved Uncle Paul back down the driveway, I left the garage and let myself into the house with my brand-new red and black key.

11

The room Aunt Helen had fixed up for me was technically the guest room, but she had decorated it with me in mind—probably the day after Mom announced we were moving and Aunt Helen began her "Keeping Dinah" campaign. It was on the second floor, closer to the stairs than Claire's, which had the big window, and it was the most "me" place I had ever seen.

Dark carpet, purple walls with black lace curtains, and furniture that looked like it came out of the Baroque period. Aunt Helen's Goth was actually Gothic.

I toed off my shoes and buried my feet in the high pile, then dug some pj's out of the dresser (peach is not the same thing as pink, thank you very much) and dragged my phone out of my bag to text Tabs. But as soon as I switched the power on, it began to vibrate in my hand and the screen lit up with a number I knew by heart.

"Hi, Mom," I answered.

"Where have you been? I've been calling you since this afternoon. Your father told me about the new phone."

Traitor.

I had switched the SIM card so I could keep my old number and files; there was no reason for Dad to say anything unless she needled it out of him. But I guess he figured it was better to mention the phone than the Mustang.

"I went to the hospital," I said. "You have to turn your phone off inside."

"Did Paul pick you up from school?"

"No."

"Don't give me the dramatic sigh."

"Is Dad home yet?" I asked.

"And don't try and get me off the phone!" She was yelling. Not quite the speed record, but close.

"All I did was ask you if Dad's plane had landed."

"I'm sure he called you first thing," she said smugly.

"My phone was off, Mom."

"I've told you that you're not to turn your phone off when you're not at home, Dinah Rain."

"Hospital rules, Mom. Cell phones screw up the equipment."

"Don't think you can use that sort of language just because you're on the other side of the continent, young lady."

"Don't" is my mother's favorite word. Most people pepper their speech with "like" or "you know" on the pauses; Mom fills in empty space with "don't." Don't make noise. Don't get dirty. Don't wear that. Don't eat on the furniture. Don't take your dolls off the shelf. Don't go outside. Don't bring people to the house if they're not her definition of normal.

Don't touch. Don't speak. Don't see. Don't say. Don't dare. Don't breathe.

I came to the conclusion years ago that she didn't really want a family so much as she wanted a diorama to drag out when people visited. That way, she could pull us out, say "look at my perfect daughter and husband," and then shove us back in the cupboard when she was done. We weren't supposed to move or talk or do anything other than serve as a conversation piece for whoever she happened to be speaking to.

And since when is "screw up" inappropriate language?

"Is Claire any worse?" she asked.

"She's the same," I said, not bothering to mention that most people would have asked if she'd gotten better. "They said it might be weeks."

"Your father told me a few days."

"Mom, you let them put me in school for the semester. They're hoping she'll wake up tomorrow or the next day, but she's still got to go through all the counseling and rehab stuff."

"The only reason I agreed to let you stay was because it wasn't going to be more than a few days."

"If she wakes up in the next few hours, they say her chances of recovery are better."

"And if she doesn't?"

"No one knows for sure."

"And, of course, you think this nets you an extended vacation."

"What?"

"She stays in the hospital and you get to lounge around your aunt and uncle's house doing nothing."

I should have left my phone off and told Mom I slept at the hospital. She was keeping this up an awfully long time; I wondered if she had an audience of sympathetic parents in the room patting her back for taking the "tough love" approach with her "difficult" daughter.

"Dad already told you. Once she's awake and out of—"

"It's been days, Dinah. Chances go down the longer someone's in a coma, not up, and if you've got some silly notion in your head that she's going to be the exception to the rule, you need to grow up."

"MOM!"

"Don't raise your voice to me!"

"Then don't say things like that!"

"Claire did this to herself, and it doesn't do anyone any good to make themselves sick hoping she'll get better. Even if she does, she'll just turn around and do it again and again until she manages to kill herself for real."

"MOM!"

"It's what people like that do, Dinah. They get off on the high of someone feeling sorry for them, so they keep trying to find ways to get pity. I expect you back here in a month. No more."

"I'm not leaving until something happens with Claire." One way or the other.

"You'll do as I say."

"Where's Daddy?"

"He's out tinkering with that piece of junk he lugged all the way out here."

"It's not junk. It's a classic."

Dad had been fixing up a 1965 Cobra—for me. It's seriously the coolest car on the planet, and was his favorite when he was a kid, because his next-door neighbor had one and let Dad drive it in and out of the driveway, even though he was way too young.

". . . so you can forget crying to him about how mean your mother is. One of us has to have some sense. I can't even imagine what he was thinking leaving you there. I won't let your aunt and uncle kill my daughter along with their own."

I wish I could say that it was an unusual conversation, or that my mother only got so awful under high stress, that she didn't know what she was saying, but I used up my lying quota on the "pretend to be nice to the killer" leg of the race. Mom's like that all the time. High drama, with her in middle of the brightest spotlight. She only cares about anything so much as it relates to *her*, helps *her*, inconveniences *her*.

When Nonie was still alive, there was a photograph that sat on her side table. It was the year Aunt Helen was born, at Christmas, and they were introducing Mom to her new sister. In the photo, Aunt Helen's asleep in her bassinet and Mom's screaming with a bright red face and running nose. On the back, Nonie wrote "But I wanted a playhouse!"

It would have been cute if Mom weren't still throwing that same fit.

"All this fuss over Claire and her mental problems . . . I guess I can look forward to you trying the same thing when you get home. Well, it won't work, Dinah Rain. I'm not going to coddle you the way—"

"I'm hanging up, Mom."

"If I find out you girls cooked this whole thing up so you'd have an excuse to—"

"I'm hanging up. Dad gave me permission to be here. I'm not truant, and I'm too tired to listen to you doing an 'is she dead yet' countdown. find another audience."

I ended the call and switched my ringer off, which did nothing to stop it from lighting up as another call came in immediately. Then another. And another. I stuck the phone under a pillow and left Mom to rail at empty space.

12

Uncle Paul and Aunt Helen hadn't always been the kind of rich that meant one phone call and three days' notice could create exceptions at one of the most exclusive private schools in the country. They hit that point about eight months ago. Six months before that, they were our neighbors in a part of town not nearly so nice or gated as their current address.

The world can change a lot in the space of two miles and a run of luck.

Back then they lived in a two-bedroom house with green siding and a basement that flooded ankle-deep anytime it rained. My house, which had one wall of brick in the front and beige-ish siding everywhere else, sat close enough that if I leaned out my bedroom window, I could lay my palm flat against their outer wall. Our basement didn't leak, but there was a brown spot on the ceiling in the hall where water dripped through. One week, Dad would help Uncle Paul fix the basement windows to protect his computer equipment; the next, Uncle Paul would be on the roof with Dad, replacing shingles that were never in quite the right place to stop our drip. In the back, their yard ran into ours without even a fence between them.

We'd lived like that forever. Dad worked on cars; Uncle Paul worked on computers. Aunt Helen did stuff for our school's parent organization and cleaned houses on the weekends, and Mom pretended she was happy so long as our house was the only one of the two with brick on it. Somehow her forced contentment was such an effort that she didn't have the time or energy for an actual job.

So maybe you can understand the paradigm shift that happened when Uncle Paul's brainchild became an online hit because some actor out in Malibu happened to sit down with his son one afternoon, stumble across it, and spend the next six hours immersed in "a virtual world of myth and mayhem."

All it took was that description in one interview and one post to his fan page, and suddenly the servers were overheating from too much traffic.

Sponsors poured in. Subscription fees poured in. Merchandising offers poured in. And in less than a year, a brick-front house wasn't enough for Mom anymore, because it took less than a year for Uncle Paul and Aunt Helen to move to a new tax bracket.

As far as Dad was concerned, it was time to celebrate. For Mom, it was time for hysterics. If she couldn't outdo her sister, then she'd move so far away no one knew it. And rather than argue, Dad did what he always does: he let her have her way to stop the screaming, and door slamming, and plate breaking. I took my cat and hid at Aunt Helen's until the storm was over, just in case Mom decided she wanted to actually hurt something. The next morning, my parents announced we were moving out of the state as soon as I was done with school for the year. Mom had tried to convince Dad to pack up and leave on the spot, but he refused to make me switch schools before summer.

The grand irony of it all was that Aunt Helen and Uncle Paul had intended for us to make the social climb right along with them. When Uncle Paul's business was getting off the ground, Dad gave him three thousand dollars he'd saved up, without telling Mom, so Uncle Paul could move to an actual work space other than his basement.

As soon as the game took off, Uncle Paul offered Dad a quarter of the company. He wasn't even going to ask him to pay for the shares because Dad's so good at fixing things. Uncle Paul handled the coding with his brain trust of supergeeks, but Dad kept the machinery working. The papers were drawn up and ready for Dad to sign, but Mom couldn't get over the "three-thousand-dollar lie," as she called it. She never missed the money, and we never went hungry or had the power turned off. All Dad did was put off buying some of the cosmetic pieces for the Cobra.

Even after hanging up on her, it was hard to get my mom's theatrics out of my head. I don't know why people think big houses are so great, because all that extra space did was remind me how empty the place was. I wandered down the hall to Claire's room and did a backward flop onto her bed.

The first night after Dad and I got in, we stayed at the hospital, sleeping smushed into plastic chairs with bars between them that meant no one could stretch out. It didn't really matter, because Claire had gone three full days in a coma by that point, and we all knew it was worse than just a bump on the head and a little blood loss. There wasn't any way to rest, between the nerves and worry, and the beeping machines that blinked with constant updates on patients' conditions. After they moved Claire from the ICU, the plastic torture seats became ugly green recliners that supposedly doubled as guest beds.

Any night that wasn't spent on vigil at the hospital, I slept in Claire's room, curled up in a ball on one end of her bed in my clothes, in case we got a call to get back to her in a hurry. I was the one who dragged out the bleach and hand towels and cleaned her bathroom floor, because Aunt Helen and Uncle Paul were too preoccupied with keeping Claire's heart beating to remember she'd left red puddles on the tile. Between the smell of dried blood and the fumes off the bleach, it wasn't a shock when I ended up retching into the toilet.

No one knew what had happened, or what was going on in Claire's head, and I'd never felt so absolutely helpless in my life.

Then I realized there was something I could do. Claire might have been unconscious, but that didn't mean she was mute. She'd kept a diary since she was ten, so her reasons for doing what she did were somewhere in her bedroom. All I had to do was find them. My only thought was that if we knew why she had cut herself, we could fix it.

Claire was never the girl who wrote with glitter pens or kept her inner thoughts under lock and key in a book with pages, and she wasn't stupid enough to keep her journal on a blog where anyone with Internet access could read it. She kept everything on a two-centimeter square tucked into the back of a snow leopard with rainbow spots.

When most people see a pile of stuffed animals on a girl's bed, they might roll their eyes and say she's too old for toys, but they'll shrug it off as cute and let it go. What they don't realize is that those fluff balls with the sound chips in their stomachs are the perfect place to hide little things like jewelry or cash or a memory card. They've already got a hard box inside them; all you have to do is open the zipper and tape what you want to hide to the bottom of the speaker. The toy will work perfectly and no one's the wiser.

I should know; I was the one who taught her to do it.

When you're fourteen, telling a twelve-year-old how to sneak her private thoughts under her parents' radar isn't something you think will ever become an important enough detail to share. You sure don't think of it as something that will come back to bite you, or nearly kill the kid you were trying to help.

I shook all the toys on her bed until I found one with a voice box, then nearly stripped the zipper trying to get it open. I almost hoped it wouldn't be there, because the idea that the explanation for Claire's misery was close enough to touch made me want to run for the toilet again. But it was there—one tiny, benign-looking piece of blue plastic. I pulled it out of the snow leopard's gut and snapped it into Claire's laptop.

I don't know what I was expecting, but it sure wasn't what I found. I bypassed the folder labeled "Diary" and clicked on "Dinah stuff," surprised to see my name on anything

Dear Dodo,

Dodo was Claire's nickname for me, the way I called her Cuckoo. It was one of those inside jokes that wasn't very funny but stuck. Dodos are extinct, and cuckoos leave their eggs for someone else to raise—we were a couple of birds who didn't belong. When we lived next door to each other, Claire would barge in and unload on me whenever she needed to talk. Once I moved, she apparently made a digital Dinah to talk to.

Mom and Dad don't poke their heads in as much when they hear typing as they do when I'm on my phone. This

way, they think I'm doing my summer "prep" homework.
(As if.)

This is what I wanted to tell you before. Last
weekend, I met Brooks Walden—who IS NOT a girl, tyvm,
so let's not even go down that road again, okay? Good.

Brooks was behind me in line at the food court. I was
a dollar short and couldn't pay for my Jilly Juice. (Daddy
won't let me have my own plastic for another year >.<)

Kicks Daddy

Brooks rescued me. Total knight-in-shiny-armor
moment.

I didn't know he was a Lowry boy at first. I mean, he
wasn't really dressed like it. Yes, I'm the stupid blond
girl who expects private school boys to wear their unis
even during the summer. (Shut up, Dodo, I can hear you
laughing.)

And you can stop worrying. I told him my fifteenth
was in a month (He thought I was sixteen!!!), so he
should be able to figure out how old I am, and . . . he
invited me to the Point on Saturday. (I told Mom I'm
going with Shauna from choir, so don't you dare rat me
out when I tell you this for real.)

Freeman's Point is the all-purpose (and often only) free
gathering place for kids during the summer. Equal parts lake,
fairground, and time warp, it's one of those weird places where
it doesn't matter what part of town you come from; everyone
mixes. And no matter how the world outside evolves, the Point
manages to keep itself exactly as it was in 1962, when the
drive-in movie theater was shut down.

They took out the parking lot but kept the screen, and when school's out, they play old movies on the weekends. You can either watch on the grass, if you want to hear the movie, or head for the lake and use the film as background lighting to make out.

The Claire I knew wouldn't have even considered the second option.

> No, I don't have a picture (yet). I got close, though—I snapped him with my phone, but he caught me. When he tried to get a look at it, he pressed the wrong button and the phone ate it. :-(
>
> Now it's like a game: avoid Claire's photo op. He thinks it's cute, but I wish he'd stop. I want you to see him. He's not as tall as Brucey, but he's got black hair, dark eyes, and . . . he's gorgeous!

She sounded so happy. It was worse that I could hear her voice chirping away in my head giving excuses as to why she couldn't send me pictures: Brooks was "Internet safe" and only posted drawings to his public profile; Brooks was camera shy. She thought I'd really like him. . . .

I looked everywhere I could think of for her phone—including unscrewing the air vents—just in case she'd managed to catch me some proof, but I never found any.

> I'm nervous, Dodo. He's a jr. and I'm just a fishstick . . . what if I end up acting like a stupid kid? If I blow this, I'll never be able to set foot in Lowry. I'll have to run away and hitch out to Oregon to find the real you, and then I'll get eaten by badgers.

Why did you have to move? You're supposed to be here so I can talk to you about this stuff!

I hate that I have to hide this thing inside my stupid cat toy because Mom snoops and Dad can open any files I save to my computer. I hate that I can't even dust off my old email account (assuming I could remember the log-in, and I can't) because Daddy has one of those parent watchdogs on my stuff. AND I HATE AUNT STACY FOR TAKING MY DODO AWAY FROM ME!

That made two of us.

There's so much I want to tell you, but every time I try to say it on the phone, I lose my nerve . . . I'm afraid someone will hear. If Mom and Dad knew Brooks was seventeen, they'd never let me out of the house. So I'll have to save it all up and tell you when we come out to Oregon for your birthday. Or maybe you could run away from home instead. The badgers wouldn't bother you.

I need you, Dinah. I don't know what I'm doing all alone here.

Every file on that card was a letter to me. They progressed from her giggly nerves over an older guy she thought was out of her league to moon-eyed infatuation with Brooks that was little more than a free-form ramble dedicated to his eyes, and hair, and too-white teeth, followed by anticipation of dates and days at Freeman's Point.

Afraid of acting her age and having Brooks shun her for it, Little Miss Can't-Do-Her-Health-Homework-Without-Blushing suddenly decided that under the pier and out of her shirt was the best way to watch *The Princess Bride*. If I hadn't known where she was going to end up a few weeks after she wrote that entry, I probably would have cheered for her loosening up. But Claire was already in over her head.

Her spontaneous strip-down was the last, steep step before topless under the pier became naked under the pier. And I bet that stupid, innocent, too-trusting kid believed Brooks when he said it wasn't his fault. He couldn't help himself—she was too pretty, and the movie was too romantic. She told me so in the letter she never sent.

It started: *I'm not a virgin anymore. . . . Please don't hate me.*

Everything that came after was a system purge of confusion, embarrassment, and betrayal. She probably didn't even notice when she wrote it out, but she kept repeating things like "I told him to stop" and "I asked him to slow down" and "I said no, but I guess he didn't hear me." She hadn't wanted to raise her voice because she was afraid someone else at the Point might hear, and in her mind things would get worse if someone caught them.

Tabs had heard about the "the new guy" in glorious crush-worthy detail, but not about this. I'd spoken to Claire a dozen times and had never heard anything in her voice to hint at how far she'd withdrawn into herself. Aunt Helen and Uncle Paul shared a house with her, knew every facial tic and nervous habit, and they didn't have a clue.

Abigail-not-Abby didn't know what she was asking for when she wished for a body that looked older than fifteen. She was so much like my cousin in every way but the physical. When everything was over, I wanted to make her read Claire's words until they sank in and she realized how lucky she was that no one hassled her.

By the next letter, Claire was doing what she always did: she brushed over anything unpleasant with a fresh coat of sunny yellow paint and pretended she'd overreacted. She actually thought the fact that Brooks hadn't called her and didn't come to her birthday party meant he was embarrassed, too. She would have called him and told him not to worry, but he claimed he'd dropped his phone in the lake.

And she believed him. The boy drove a Beemer, and she believed he didn't have access to a cell phone.

Claire acted like the real world worked the same way as a musical, where even the bad stuff wasn't so terrible. She restructured things in her head so that what happened at Freeman's Point worked into her big-picture plan. She was going to surprise Brooks, likely the first day of school, when she started Lowry, like the first scenes in *Grease,* and she expected just as happy an ending, spontaneous choreographed dance numbers and flying cars included.

But reality didn't play along with her fantasy. Brooks kept not showing up and not calling. Her vision for how they'd spend the last few weeks of the summer never came true. It took a while, but she finally got the message that her beginning had been his ending—he was through with her.

Claire didn't get angry like a normal girl who'd been dumped; she got scared.

Poor little rich girl, good enough for a roll under the pier if you don't mind used goods.

In Claire's overactive imagination it had already happened. Everyone at Lowry was waiting with a hot branding iron to burn a red "A" into her chest the first day of school. No, a red "F," she said, because "A" was only for "adulterer," and she, at least, hadn't cheated on anyone. It never occurred to her that "rich girl" was the default setting for people who went to Lowry, or that maybe she wasn't alone in the Brooks Walden Disposable Girlfriend Club.

The last entries before her not-suicide were dedicated to talking herself out of and then back into cutting herself. She'd gotten frustrated enough to break a mirror with her fist, and letting the pain out had made her feel better.

She fell apart and I wasn't there to help her hold it together (or tell her just to find him at the mall again, dump his Jilly Juice on his head, and give him a swift kick to the crotch).

There was so much in those letters it took me days to get through them, and I'd been coasting on adrenaline and raw fury since that first night I'd found out who had made the most perfect person I'd ever known see herself as so worthless she wanted to disappear. Meeting Brooks in the flesh and making the monster real finally put me over the edge. I was wiped out.

I lay in Claire's bed, hugging that hideous snow leopard while its voice box purred. I closed my eyes, and all I could see was the macabre light show of LCD displays from the hospital. The beeps and pings echoed in my head, refusing to stop. They morphed into the ringtone I had set to warn me when my mother was calling and I fell asleep, dreaming that the cold water at Freedman's Point was closing over my head, drowning everything out and pulling me down into sweet oblivion.

13

You know the cartoon version of a teenager clinging to the bed at two o'clock Saturday afternoon, pillow over their head and scooting farther away from the window as the sun moves, until they finally fall off the edge in a tangle of sheets? That's me. Seriously. I've got the scar on my chin to prove it.

I hate alarms. At eight o'clock in the morning on a Saturday, I hate clocks period, but the morning after my recon trip into killer-infested waters, I didn't even need the alarm. I was up and waiting for Tabs with time to spare before she rang the bell.

"This wasn't my fault," she blurted as soon as I pulled the front door open.

I knew that look.

"Who did you tell?"

"No one. At least, not intentionally . . ."

Grimace sat parked at the base of the stairs in front of the house, and a very familiar, very tall, very thin, and very pale person climbed out of the passenger seat.

Everything about Brucey requires a "very" in front of it; he doesn't have a lower setting.

"She doesn't write; she doesn't call. I was beginning to think our dodo bird had really gone extinct."

"Tabs!" I'll admit it, I shrieked. There may have even been slapping involved. "You told Brucey!"

"No?" Whenever Tabs lies, her statements become questions.

"How much does he know?"

"You know, a fella could get the impression that perhaps no one wants him to help destroy the life of the next generation's social elite. Even though I've more than proven myself as an evil genius in training through our countless joint endeavors—"

I stuck my hand over his motor mouth.

"Why is he talking like this?" I asked Tabs. "He sounds like someone rebooted his brain with an upgrade."

"Technology puns!" Brucey beamed. He lifted me off the ground so we were at eye level and twirled me into the house. "She still loves me! When do I get to see you in your disguise? Is it plaid? Are there knee socks? Barrettes?"

"He's in one of his weird moods."

Yes, he was. Very weird. He'd pulled his hair back into a (brushed!) ponytail, and the only piercings I could see were the black spacers in his ears; all the polish was off his nails. The way he was dressed, he could have passed for the film student he liked to pretend he was.

"Don't blame dear Tabitha, my lovely vigilante. 'Tis not her fault."

"Are you on something?" I pulled his eyelids down at the bottom for a better look. "You tested the orange powder on him, didn't you?"

"I am in character, and high on the prospect of mayhem for a good cause," he said as he set me down. "When do we get to synchronize our watches? How about reconnoitering? Do we get to reconnoiter?"

Ah. There was my Brucey. He slouched, knocking three

inches off his height, and jammed his hands in his pockets. His eyebrows waggled up and down in what he called his "sneaky look."

"How do people stand up straight all day?" he asked. "It's painful."

"Only for you," Tabs groused. "Normal people can't have an eye-to-eye conversation with a giraffe."

"It's only easy for you because you've got a counterbalance." He smirked. "Two of them."

"Pervert." Tabs scowled, crossing her arms over her chest.

"At your service."

Brucey gave her a dramatic bow.

"Guys, please . . . *focus!*" They snapped to attention. "If Tabs didn't tell you about me and Brooks, then how'd you know?"

"Remember how I said we were going to get caught?" Tabs asked.

"Yeah? So?"

"We got caught."

"What happens in Vegas stays in your call log, doll." Brucey vaulted himself over the back of the sofa, landing with his long legs out in front of him across the cushions.

"He synched my phone," Tabs said apologetically.

"Tabs!"

"It's not my fault. I had to pee and I left it on my desk."

"You know you can't leave Brucey alone with any kind of tech. He can't control himself."

"There's a fine line between insult and playful banter, dear harridans. I'm tempted to take your snarking as character assassination, and then I'd have to do something unpleasant with your photographic evidence."

Brucey waved something in the air over his head.

"My phone!"

I launched myself over the sofa to take it back, but Orangutan Arms held it out of range.

"This the guy?" he asked, calling up my lunchroom snapshots of Brooks Walden's smug, smiling face.

"Yes! Now give it back, you friggin' klepto."

Yes, I said "friggin'." You'd have to actually enter my aunt and uncle's house to understand what happens there, but it's impossible to use real curse words in that environment without being slammed by the feeling that you've just kicked a puppy in front of a five-year-old. Eventually, you start to censor yourself. (I suspect that one of Uncle Paul's many secret projects includes a box like the kind people use to recut R-rated movies, only it works on real people and makes them all nice against their will.)

"Kleptomania is a medical condition beyond the afflicted's control. Picking pockets is a legitimate trade, thank you very much. I only pinch what I intend to take and nothing more."

"Fine, fork over the phone, you friggin' legitimate thief."

"Smoochies?"

I glanced at Tabs, who'd positioned herself on the other side of the couch.

"Get him!"

We grabbed the couch pillows and pounced—just like Kyle Smith in kindergarten, only with less intent to maim.

"Dinah? What's going on in—" Uncle Paul came into the living room from his morning coffee run in the kitchen. He was still wearing the clothes he'd had on the night before, so he must not have slept at the house. "Oh, you're smothering Brucey. There's superglue under the sink if you break something."

"Morning, Mr. Reed." Tabs put her weight on her elbow so she could hold Brucey down with one arm.

"Hello, Tabitha. Okay there, Brucey?"

Brucey waved with his free hand and gave Uncle Paul a thumbs-up. He shoved Tabs' pillow off his mouth and said, "Death by pillow fight is every guy's fantasy." Which only made her press down harder with her elbow.

"Don't worry, Uncle Paul, we'll dispose of the body when we're done. Then we're going to the mall."

"We'll find an extralong bedsheet to bury him in and everything," Tabs promised.

"Wipe the place down for prints before you go," Uncle Paul said. "I think your prisoner's escaping."

Brucey had stopped fighting back and was inching his way to the far end of the sofa, caterpillar-style, to try and make a break for it.

"Stay out of my office, Brucey," Uncle Paul warned as he left.

"Scout's honor. You know me, Mr. Reed."

Uncle Paul froze midstep and turned back toward the hallway that led to his office.

"I'm setting the keypad."

Twenty minutes later, Uncle Paul had gone back to the hospital, and Tabs, Brucey, and I had turned the kitchen into our base of operations. I might not have wanted Brucey involved originally, but I had to admit, he took to the idea of torpedoing Brooks' social standing with aplomb.

St. Michael wasn't the only avenging angel Claire had on duty.

Brucey had retrieved his computer from Grimace and built a techie nest on his side of the table. He was also horrified to discover that I hadn't updated (or, as he said, "scrubbed") my online profile. I'd been a blond less than a week, and my mind hadn't exactly been centered on taking new pictures to replace the ones I had posted. Brucey set to work, Photoshopping Lowry Dinah into old scenes of the real me.

"This is why you should never leave me out of the loop," he said as his fingers flew across the trackpad, giving photo-me a makeover. "You've got half a dozen friend requests already. If you hadn't had your profile locked, you'd already be busted. These albums have to go—Claire's in them."

I moved around the table so I could peek over his shoulder to find out who had friended me; seeing Dex at the top of the list sent ripples through my stomach.

Considering Dex had already figured out that my Lowry persona wasn't the usual me, I wasn't too worried about him seeing the profile picture of me with Tabs and Brucey, with my usual black hair and not-at-all uniform appearance. But Brucey was right—I'd made a huge mistake by jumping into this without thinking. Jordan-from-homeroom, Abigail-not-Abby, even the school itself had me on standby (Tabs' "spy on thy neighbor" theory was spot on, I guess). Two of the names I thought I recognized from one class or another and decided they were the kind of people who friended everyone whether they knew them or not. Chandi was a surprise, and I wasn't sure I'd accept her request once Brucey gave me the all clear. Sure, her profile and the secrets it held were potential ammunition, but earlier antagonism aside, I was uneasy about using Brooks' girlfriend like that. Manipulating her private life felt too close to what had happened to Claire.

Brucey finished my pictures pretty quickly and moved on to changing my favorite movies and music.

"Add *The Princess Bride*," I said.

"As you wish . . ."

Brucey was entering his comfort zone, where there was a movie quote for every situation. This required redirection, and fast, or else he'd recite the whole thing from memory. (Or just shift straight into the Oompa-Loompa theme from *Willy Wonka*.)

"When he's done, you should send a request to He Who Must Not Be Named," Tabs said; she must have had the same idea.

She was also right, and I hated it. I didn't want to friend Claire's tormentor, or have a link to him that others could follow with a quick click, but there was no other way. I couldn't snoop without him friending me.

"Now that the groundwork is taken care of," Brucey said, cracking his knuckles, "have you decided how you want to do this?"

"I'm pretty much winging it," I said as my mind drifted back to Wonderland. *If you don't know where you're going, any road will get you there,* or so says the Cheshire Cat.

It wasn't like Amazon had a bright yellow *Vengeance for Dummies* manual I could download. (I checked.)

"Give me ten minutes with your uncle's equipment and I can make him a ghost."

"Ten minutes with Paul's equipment and you'd crash the IRS," Tabs said.

"You make that sound like a bad thing."

"Go sit in the car." I pointed toward the door. "Now. You've lost inside privileges."

Brucey stuck his tongue out at me, reminding me yet again that I no longer had my barbell. His was blue.

"I checked Mom's pill cupboard last night," Tabs said, pulling us back on point.

"It's a cupboard now?"

"And two of those ugly green storage boxes. She hasn't touched the bitter orange or ma huang in months. The bottles were still sealed, so I grabbed one of each . . . but there's a problem. No way can you disguise the taste of either one of them with drink mix. They're awful."

"Great. I had all of one idea and it's a bust."

"Actually, it's a piece of cake."

Tabs reached for her bag where she'd stashed it under the table and pulled out one of those plastic bowls people use to take food to parties. When she took off the lid and tipped it my way, there was a fudgy cat cupcake with licorice whiskers—just like the one from the hospital magazine.

"I looked it up online," she said proudly. "Chocolate's used to hide the taste of medicine for kids or poison at assassination dinners. It'll kill the taste of anything. Try one."

Maybe it was me, but knowing Tabs now possessed the skills to conceal arsenic at will didn't make me want to be her official food taster.

"I put pudding in it," she added as Brucey devoured our prototype, whiskers and all.

He mumbled something that, based on the okay sign with his fingers, was probably "It's good."

"I tried it with both of them and you can't taste either one. I'm not sure we should use both, though. What if it's too much for his heart or shuts his kidneys down?"

"Good point."

Death was too fast.

I wanted to make him as miserable as he'd made Claire; it was no good if he had a heart attack. Things like that led to autopsies and overly sympathetic views of the guy who died. No way did I want him painted as the tragic boy with a bad heart who was cut down in the prime of life. I wanted Brooks to forget what happy felt like and stay healthy enough to regret his mistakes for many, many years.

"Which one do you want?" she asked.

"Isn't ma huang a hormone?" Brucey asked, still trying to unstick the chocolate fudge from the roof of his mouth with his tongue. "Use that one. Make him grow boobs."

"That's Dong quai, moron." Tabs hit him with the lid of the cupcake bowl.

"Oooh . . . you should turn his pee blue." Brucey bounced up and down in his seat.

"See? This is why I tell you not to feed him sweets."

"Sorry," Tabs said.

"I'm serious." Brucey pouted. "There was this show and they used a chemical, and you can put it in soda, and he'll pee blue, and you can make him think something's seriously wrong."

"I thought we all agreed you would stop watching reruns of anything made before you were born."

Brucey had been taking his cues from old TV shows since his dad got cable when we were nine. If he hadn't had such a low tolerance for pain, *Jackass* would have done him in.

"Just because they did it on TV doesn't make it stupid," he said, sulking.

"Let's stick to things anchored in this millennium."

"Fine." He tapped the trackpad on his laptop. "Here you go." Brucey spun his computer around and showed us what he'd been working on besides my profile. Brooks Walden's head was now sitting firmly atop the shoulders of some other guy in a boy-clench. "Say the word and I'll mass email Lowry's class list with my masterpiece. I doubt there's too many guys at Lowry coming out of the closet."

"Not helpful, Brucey."

"What? You said you didn't have any ideas. . . . This is an idea."

"A stupid idea," I said. "And where did you get that picture?"

The photo he'd used of Brooks wasn't one I'd snapped at lunch. He couldn't have snagged it from Brooks' profile, either. Brooks had everything on lockdown; I'd looked for a picture of him after I found Claire's letters, but the only thing I found was a drawing of an insanely detailed futuristic sports car with a stick-figure man behind the wheel.

"I used the password the school gave you and skimmed their archives." He shrugged.

Lowry had archives? Who knew?

"If emailing the whole school is too much," Brucey said,

"I'll aim smaller. This guy's one of those WASPy types, right? Find out where his family goes to church—I'll send it to his pastor as an anonymous concerned parishioner."

"No."

"I can make an official notification stating he's got twenty-seven STDs and post it to the school's bulletin board for public health reasons."

Brucey with a password was a dangerous thing.

"No."

"Do the fish-in-the-tire-well thing! It'll rot and he'll never figure out where the smell's coming from. Or instead of putting the powder in his orange drink, you could mix milk and juice to make him sick, or—"

"So help me, if you start quoting *Heathers*—" Tabs looked like she was considering hitting him again.

"Do *not* mock the cinematic classics."

"Brucey, this is serious. I need some real ideas," I said.

"No, you need real information," he corrected. "What does he want? Find out and take it. What's his dream? Find out and crush it. Who does he love? Find out and make them hate him. You have to crack whatever wall he's got around him and get on his good side."

There's no way to describe the evil look that took over Brucey's usually placid face, but it gave me goose bumps, and I was suddenly very happy that he was on my side.

14

The food court at the Five Points mall always filled quickly. It was worse on the weekends, when the mall's major design flaw showed through—they'd built it half as big as it needed to be to hold the number of people flooding out of the stores when their blood sugar crashed. Tabs, Brucey, and I got there early and claimed a strategic table before the retail pilgrims descended for tacos and pizza.

Since this was Brooks' meet-cute with Claire, and he'd said he'd be here today, I figured the mall was his hunting ground of choice. But he stubbornly refused to make an appearance.

"Remind me again why calling the cops on this guy ranks below your almost-sure-to-fail plotting skills?" Brucey asked. Armed with my Lowry-issued password, he'd combed through the school's old newsletters and yearly reports and was currently building something he referred to as a dossier on Brooks Walden. Apparently Brooks hadn't been lying about the extracurriculars. He'd won all sorts of awards and medals for the school and on his own. It was also worth noting that there was no mother listed as an emergency contact for him, only his dad and a set of grandparents who lived in Wisconsin.

"What's she going to tell them?" Tabs asked. "She found the diary of a girl with mental issues who decided to strip down and follow a guy under the pier, then *didn't* scream for help?"

"The Cuckoo bird was fourteen, right? It won't matter whether she said yes or no."

"Forget it," I said. "If I turn Brooks in without a confession from him, then all the cops will do is *maybe* question him. Claire can't speak for herself, so they'll fill in the blanks by making her out to be some kind of slut. She doesn't need that waiting for her when she wakes up."

Rumors wouldn't die just because Claire refuted them later. Brooks would get the benefit of the doubt—and his dad's bank account—and the whole thing would be forgotten by the time he was ensconced in whatever Ivy League school his dad bought him a place in. Claire would still be seen as trash.

"I'm not letting them destroy what's left of her by making this her fault. We stick to the plan: make everything Brooks touches wither until he's so off center he thinks his own karma's got it in for him. He'll either confess to try and get some peace or he'll go crazy."

"Gimme your phone," Brucey said. "I want to see the pictures you took in the cafeteria."

"You've got a half-dozen photos of him."

"I want to see him in the wild, not posing for the school newspaper."

I pulled my phone out of my pocket but held it out of his reach.

"Swear you won't send any emails without asking first."

"I sw—"

"On your celluloid collection," I added. "Any unauthorized messages and I'll melt them in their cans." Brucey has about two hundred flat, round cans of movie film like they use in the projectors at the old drive-in. He's also got an unhealthy attachment to every one. They live in his dresser and closet while his clothes get piled on the floor.

"When did you get so mean?"

"Five minutes after Claire cut her wrists."

"Fair enough—I promise all I want is another look."

I handed him my phone and let him scroll through the pictures.

"This is the fallback girl, right?" he asked, pointing to Chandi.

"Yeah."

"How boring. Barbie-blondes are so last decade. Her bestie's hotter."

"Bestie?"

"One of your new friends: pixie haircut, twenty pounds soaking wet, built like a mini Victoria's Secret model."

He turned my phone around to show me Jordan-from-homeroom.

"What makes you think Jordan's her best friend?"

"Look at her," Brucey said as he zoomed in to get a better look at Chandi. Tabs and I leaned closer, but all I saw was a packed cafeteria table.

"What are we staring at?" Tabs asked.

"Body language," Brucey said. "The girlfriend's Miss Painted Perfect, but it only goes as deep as her topcoat. Look at the way she's holding herself—arms bent in at the shoulders, hiding, body leaned toward our nefarious villain, eyes down. She's trying to appear angry, but she's biting her lip; she's embarrassed, and terrified. See the way she's picking at her sleeve cuff? It's a nervous habit for people trying to control social anxiety."

"You got all that from a snapshot?" I asked. It still looked like lunch to me.

"And six years of therapy with Dr. Useless." He flipped the phone sideways to stretch the picture. "Look at your other girl. If anyone's angry, it's her. The others are watching the blonde, but her eyes are on that guy with the stupid grin. Whatever he did, she's pissed about it."

He was right. I'd missed it, since my focus was homed in on Brooks, but if looks could kill, Jordan and Dex would have both been dead—the kickback would have dropped her. In my mind, Jordan inched away from Tweedle status to possible enemy.

"What'd he do to her?" Tabs asked.

"He was just being himself," I said. "Dex and Chandi don't get along. It's almost like the two of them are competing for Brooks' attention."

"You think this Dex person is jealous? He could be pretending to hate the girlfriend when he'd really rather hook up with her. . . . Maybe you could help him get what he wants."

"I saw them all day—it wasn't an act. He picks at her and she loathes him for it."

"Either way, they're your weak links," Brucey said. "The point of contention is the easiest broken. Pick one and wear them down."

Chandi already hated me, so that left me with Dex.

Dex, who I was truly beginning to think had me LoJacked, because he had just entered the food court. His Lowry blazer and slacks had been replaced by an untucked T-shirt, flannel, and worn-out jeans. Rather than the regulation combed-back horror the school required guys to maintain as a "respectable and nondistracting" hairstyle, he looked like he'd walked here straight from the shower and let his hair dry on the way. I was forced to retract my initial opinion of "not handsome."

Lowry Dex wasn't handsome. Real Dex could have set fire to a glacier.

"Who's that and why are we watching him?" Brucey whispered.

He and Tabs moved their chairs around so that I was in the middle and their viewpoint was the same as mine.

"Yum," Tabs said.

"That's Brooks' best friend."

"I want one."

"That's the grinning idiot?" Brucey asked. He checked my phone again. "Nah—can't be."

"Leave," I told them quickly.

"I think she's ashamed of us, Tabby Cat." Brucey sniffled. "She doesn't want us meeting her new friends."

"I'm serious. Get out of here. I can't operate as Lowry Dinah with the two of you here to make me fall back into my real self." I wasn't trying to hide who I used to be—it was no secret, as Dex pretty much knew where I'd come from—but I couldn't keep my personalities straight with Tabs and Brucey nearby. (Once upon a time, I'd only had one personality to worry about. . . .) "Stop looking at him!"

"How about gawking? Can I gawk at him?" Tabs tried to weave around my hand as I turned her head away. "Is ogling allowed? Eyeballing? Gaping with intense interest? Give me something to work with, here."

"Stop it," I snapped. "Dex has some kind of weird sixth-sense thing. He'll know you're staring."

"And now I'm waving," she said through a phony grin. "He's looking right at us."

"Dinah?"

Dex left the line where he'd been chatting up a girl wearing a track jacket. He cocked his head to the side, trying to fit my non-Lowry self to my face. Ratty shorts and an old sweatshirt didn't scream "private school" any more than his scuffed Converse did.

"Hi," I said, then started praying for a freak meteor shower to shatter the mall's glass dome and knock me through the floor.

Dex grabbed the free chair at our table, spun it around, and sat with his legs straddling the back. I cringed, anticipating Brucey's usual tirade against people who sit backward. (He claims it's a sign of social deviance, but considering his habit of taking things that don't belong to him, I tend to ignore his assessments of other people and their quirks.)

"She said hi." Brucey scowled. "She didn't say you could steal our seat without even introducing yourself."

"Maybe I'm shy," Dex said. "You should introduce yourself first."

"Bruce Wayne Bateman."

Crap. That's Brucey litmus test number two—the one he uses whenever someone makes a bad first impression on him. Depending on their response to his full name, he can sprout wings and a halo or horns and a tail.

"Marcus Norwood," Dex said, and stuck his hand out.

"Guys, this is Jackson Dexter," I corrected. "Dex goes to Lowry, too. Dex, this is Tabs and Brucey."

"You were serious about the name?" Dex asked. "My bad. I thought maybe I needed a secret identity to sit here."

Brucey relaxed. The last time he'd told someone his full name, the kid had come back with "Holy evil parents, Batman." And since Brucey had actually watched enough old reruns to get the joke, he hadn't been amused.

"You know they kick you off the tables here if you don't eat," Dex said.

"Urban myth," Tabs said.

"If you say so." Dex cut his eyes from side to side in a comical rendition of suspicion. "But I used to work here, and I'd rather not do the escorted walk of shame to the escalators for being a 'nuisance' to the police academy dropouts."

"Then maybe you should leave before they decide you're guilty by association," Tabs said sourly.

"Not me." He pointed to his T-shirt, which was likely the only thing he was wearing that was new. "Sixth Street Shelter" was stenciled across the front in giant block letters. "We're having a toy drive for the trauma center. I'm one of the good guys today."

"Only today?" Tabs asked.

"It's no fun being the good guy all the time." He flashed that same smile that had nearly melted the soles of my shoes to the floor of not-trig the day before.

His head popped up higher, like he'd locked eyes with someone across the crowd, and he raised his hand to beckon them over.

Double crap. All that time waiting for the devil to show and he found me as soon as I stopped looking. Brooks approached our table, wearing a flaming orange shirt identical to Dex's.

"'Scuse us," I said, hauling Brucey away. When Tabs didn't move, I hooked her arm and dragged her behind me.

"Stop staring at them," I said.

"I can't help it. Your friend Dex looks familiar, and it's driving me crazy."

"The two of you are driving *me* crazy, and he's not my friend." I was also starting to hate Mr. Tripp for imprinting Alice on my frontal lobe. Everywhere I went, my world slanted through the looking glass, and now I was hearing the Mad Hatter cackle about how we were all going mad. "I can't handle both of them with you trying to psychoanalyze their nacho-eating skills. If this is going to work, then I have to at least act like the person they think I am. Which means you two need to stick to the background unless I need a bailout."

"Aye, aye, mon admiral—run silent, run deep." Brucey stood up straight and saluted.

"What does that even mean?" Tabs asked.

"Go!" I ordered, shoving my keys into her hand. "Take the Mustang. You've just ditched me, so I have to beg a ride home."

"Have fun—so long as there aren't any witnesses." Tabs grabbed a fistful of the front of Brucey's shirt and pulled him away.

".Later," Brucey said.

As he and Tabs left, Brucey angled just close enough to Brooks to make me certain he'd lifted something while Brooks was busy talking to Dex. Then Brucey and Tabs ran off toward the escalators, leaving me to wonder how much trouble he'd managed to pick out of Brooks' pocket.

"Did I scare your friends off?" Brooks asked when I sat back down.

"Not really," I said. "They're headed for the cineplex."

"Without you?"

"I told them to go. Dex was telling me about your toy drive and I thought I'd see if you needed a hand."

For the first and only time in my life, I found value in my failed-pageant past. Drilled-in lessons about how to stand and smile in order to create the best possible image flooded back, as some sort of latent secret power I never knew I possessed. Like Dex said, there was no better cover than pretending to be one of the good guys. If the snake could pull it off without shedding his skin, then so could I.

15

It took exactly twenty-six minutes to figure out what Brucey had stolen, because twenty-six minutes after I chased my friends off our table, Brooks finished eating and tried to use the phone that was no longer in his pocket. And it took exactly one minute longer for Brooks to begin retracing his steps from the moment he entered the mall to see if he could figure out where he'd dropped it.

Dex had neglected to mention that both he and Brooks were on the morning shift for the shelter's charity drive, and it was now over, which meant that if I wanted to stick close, I had to go with them and look for a phone that wouldn't be found unless Brucey decided to give it up.

"I need someone to dial it," Brooks said. "Maybe it's close enough to hear the ring—or someone could find it."

"Can't call without a phone," Dex said. He turned a bit red, crossing his arms and looking at his feet as he ground his toes into the floor.

"I've got mine," I said, quick-scrolling through my very short contact list to find the number Brooks had put into it after Cavanaugh's class. I pressed the button and prayed my mad genius of a best friend was either out of range or had thought to turn the ringer off.

I was also praying neither Brooks nor Dex could tell I was

holding my breath until I was sure there wouldn't be a ring-tone.

"Where'd you get that?" Dex asked while I pretended to be searching the food court for a hint of sound.

"Uncle Paul," I said with a shrug, then hung up. "He wanted to make sure any news got through, so he gave me a new phone."

"Who are you related to? Seriously?"

"Just Uncle Paul," I said, turning to Brooks to add: "No answer, sorry."

Dex was practically salivating. My phone wasn't the prepaid from-the-drugstore piece of trash I was used to. It was a gift from one of the companies with a buy-in on Uncle Paul's game—a beta version of a model that wouldn't hit stores for another three months. They were hoping he'd give them special consideration on an app or something to increase their audience base. (I'm sure the company suits would have passed out if they knew Uncle Paul had handed their Next Big Thing to his teenage niece, who then dragged it around the city on her quest to skirt the line between misdemeanor and felony.)

I slipped the phone back into my pocket, and for once I was fairly sure hormones had nothing to do with why Dex was staring at my backside. He looked like a starving man forced to sit at a banquet with his hands tied. At Lowry, he had a well-polished suit of social armor in place—no different from making sure his tie sat straight—but in the open, when he didn't have to conform to a set way of acting, the desire for things he couldn't have showed. It made the moment uncomfortable enough that I was happy to join in on a physical, if pointless, search where we had to split up to cover more ground.

We came up predictably empty in the food court. We scoured the shelter's area and all of the bags and boxes of toys, but of course there was nothing there, either. Brooks' final, desperate idea was to backtrack the route he'd taken from his car to the charity tables, which led us through a large department store with one of the main parking entrances.

"I'll go right," I said, turning toward the nearest cashier.

Dex and Brooks divvied up the left side and center of the store, and we split for the time it took to ask if anyone had turned in a phone.

"Sorry, honey, haven't seen it," said a woman in a lavender suit. "I can give you one of our gift bags if it would make you feel better."

I shook my head. All I needed to feel better was to breathe. When we entered the store from the mall, that familiar air compressor scent that used to ground me had only made me think of the unit in Claire's hospital room, so it was a relief to pass the cosmetics counter, where competing trails of perfume beat it back.

"I got nothin'," Dex announced when we met on the other side of the store.

"Me either," said Brooks, and when he looked to me for better news, I just shrugged, twirling my gold.bird necklace on the end of its chain the way I always did when I got nervous. "Maybe I left it in the car," he said.

Brooks headed for the door but ended up bouncing off a six-and-a-half-foot twig with shaggy black hair before he made it out—*Brucey*.

Brucey mumbled sorry as he jostled past us and shoved his hands in his pockets. It was a very specific physical tic that no one aside from one of his friends would recognize. Just like only Tabs or I would know the version of Brucey standing there in that store compared to the one Brooks and Dex had seen earlier. He'd ditched his jacket, and with his hair drawn forward, there wasn't a face to be seen, much less remembered.

"You didn't," I mouthed as he pushed his hair out of his eyes.

He danced his eyebrows up and down, grinning back.

I was about to warn Brooks what was coming when—

Bwaaaaaaaaaaaaaaaaaap!

The store's alarm started screaming as soon as he put one foot out the door and his pocket passed the sensor.

Brooks froze, confused by the sound, having no idea what had triggered it or the flashing lights on top of the door panels. People stopped to stare at him while a pair of mall cops with store badges popped out of a door camouflaged into the wall. I took a step back and did my best to look like I didn't know what was going on.

"What'd I do?" Brooks asked one of the mall cops.

"Empty your pockets, son," he said.

"Sure, but I didn't—" Brooks shrugged and reached into his pockets. I knew the exact moment he realized he was sunk, because his face bleached whiter than Brucey's. When he pulled his hands back out, there was a necklace dangling from his fingers.

"You're going to need to come with us to the security office," the mall cop said before turning to me and Dex. "Are you three together?"

"Yeah, but—" I started.

"We just bumped into each other." Dex cut me off. "We go to school together."

"Turn out your pockets," the guard ordered.

We did as he said, pulling everything out for security to see, but there was nothing of interest to them.

"Names?"

"D—"

"Daley." Dex cut me off again. He took my sleeve and pulled me toward the mall exit. "We'll get out of your way, sir. Let's go, *Daley*."

"And what about you?" the mall cop asked.

"Courtney D'Avignon, and that's all you get to ask— remember your right to remain silent," Dex said to Brooks.

The guard watched us until we had cleared the security scanners. When they didn't go off again, he lost interest and set his focus back on Brooks.

"I didn't take anything," Brooks said.

"You can tell us about it in the back; we'll need a statement to give the police. Are you seventeen?"

"Yeah, but—"

"Then we don't need your parents."

The mall cops flanked Brooks, marching him toward the back of the store while everyone they passed stopped and stared. He glanced back over his shoulder; the easy confidence I was used to seeing on his face disappeared, replaced by wild-eyed panic.

I wondered if that was how Claire's face had looked when she stood in front of her mirror that last day. Had her eyes been so hollow in the moment before she cut into her own skin, or had she looked at herself and seen fear so deep she couldn't run from it?

"We should get out of here," Dex said. I had stopped just outside the door and he was getting nervous.

"Why did you lie about our names? Courtney and Daley could get in trouble."

"Courtney's mom works for the biggest law firm in the state; no one's going to get near him. Daley's grandfather's in Congress. Wherever they are, it's not here, and they most likely have witnesses to say so. Now let's go before someone wonders why we're still lingering."

He headed for the mall's main doors, but I hung back. The thrill of knowing Brooks was finally getting to experience the smallest fraction of the misery he'd inflicted on others lasted only as long as it took me to realize that at seventeen, he could be locked up and out of my reach.

"What about Brooks?" I asked.

"Brooks' old man is made of Teflon—nothing's going to stick." He started walking again. "Are you coming?"

"I don't bail on my friends."

"Suit yourself, but do you really think he'd do the same for you? If you change your mind, I'm at the fairgrounds. Ask for me at the front gate; they'll let you in for free."

Dex sped up to a lazy jog until he was out of sight. As soon as he was gone, Brucey came out of hiding, grinning like the idiot I suspected he'd become.

"I did good. I did good." He started doing a stupid dance right there in the middle of the mall. "That's two points for me and none for you. I think I'm better at this whole revenge thing than you are."

"Brucey!" I slapped him as close to the back of his head as I could reach. I'd do worse than that to Tabs if I found out Brucey had escaped while she was on another bathroom run. "Shoplifting was *not* part of the plan! Observation and information—not incarceration!"

At the rate he was going, my long-term-vengeance scenario would be over in a matter of days. Shoplifting was nothing in the course of someone's life. Brooks might even get it taken off his record when he turned twenty-one, assuming the charges stuck at all. After that, he would get to live like nothing had ever happened. He deserved worse.

"I improvised—modified Wookiee-prisoner gambit," Brucey said.

"English, Brucey. I don't speak Star Wars."

He held his hands out in front of him, wrists together like they were handcuffed.

"I confess," he said. "Take me away and go bail out the bad guy."

"You got him arrested so you could turn around and get him unarrested?"

"He's not arrested yet."

"They've probably already called the cops; you'll get arrested if he doesn't."

"They can't arrest me. I never left the store with their property—all I did was move it to a new location within the store itself. That's not theft; I've checked. Besides, they know me here."

"Define 'know.' "

"I *might* have used a certain store or two to perfect my pick-pocketing skills, and I *might* not have been so good at it the first few times out. They won't even question it if you tell them I took something. All I have to do is claim I panicked; Dr. Useless will back me up. That's the beauty of a compulsive diagnosis—it's compulsory. Don't you know I can't help myself?"

Dr. Useless is the psychiatrist Brucey's parents make him see because, so far as they know, his habit of "reallocating resources" (his pet name for picking pockets) is something he does subconsciously. According to her, he feels helpless in his own life, so he reaches out to take the things he knows he can't have otherwise.

Brucey's got the exact wording framed on his wall between the street signs he stole when we were in seventh grade. There should really be a law that says any shrink treating a patient should have to have a higher IQ than said patient. Brucey's been leading Dr. Useless down trails of false diagnoses since he was eleven and discovered he could look up symptoms online. He considers it real-life experience at Method acting.

"Tell the rent-a-cops you saw me bump into your guy and that I confessed to taking the necklace. The Omen gets released, and you're his new hero." He stuck his hands out farther and shook them at me. "Just do it. You don't have time to think about it. Oh, and Casanova's phone is in my back pocket. I'm done with it, so you can tell him someone turned it in at customer service."

"Please tell me this at least worked in the movie," I said as I shoved him back into the store.

"I did mention it was modified, didn't I?"

Tabs was right. We were all going to end up in jail.

16

The door to the mall's security office stood slightly open to the hall. One of the mall cops sat at a desk with some kind of form pulled up on his computer. The other was on the phone, most likely calling the real police. Brooks was in a chair beside the desk, scowling straight ahead with his fingers clenched around the edges of the seat. His face kept waffling between red and white as anger and fear fought for control of his complexion.

"What's your name?" the mall cop asked.

"My dad's attorney is Ryland Hamilton. His office is in the Briars. I'll give you his phone number."

"*Your* name, son. I have to fill out the form."

"My dad's attorney is Ryland Hamilton. His office is in the Briars. I'll give you his phone number."

"How about your address?"

"My dad's attorney is Ryland Hamilton. His office is in the Briars. I'll give you his phone number."

"Which display did you get the necklace from?"

"My dad's attorney is Ryland Hamilton. His office is in the Briars. I'll give you his phone number."

Brooks was pretty good with the whole name, rank, and serial number act. I wondered how often he'd needed Ryland Hamilton from the Briars to bail him out before things actually escalated to a point that required bail.

"You aren't doing yourself any favors, kid," the mall cop

said, exasperated. "You aren't a minor, and this store prosecutes shoplifters. You look like a decent young man, well-off . . . . Was it a dare? Is that it? You thought it would be fun? Or you wanted to see if you could pull it off? If you tell me what happened, I can word it so things aren't so bad."

"My dad's attorney is Ryland Hamilton. His office is in the Briars. I'll give you his phone number."

"Fine, kid. Have it your way, but this isn't—"

I knocked on the door before he could finish his useless attempt at intimidating the devil.

"Excuse me," I said.

"Is there a problem, miss?" the mall cop asked. "I'm in the middle of . . . Oh, you're the girl who was with him, aren't you?"

"Yessir," I said, nervously slurring my words.

"Good, then you can tell me his name. Your friend is refusing to see sense."

"His name's Brooks," I said. "But he didn't take the necklace." The mall cop sat up straighter and gave me his full attention. Brooks gave me the most pathetically hopeful face I'd ever seen. Brucey was brilliant. I was about to hand Brooks his life back. "I was standing right next to him; he didn't take it."

"I know you want to help him out, but lying isn't—"

"She's not lying," Brooks snapped. "I didn't do anything."

"Brucey, get your kleptomaniac keister in here."

Brucey slunk in, the personification of shame with a capital "S" to match the crooked bend of his spine. He shuffled his feet, forcing me to push him the last few steps to get him all the way through the door. His acting skills had definitely improved (hopefully without too much loss of property to anyone else).

"Brucey took the necklace, not Brooks. He dropped it in

130

Brooks' pocket when they bumped into each other near the door."

"Bateman?" the mall cop asked.

"Hi, Officer Ward," Brucey said. He kept his eyes on his hands and picked at his fingernails. "I didn't mean it. I was walking toward the door and the necklace was just there in my hand. I panicked. I ran into that guy and stuck it in his pocket when we separated."

"Bateman, you know you're not supposed to come here anymore. I thought the store made that clear the last time this happened."

"I know," Brucey said; he managed to widen his eyes enough for a pleading effect. "But I came with my friends. I thought I could handle it, Officer Ward, but I screwed up. I'm sorry. Please don't call my mom."

"You know I have to, Bateman." The mall cop's voice and manner had softened considerably, more so each time Brucey called him "Officer." "Take a seat, son."

Brucey bowed his back even farther, with a resigned sigh, and headed for an empty chair near the wall. His posture when he sat was carefully constructed: hands in his lap, toes turned in, hair falling in stringy cords to hide his face. He held it until the mall cop looked away, then brushed his hair back, grinned at me, and made a shooing motion with his hands.

"Does this mean we can go?" I asked.

"Leave me a contact number, but other than that, both of you can get out of here."

Brooks scribbled his phone number down on the notepad beside the computer and headed for the door. He held it open for me and slammed it when I was clear.

"You okay?" I asked.

"They could have at least apologized." He ran his hands over his hair, then did it again and again. What I had taken for an anger-fueled calm in the office now seemed like something else entirely. He couldn't stay still, but fidgeted with his hands and clothes and hair the whole way down the hall and out of the store. The pale cast to his face hadn't changed.

"I'm sorry," I said.

"You didn't do anything."

"I'm sorry about Brucey. . . . It wasn't an accident. He did it because of me."

"You told him to get me arrested?" Brooks stopped and stared at me, a bit of the edge creeping back into his features.

"Nothing like that. He's . . . well, Brucey's weird. He's like the overprotective big brother I never wanted, and that was his idea of a high-five. He likes you; he wanted to see how you'd react."

"What's he do if he *doesn't* like someone?"

"Forgets to confess."

"Terrific." He gave me another one of those puffed-out laughs like in class, only this time it was a dark sound, more tears than laughter. "My dad's not going to believe that."

"But they didn't call your dad," I said. "You didn't give them your name."

"I gave them Ryland's. Dad's the only one of his clients with a teenage son. If they called him, he'll call my dad. Which means that Dad will be waiting for me when I get home."

"I could go with you and explain what happened if you think it would help. I sort of need the ride anyway. Tabs took my car."

The rest of my plan solidified the second he accepted my offer. If Brooks' dad was that easily swayed to disappointment or disapproval of his son, then it wouldn't take much to inflict maximum damage. If I was lucky, his dad might even cut him off, so he'd get to see what it was like to live like one of the people he thought he could throw away. Maybe a taste of life without a safety net would do him some good.

Maybe it wouldn't. I didn't really care.

17

Brooks' house was definitely the home of someone who belonged at a place like Lowry. Green ivy ran up two exterior walls of a mansion that would have swallowed Uncle Paul's as an appetizer, as though the grounds were trying to reclaim the stones by pulling them down. Dense, dark clouds blocked any direct sunlight, creating the illusion of twilight in the middle of the day, and a chill wind twisted around my throat with the feel of a tightening cord. The closer we came to the front door, the slower Brooks moved.

In old movies, this would have been where the orchestra cued up something heavy and mournful, set to the cadence of running feet or a hammering heart.

"Your dad will understand." It took mentally superimposing Brucey's face over Brooks' to make myself sound sincere, but I managed.

"You'd be surprised what my dad can misinterpret when he wants to."

"We could call Dex for backup. Two have to be better than one."

"Dad wouldn't believe Dex if he was strapped to a polygraph on truth serum."

"Why not?"

"He's not allowed on the property, for one thing, so the chances of his being able to help are pretty slim. And if Dad finds out that I was anywhere near Dex this morning, it'll be worse."

"So we won't mention him," I said, careful to keep my voice and mannerisms as Claire-like as possible. "And if your dad doesn't know about the mall, we'll just tell him I came by early for our study session. It'll be fine."

Brooks didn't answer other than a nervous nod as he put his hand to the door and pushed, showing me inside, where the wood grain and wallpaper made what sunlight there was nearly disappear. The haunted storybook atmosphere deepened. Chandeliers and lamps made of colored glass turned the space into something with all the warmth of a library's antiquities stack.

I followed Brooks down the first hall, turning toward a closed office door when he did. His shoulders got tighter and tighter, and before I realized what I was doing, I'd bunched closer to him, like the dumb blonde in a horror movie. He raised his hand to knock but stopped.

"I'm sorry," he said. "In advance, for whatever my dad does or says . . . I'm sorry."

Then he knocked.

"Come in," said an accented male voice.

Brooks closed his eyes, breathed out, and pushed the door open.

"Dad, I—"

"I've just been on the phone with Ryland."

"I know—"

"He told me something disturbing."

"I know, but—"

Brooks' father stood from his seat behind the desk. He was

taller than I expected, and older—probably twenty years older than my dad—with silver hair and posture so straight he must've been bolted to a yardstick. The way he spoke, and then moved as he slid around the desk to face us, made me want to check for fangs to match the crystal blue eyes.

Behind him, high on the wall, hung a life-sized painting of him when his hair only had a few silver streaks in it. A beautiful young woman with dark hair and Brooks' smile stood beside him, and he held a small boy in the crook of his elbow. I supposed that was Brooks; it had to be a family portrait.

"I told him he had to be mistaken," he said. "That it had to be someone else's teenage son accused of theft, because mine knows better. *My* teenage son would know the consequences of something so foolish."

"He didn't do it," I said, not sure at what point I'd hidden behind Brooks' shoulder.

Brooks' dad stiffened and stood taller, though I don't know where he found the extra inches; he somehow managed to look like he was crossing his arms even though they were straight down at his sides.

"I was with Brooks this morning, Mr. Walden," I said. "He only gave security your lawyer's name because they wouldn't stop asking him questions."

"I didn't realize you had brought company, Brooks."

"She's not company."

"Then who exactly are you?" he asked. Claire would have melted under that laser stare of his, but I let a bit of myself bleed through the impersonation and stared right back. Stodgy aristocrats in suits were nothing compared to the sort of fear you feel when you find yourself in your underwear in a locker

136

room with fifteen other girls who think you're a freak because you'd rather dye your hair black than blond.

"I'm Dinah," I said. "I'm in Brooks' class at Lowry."

Brooks' father looked me up and down without bothering to hide his opinion of the way I was dressed. Maybe there wasn't that much difference between a crusty aristocrat and a teen queen with a padded bra after all.

"I wasn't aware the Board of Regents had approved another scholarship for this term."

Brooks winced, but this was something I could handle. He was nothing but my mother made into a man.

"Actually, if I knew enough to get a scholarship, I wouldn't need your son to tutor me."

And just like that, the old man's mood changed; I became invisible.

"You didn't tell me you had decided to reinstate yourself as a tutor, Brooks."

"It wasn't planned," Brooks said; it sounded like his throat had gone dry. "Dinah's new, so I told her I'd help her catch up. It's not that big a deal."

"On the contrary, it's one of the few sensible decisions you've made in months. Your mother would approve."

An interesting way to put it, I thought, especially knowing that Brooks' mom didn't exist in his school records. I had assumed a divorce, but that wasn't likely if Brooks' dad still considered what she would and wouldn't like about her son's behavior.

Brooks' dad went back to the green leather chair behind his desk and reached for the phone. "I'll inform Ryland that his services won't be required. You may go."

I'm in.

I texted while I waited in Brooks' room for him to shed his "charity superstar" persona and turn back into the evil villain/trig tutor version of himself I knew and loathed.

Dropped into hot zone--Brooks' house.

His profile picture and obsession with doodling made a lot more sense after seeing his personal space. There were concept sketches of houses and high-rises, even sci-fi-style future palaces scattered over his desk, the one place not kept completely spotless. Tubs of high-end colored pencils and markers divided the top into sections dedicated to drawing and schoolwork. A charcoal-stained tablet and stylus had been shoved under a pile of discarded papers, leading me to make another mental note about Brooks' personality—he was more analog than digital.

And he absolutely could not draw people. Any time there was a person in one of his pictures, it was a stick figure used to hold a place, or a cutout from a magazine.

Bad guy in sight?

appeared on my phone.

Bathroom.
Hide panties under bed. Tell girlfriend.
Shut up, Brucey.

Brucey still in trouble, it's Tabs. Lose the undies.
Tabs!

If I'd had on a skirt, it would have been possible, but in shorts, I'd have had to strip. And despite Tabs' opinion that being caught bottomless would speed things up on the getting-Brooks-to-like-me front, I wasn't planning on that sort of tutoring session. What good would it do to add one more pair of panties to the collection of a guy who'd probably already taken possession of underwear from every girl in class?

Computer close?

she asked.

Yes.
Email me so we can backtrace IP.

I actually hesitated on that one. Hacking someone's computer could lead to serious trouble if we got caught, and it was one more digital trail, but she was right. If we wanted to really ruin Brooks, then any messages or emails had to look like they came from him. To do that, we'd need his IP so Brucey could work his magic.

I shut off my conversation with Tabs and ran my finger across the trackpad on Brooks' laptop where it sat open on his desk. All of my muscles tightened, anticipating, maybe even hoping for, a locked screen or alarm. I was already running through viable excuses to explain away why I'd been on his computer when it switched on, no password required.

So much information right there for the taking . . .

It was too tempting not to try and scan for anything useful, so after shooting a blank email to Tabs' phone, I went exploring.

For a guy with no extra security on his system, Brooks was meticulous. He'd wiped his chat logs when school started, and the only photos were of people at Lowry—mainly Dex and Chandi, but almost never at the same time. And despite appearances to the contrary at school, it seemed that Jordan was as much a part of the inner circle as the other two. Considering how antagonistic she was to Dex, and how often Dex's eyes were glued to her chest or her butt, it was possible that they had once been a happy foursome, with she and Dex being an item. That was an information gap I needed filled, and quick. Angry exes of best friends were gossip gold mines.

"What are you doing?"

Brooks stood in the door, staring at me in his newly changed clothes. The greenish halo of a nearly healed bruise was now visible on his leg where he'd changed into a pair of shorts, and it seemed that the scratches on his face were part of a matched set that went with the ones on his arm.

"Making Dex regret running out on you at the mall," I said, switching the screen to something that would back me up. Thankfully, he couldn't see it from the bathroom.

"With my computer?" he asked.

Brooks came closer, circling around for a better look, so I showed him my cover story. The home page for Uncle Paul's brainchild filled the screen with a superpowered avatar in the "launch" position.

"You said he's a Meta nut, right?" I asked. "He plays Empyrean?"

"Since before the game went global, but I don't—"

"As of now, you're immortal and carry a bottomless bag of ambrosia chips. Challenge him to a duel; he'll last ten seconds. I can give you the kill code if you want to cut that down to two."

"Isn't this the sort of thing that gets people banned?"

"My uncle created the game. I used his override code."

"Your uncle Paul is Paul Reed?"

"Yeah, and I'm *still* not used to that reaction." I cringed, certain he was about to add me to Uncle Paul and come up with Claire. But it seemed that her enrollment in Lowry wasn't the only secret she never told him.

"You might want to keep that to yourself," he said. "Otherwise, Dex will never give you a moment's peace for the rest of your life or his."

Brooks took the seat I yielded at his desk and started playing with his new avatar. A slow smile spread over his face as he took it through some basic test motions in the game's training area.

"You like?" I asked.

"Definitely," he said, then lopped the heads off a row of goblins. "Dex'll be furious. I've never gotten a single point off him . . . this'll kill him."

He laughed.

It must have been terrible for the little prince to not excel at something by virtue of his reputation, especially when the guy who was beating him didn't need cash to win. I felt a pang, remembering Dex's caution that just because we all wore the same uniform, it didn't mean we were equals.

I took a seat on Brooks' bed, as there were no other chairs, and crossed my legs.

"Did you tick off a feral cat or something?" I asked, pointing to the marks on his arm.

He glanced down and flexed, as though he were testing the muscle.

"I said Chandi *hardly ever* draws blood—not that she *never* does. You get used to it."

Another block of ice dropped into my stomach. He said it so casually, and without stopping the test slaughter on-screen, as though provoking a girl to physical (and most likely self-protective) violence were a normal part of life. That thought dovetailed with another, darker one: for Brooks, maybe it was.

Maybe evil didn't look like the half-mangled ghoul in a slasher movie. Maybe it didn't come with any sort of obvious sign that screamed "Run from me or I will destroy you." Maybe it came in designer clothes, and wore the face of a friend because the slow fall paid off better in the long run.

I'd seen the way Chandi stuck to Brooks. . . . Real evil didn't need to chase someone down with a chain saw. Its victims were volunteers.

18

The threat of Brooks' father being so close put him on his best behavior and got me stuck having to endure an early trig-tutoring session for real. For forty-five minutes the only thing we discussed involved numbers and angles. I was at the point of reconsidering Tabs' panty drop when he shut his book.

"Are we done?" I asked.

"You've got the idea well enough to make it through next week," he said, "and I'm fried. If I don't switch gears, my brain's going to toss one. We can take a break. Dad should be gone by now."

Finally. Progress.

Brooks stood up and stretched. I set my borrowed paper and pencil on his bed and did the same, while trying to mimic the sort of innocent, bewildered look I'd seen on Claire's face a million times. This had to be the setup he used. Empty room. Empty house. It was perfect . . . which is why it was such a shock to hear him say: "Wanna stretch your legs?"

He twisted his head far enough to the side to pop it and headed for the door.

"Where are we going?"

"Away from anything trig-related. I hate being cooped up in here. Come on, I'll give you the tour."

I followed him out the door into a second-story hall that started with his bedroom and led to what were apparently a lot of empty ones for guests. (Though if Brooks' dad was so averse to having people over, I couldn't see why he needed them.)

It was very nearly like my first impression of Lowry, the way the scale and grandeur eclipsed the more interesting details of the place. I'd first noticed things like how the hall was so long it could have been used for a perspective study in some art composition class, but not the way the rug was only worn from the space between Brooks' room and the stairs, as though he was the only who ever walked on it.

I'd noticed how all the pictures on the wall were framed in the sort of gold gilt that belonged in a European museum with thick red ropes to protect them from the fingerprints of anyone who got too close, but not how they were actual paintings.

I'd noticed the stained-glass window at the end of the hall with its swirls of pearly color, but not how clouds banking up outside had turned iron-gray to say a storm was coming.

Brooks cleared his throat to draw my attention away from the portraits.

"Awful, isn't it," he said. "Now do you get why I hate all that blue-blood insanity?"

"Wait . . . you mean these are relatives? They're not just paintings?"

"Paintings? Mademoiselle, I am highly insulted. This is the pedigree of kings." He did a dead-on impression of his father's accent and straightened his spine until it looked almost painful, taking on the bearing of some snooty museum docent. It didn't exactly fit the T-shirt and shorts, but it definitely made an impression. "You're lucky they're all dead, or else they would be highly insulted as well, and then they would be forced to pay someone to mock you or smite you or something else they couldn't be bothered to get off their cushioned seats for."

I hadn't snorted a laugh since I was ten and doing so sent chocolate milk through my nose, but right then, I snorted from trying to hold back, and had to slap a hand over my nose and mouth.

Brooks took the sound as his cue to make things worse and give me the introduction to a seemingly endless list of people with too many names and too many titles. There were earls and ladies, and dukes and duchesses, and even something called a viscount (which, apparently, is not the same as a count). When I said a marchioness sounded like she should have a baton to twirl, the glaze over Brooks' features cracked and he laughed, too.

I was falling back into that space I'd landed in during class when something about him tamped down my defenses, so in my head I kept repeating "He really is a royal pain in the ass" until I was able to get a grip on myself. It was preferable to thinking how he probably spun things with girls like Claire to paint himself as an authentic Prince Charming.

"I don't get the hate," I said. "What's wrong with knowing where you come from?"

"Nothing, so long as there's not someone trying to drag you back into the Dark Ages. Dad puts way too much emphasis on this stuff. I've yet to figure out why he moved to a country without royalty."

"For your mom?" I guessed.

"Then that would make it the first and only concession he's ever made."

Just like that, the light mood broke and Brooks headed for the stairs as a perfectly timed thunderclap rattled the chandeliers.

Brooks was starting to remind me of a puzzle I had when I was little—one of those cubes with the different-colored squares scattered over the sides. Every time I'd come close to solving it, I'd make the last turn only to realize that the corners didn't match up the way I expected. I'd missed a step somewhere.

I was no better at backtracking with that thing to find my mistakes than I was at trying to figure out where I'd gone wrong in anticipating Brooks' next move. Mainly because I kept waiting for moves he never got around to making. He didn't even take his hands out of his pockets until he needed them to open the door and let us outside.

We left the house through a different door from the one we'd come in, so I figured that unless he was kicking me out the servants' entrance or something, he wasn't planning on taking me home yet. The door he chose led to the back of the property, where the mansion's shape created a courtyard framed by stone walls covered in ivy, and an unquantifiable heaviness to the air itself that defied anything living to move through it.

A cobbled path lined with flowers and old-fashioned iron lanterns weaved through a place that could have been an exhibit at the botanical gardens. It even had a bridge and a shallow pond full of oversized goldfish.

Brooks ignored the marked walkway and turned past a set of stone benches, cutting through a hedgerow. I followed, not sure where we were going but hoping that if I kept up with him, we'd end up somewhere productive or informative.

But we weren't really going anywhere, and we were getting there at light speed. He stopped, as though he'd hit a wall I couldn't see or reached the end of an invisible choke chain, pivoting on his heel and heading back the way we came. He'd only gone a few steps when he did it again, pacing the same line over and over.

"Are you okay?" I asked.

"I'm perfect, haven't you heard," he snapped back. "No problems in my world."

Piles of dark steel clouds painted everything with the surreal, hyperpigmented appearance that happens right before a storm, so the trees were a little greener, the stone a little brighter. Brooks stood against the sky with an outline to his clothes and skin as though he'd been cut out of reality.

He kept pacing, tightening the line as his movements grew more erratic. He couldn't keep his hands still; they clenched and unclenched, pulled at his sleeves, wiped at the back of his neck. I think if there'd been something handy other than me or walls that would have broken his fists, he'd have punched it.

"Everyone's got problems," I said. Though to be honest, I wouldn't have believed that before seeing him with his dad and feeling how one look from the man could knock the wind straight out of your lungs and the warmth off your skin. Brooks really did seem perfect when he wasn't at home . . . if I discounted everything I knew about him and Claire and who knew how many girls just like her, of course.

"Sometimes that house is so dense I can't breathe," he said.

"I have to get out and into the open air or else I'll suffocate under the shellac."

"At least you've got a good place to think when you want to get out," I offered. "This place is gorgeous."

Everything was pristine, fairy-tale unreal with the added effect of the prestorm lighting, and expertly manicured. The flowers grew in neat rows, color-coordinated so that they were darkest to the back, toward the house, and lightest in the front, creating a cascade. The last blooms of the summer's trumpet vines still stood out in bright orange and white against the climbing ivy, and all the different floral scents mixed with the first hint of a coming rain. Things couldn't have been more exact if a genie had popped up and someone wished for a secret garden.

"He built it for Mom, but it's nothing but another image that has to be maintained," Brooks said, grabbing the nearest flower and yanking it off its stem. "These plants, this lawn, those stupid paintings upstairs . . . are all meant to remind me who I'm supposed to be. Everything here is arranged and pruned and groomed and so perfectly placed that sometimes I want to break a window just to prove to myself it's real and not some never-ending nightmare I can't snap out of."

He crumbled the flower in his hand and let it fall in a browning clump of ruined petals.

"I can't figure him out. Sometimes he acts like he hates me; others it's like he's forgotten I exist . . . and I shouldn't be dumping any of this on you. Sorry. You've got enough to deal with."

"I don't mind listening." I could taste the betrayal on my tongue as I said it. I *didn't* mind listening, and I couldn't quite convince myself it was because I wanted to hear him run his mouth about everything wrong with this life. The offer was real, and I hoped Claire would forgive me for it. "And I doubt your dad hates you."

"Let me put it this way—he was using his nice face because there was a stranger in the room and he didn't want to be rude."

I nearly choked. Not from what *he* said, but because of what *I* almost said. It was a Brucey response, an inside joke, actually, from one of his old black-and-white movies where the censors operated like Uncle Paul and wouldn't let people use real curse words. Something like "jeepers" or "yowza" wouldn't have made sense to Brooks, except maybe to make him laugh, but to me it was a warning. Either I was slipping too far into character, or he was breaking through my best efforts to maintain nothing but contempt for his existence.

"He can barely look at me most days; the others he avoids me altogether. I know why . . . I mean, it's no secret I look more like her than him. Everyone who knew her says it." He bent down, scooping a few small rocks into his hand, and started throwing them at the side of a garden shed painted like a cottage. One would hit and clang off the side and he'd throw the next one harder, until he looked like someone pitching the World Series.

"How long's she been gone?" I asked as my nerves knotted up. I let my eyes stray back to the bruise on his leg and the scratches on his arm and face. Brooks was about the same size as Dex, and I already knew how difficult it was to get away from Dex when he wanted to follow. If Brooks really did have a temper, and decided to act on it . . .

Having his dad around wasn't such a bad idea anymore.

"Almost five years, and he still acts like she's going to join us for dinner. I think that's why he's made it his life's mission to make sure I'm never happy. He can't stand seeing her smile on someone else's face; it ruins his illusions."

Something clenched inside my chest. My hand was reaching out to touch his arm before I could remind myself he didn't deserve my pity. The barrier I'd put up in my brain to keep track of all Brooks Walden–related information had begun to collapse, and he was bleeding into the part reserved for people who weren't sociopaths in the making. I should have been cheering for the knowledge that his life wasn't the nonstop carousel of sunshine and rainbows everyone thought it was, or that the universe hadn't completely let me down and he was paying for the things he'd done.

Instead, I nearly hugged him.

Hate's a difficult thing to maintain in the context of actual events that blur the black-and-white lines. Absolutes are easier.

"He can't hate you," I said. "If he did, he wouldn't have stayed here. He'd have packed you up and shipped you back to wherever it is he came from."

"I used to think that, too. Then I realized doing that would mean showing up in public with his American son, and he wouldn't do that. My voice grates his nerves. He says it's unrefined."

"I like your voice," I said—another cringe moment.

Brooks must have taken my self-flagellation as embarrassment because he looked down, too, and grinned. His ears turned pink.

As he started to speak, likely to tell me what a bubble-brained idiot I'd turned into, the color that had crept into his face left it, leaving him pale and blank. A cold, fat raindrop landed square on my forehead; another hit my hand when I opened it flat to make sure the first one was rain and not me getting dive-bombed by a bird.

"We need to get back." Brooks slipped past me and walked quickly back toward the house. "Storm's coming. We should get inside."

"It's barely sprinkling."

"Come on."

The few intermittent drops picked up into a steady pitter-patter against the grass and stone, with just enough space between impacts that what fell dried on contact before the next drop could reinforce it. Still, Brooks sped his pace to a jog, turning toward the nearest door and ducking inside just as it started to pour. He shut the door behind us, leaning against it, shaking and unable to catch his breath.

"Brooks?"

"I'll be fine, just give me a minute."

Beneath his feet, where he was leaned against the door, water began to pool, darkening the cement floor. It touched his shoe, and he launched backward, farther into the room.

"Is this seriously because of the rain?" I asked. Even the Wicked Witch of the West didn't hotfoot it away from water that fast.

"I told you—I don't like water."

"Yeah, but I didn't think you were serious about the whole skipping puddles part of it."

"Well, I was! Sorry. Let me catch my breath, okay?"

This was more than someone needing a pool float to go in the deep end; this was serious, book-a-spot-on-the-couch, psychiatrist territory. That annoying sting pricked my chest again, and there was no sense hoping for a heart attack. I felt sorry for the creep.

"I know how this looks," Brooks said. "And in my mind, I know it's stupid, but I can't help it. I almost died in that hospital when I was a kid, and somehow that rewired my reflexes to treat water like poison. . . . Go ahead and laugh."

"I don't find it funny."

"You probably want to leave now, don't you?" he asked. "I don't blame you."

"That would require going outside, and I'm not going to be the one responsible for your going into cardiac arrest."

How's that for irony? I had a perfect, believable, excusable means of dealing with Brooks, and I wasn't going to take it. If I felt sorry for him, anyone else would, too.

"I guess this means you don't spend too many summers at the Point, huh?"

"There's other stuff to do there. So long as I stay out of the lake, I'm fine."

And the pier was definitely out of the lake.

"Chandi and I used to catch the movie there every weekend. It was our own silly tradition."

"But not anymore?"

"This year's been rough on her. Family drama, you know?"

"I'm acquainted with the concept."

"Thanks," he said, "for the distraction. I can drive you home. If I'm in the car, it's— Oh no . . ." He rushed to the window and pressed his hands and forehead against the glass, straining to see something in the distance. "I think I left the top down."

"Maybe it won't last long."

"I hope not. Otherwise, we'll have to take one of my dad's."

I hadn't paid any attention to where we'd actually ended up when Brooks all but locked us in out of the rain. I assumed it was another part of the house I hadn't seen yet, but the cement floors should have been a clue. It was a garage—twice as big as Uncle Paul's and just as full. Only, where Uncle Paul had classic fixer-uppers for Dad and off-road toys for himself, these were all high-end, and mainly European, sports cars.

"The Beemer's the only one that's really mine, but the keys to the others are on the wall if I want to use one. Dad couldn't care less."

Brooks' voice droned in the background while I went into a daze. Side by side, the cars in that garage represented the net worth of a small country. Any one of them could have paid for our old house. And one of them . . . one of them . . .

"Oh my God . . . this is a Bugatti Veyron." I reached out to touch the two-tone black and silver piece of art on wheels but couldn't quite convince myself that laying skin to paint wouldn't make the whole thing burst and disappear like a stray thought bubble. I settled for drooling in awe. "My dad would kill just to be in the same zip code as one of these."

"You've never seen one?"

"Mechanic shops in the-middle-of-nowhere western Oregon don't service too many cars with sticker prices out of the five-figure range." Most of them were in the four-figure range, actually. "Uncle Paul's the only one in my family with money; once things with Claire are settled, this Cinderella's going back in the ashes."

"Your cousin Claire? The one in the hospital?"

"Yeah," I said, carefully, and probably too quickly. "Does your dad actually let you drive this?"

"No one's ever driven it, but he wouldn't care if I did. He sort of went off the deep end after mom died and bought all this stuff. I don't think he's thought about it since. He says money's meaningless, as there's always more of it, and it's worthless in the long run if you can't use it to accomplish the things you really need it to do."

I wondered if the thing it couldn't do was save Brooks' mom. Money sure hadn't done Uncle Paul or Aunt Helen any favors with Claire.

"What's that look?" he asked.

Inside, I was screaming at myself for not keeping my emotions on a tighter rein. I didn't know what look was on my face, whether it was a smile or a frown or a thinly veiled desire for Brooks to fall headfirst into a vat of boiling motor oil, so I said the only thing I could. "You're not what I expected."

He couldn't say everything I told him was a lie.

19

"Kill the car."

I had been right about the rain; it didn't last long—barely ten minutes, in fact. Ten long, grueling minutes that tested my sanity and forced me to hang on to my anger by sheer force of will under the onslaught of a perspective I never wanted. They were also ten minutes that produced a surprising stumbling block to my ultimate goal of turning Brooks Walden into a shell of his current self, because for those ten minutes he continued to make me wonder if the Brooks Walden everyone saw wasn't a shell already. Learning his weaknesses was supposed to give me leverage, not second thoughts.

He knew who his father expected him to be, and who his friends needed him to be, and maybe even who he wanted to be, but the longer I sat on the cold cement of his garage floor, the more painfully clear it became that he was fast losing his ability to juggle the different personas or even find common ground between them.

Maybe that was what made it so easy for him to slip into someone so awful.

Once we noticed the rain was no longer pinging off the roof, I told him I needed to get home. We checked on the BMW and found that the port cochere had covered the interior, so it was dry enough for Brooks to drive me home. Tabs and Brucey (freshly rescued from the mall cops by Dr. Useless)

155

were waiting for me, and the sum total of their input since we'd started combing through the afternoon's events was "Kill the car." It was most likely my fault, as I may have—momentarily—let my focus slip off our brainstorming and back to the Veyron. Once or twice. (Twelve times, tops.)

I'm a car guy's kid, what can I say?

"I'd kill *you* before I put a dent in that car," I said.

Brucey popped his eyes up over his open laptop.

"This is becoming a nasty habit—threatening violence and planning demises. Once is temporary insanity; twice is a career path. Not saying you shouldn't go with your strengths, but think how it's going look on a job application under 'experience.'"

We were back in Uncle Paul and Aunt Helen's kitchen with Brucey once again trenched in behind his computer (and supposedly data-mining the haul from Brooks' phone). Tabs was pure *Twilight Zone* material, standing beside the oven wearing Aunt Helen's duck apron while she stirred what she had started calling "the secret recipe" (basically, Betty Crocker mixed with a bottle and a half of her mom's capsule stash). I was in charge of dying icing with food coloring, which would have been easier if Brucey hadn't poked his fingers in the bowl every twenty seconds.

"Kill the car," Tabs said again. "It's a big-ticket item; seeing it destroyed will draw a lot of attention. Remember that wreck two years ago? It made the news just because there was a pair of Porsches in it. That thing he's got would make waves if he chipped the paint. If it looks like our social deviant is to blame, then all the better."

"You're not touching the car. End of discussion."

"We don't have to destroy it," Tabs said. "We could use it as a set piece. A pair of underwear, a bottle of booze, maybe some pills under the backseat . . . then we get him pulled over."

"No! What is it with you and my panties today?"

"I never said they had to be yours." Tabs wiggled her butt and reached for a set of hideous oven mitts shaped like trout.

"Can I please put a fish in the wheel well?" Brucey asked. "I've always wanted to see if that would work. Pleeeeease?"

"How much of this have you eaten?" I slid the bowl of frosting out of his reach.

"Four fingers' worth." Brucey held up his hand, which was stained with splotches of the blue and purple coloring I'd been using to make black, then hooked a finger in the frosting bowl to scoot it back to his side of the table.

"Did you spike the frosting, too?"

"Fine." He pouted. "Then what about the Ping-Pong ball thing like with Mr. Weir? No damage to the car, just a lot of annoyance."

He was referring to a prank we had pulled our freshman year. We had a shop teacher named Mr. Weir, who was a total caveman. For two weeks he kept telling me that he was sure a slot in home ec would open up soon, no matter how many times I told him I had signed up for shop on purpose. When he refused to accept my class project, claiming I must have had my dad do it for me, I got Brucey to bump the lock on the shop garage after school and dropped a Ping-Pong ball into the fuel line of the senior class's year-long restoration project.

The first time Mr. Weir took it out on the road, it drove fine . . . for a while. Once the ball got sucked into the fuel line, it would clog and stall. Without the car running, the ball would drop, so there was nothing wrong with the line when he checked it. As far as I know, he never figured out what was wrong or who had done it. I certainly didn't volunteer any information; by that time I was across the hall playing with my Easy-Bake Oven like a good little girl.

Like I said, I'm a car guy's kid.

"That only works with classics. New cars have filters that prevent things from falling into the line and clogging them—and don't bother mixing the gas with sugar or linseed oil. It's not reliable, and it could damage more than Brooks' reputation. We don't want collateral damage. Besides, the car's locked up inside the house's security system in the garage. We can't get to it. What are you playing with? Putting his head on someone else again?"

Brucey had tuned me out, focusing squarely on his screen for longer than I thought his attention span was capable of lasting.

"I am not a one-trick pony," he said. (I assume that was another of those weird expressions he picked up from watching old movies in his sleep.) "I have new wallpaper. Check your phone."

His ringtone went off in my pocket, earning me a high-pitched and half-sung "Yay, it worked!" from Brucey. I opened the incoming message to a phonecam video of Brooks' perp walk with security at the mall. The whole thing lasted less than ten seconds, but it was a perfect shot of Brooks' face with that "Busted" look.

"I made an avatar-sized one, too, if you're interested."

"I'll be interested when you tell me you've done something

useful." As much as I loved the camera work, it wasn't getting me any closer to my goal.

"Trust me, it'll be useful, but not until Monday. For now, your guy's got an interview with a college representative on Wednesday."

"He's not *my* guy," I growled. (Literally. I felt the rumble in my rib cage.)

"No, your guy is the hot one who practically lives in my backyard."

"Stop trying to set me up with your cousin, Tabs. I've been telling you no since he set the front yard on fire and called it a valentine."

"I'm not talking about Greg," Tabs said. "And it *was* a Valentine. It was shaped like a heart. I'm talking about your man of many names from the mall."

"Dex?"

"I figured out why he looked so familiar—he lives half a block over from me, right on the other side of the Massey/Peete dividing line. Three houses closer and he'd have been in middle school with us. I could hop the back fence and spy on his room."

"You didn't."

"Of course not," she said. "He's got curtains. I could sneak you in the back door if you want, though. He actually hid a key under the mat. Who does that?"

"Step away from the stove, Tabs. You've inhaled too many fumes."

The oven timer dinged and she pounced before the cupcakes had a chance to overheat by even a second. If they tasted like they smelled when she opened the oven, this plan had a real chance of success. The whole kitchen filled with the scent of warm chocolate, without a single note of anything extra.

"Speaking of changing the subject," Brucey broke in without bothering to look up. "Are we back on track? Yes? Good. As I was saying, our maniac in the making has an interview on Wednesday, and another on Friday. I'm thinking we send each a note and switch days so he shows up at the wrong one."

One of those "very" things that defines Brucey is also his ability to be very annoying. It doesn't help that he's usually right.

"Better idea—leave his calendar alone. Email them both and say something's come up and could they please reschedule for Monday afternoon. With a big shot like Brooks' dad paying the bill for whatever college he signs on to, they'll do it. They'll think he blew them off, not to mention ruining whatever they moved off their schedule to clear the time slot. His dad should love that."

"Nice."

And Brucey was off again, clacking keys in whatever zone he entered when there was a computer screen in front of his face.

"The idea that you might someday be responsible for the well-being of your own children is terrifying. Really, it is," Tabs said.

"Like knowing how to make 'special' cupcakes makes you mommy material."

"Meanwhile: boys don't make passes at girls who kick asses." She jabbed a trout at me.

Brucey quotes movies; Tabs generally sticks to things she's read on T-shirts and bumper stickers.

I would have done more than stick my tongue out at her, but my phone picked that moment to ring with the tone I'd assigned to Uncle Paul and Aunt Helen.

"Pick it up," Tabs mouthed as she fanned her cupcakes with her fish hands.

Brucey was sitting up straight; he shut his computer so he could watch. Everyone knew that tone by heart now.

There was nothing so simple or difficult as answering that ring. Over the course of my stay, the phone had become both my nemesis and my lifeline; it made me so nervous I didn't even want to handle it unless it rang. Uncle Paul would only call if he wasn't in Claire's room, because cell phones weren't allowed up there. And if he'd left the room to call, then something had happened he thought I needed to know. Whatever news waited on the other side of the Talk button was either very good or very bad, and I didn't trust my luck or my karma.

I let the phone ring again, staring at the photo of my aunt's and uncle's smiling faces that popped up on-screen with the tone, and took a deep breath before answering. Every possible piece of news had already passed through my imagination anyway. Worst-case scenario, he was only repeating something I'd already told myself.

"Hello?"

The block of ice that had been growing in my stomach started to thaw as I listened to my uncle's voice. My cheeks grew hot until I knew they were turning red, and I felt the sting in my eyes that meant they were likely heading that way, too.

"Okay, bye," I said, and hung up the phone. I laid it on the table, daring it to ring again.

"What?" Tabs asked, cringing against what I suppose my

reaction made her think was bad news, but it wasn't. I was so jumbled up and turned around inside that I'd responded with tears instead of a smile.

"They say she's showing signs of moving toward consciousness." I parroted back my uncle's words just as he'd said them, barely believing they were possible. While my luck was on a downward slide, Claire's was holding steady. "One of her monitors is picking up increased brain activity. . . . They think Claire's got a chance of waking up."

All the tears I'd stopped crying when I first read Claire's diary rushed to my eyes at once, and I was hit from both sides by sets of arms in black sleeves. Tabs' fish mitts crossed under my chin, while Brucey had us both surrounded.

It wasn't until that exact second that I realized that in my head and my heart, I'd already seen her as dead. I'd written her recovery off as impossible, and I was trying to make up for her not being there anymore, because I couldn't convince myself she would be. I was avenging a death that might not happen.

But now, there was a real shot of her opening her eyes and her mouth and telling people what I was trying to force Brooks to confess. If we were lucky, maybe she'd snap out of it in time to see his future go down in flames as hers pulled out of them. It could even speed her recovery if I was able to tell her there was one fewer obstacle waiting for her outside the hospital. All I had to do was hang on a little longer.

The rest of the weekend crawled by between calls to Oregon to give my parents updates on Claire, even though most of the time it was just me saying "Nothing's changed" or "They're still waiting to see what happens." I should probably say to give my *dad* updates, because despite my mother's continuing to fill my in-box with messages I didn't open, she never once answered the phone at home. She also never asked to talk to me when I was on with Dad and she was in the room—speaking loud enough that I could hear her.

While Uncle Paul barely spent enough time at the house to make sure I hadn't somehow knocked it down, Brucey, Tabs, and I finalized our plans with a to-do list full of problematic emails and a possible means of reaching Brooks that didn't involve destroying the Veyron. One last trip to the hospital to assure Claire that everything was going well, and I set out for school Monday morning with a real smile and a plastic-wrapped chocolate cat cupcake. (I had to confiscate the recipe magazine for Tabs' own good. We were nearing the point of sprinkles and/or glitter, and that was a step too far, even in the name of righteous vengeance.)

Reality had settled firmly into a new normal. When I pulled through Lowry's security gate, no one snuck looks at me while pretending to read things on their clipboard. No one showed the annoyed, glazed suspicion that questioned whether I'd pulled off the highway to ask for directions. That was the kind of thing reserved for used-to-be public school girls being dropped off in their father's circa 1976 Ford pickup or being picked up by an overpierced and undertanned Goth whose attitude counted as a visible accessory. I was just another bleach-blond Lowry girl in a nice car. The only reason I even rated a blip on the guards' radar was because one of them had to step out of the guardhouse to stick a permit on my windshield.

But on the inside . . . on the inside I was still me, and I was far more confused than I should have been.

No matter how many pep talks I gave myself, that annoying seed of . . . I don't even know what to call it. Maybe compassion, maybe understanding, or maybe it was the first hint that I was falling off that ledge Tabs kept warning me about, but it was the same feeling that had manifested when I was sitting next to Brooks in his garage hiding from raindrops. I actually felt bad about what I was planning, and that was a feeling I couldn't tolerate. It made me want to toss the cupcake in the nearest garbage can and tell Brooks he needed to contact those two college recruiters before he missed them both and had no way to escape his dad.

I pulled my Mustang into an empty spot near the fence and slammed the door, hoping if I chipped the paint it would generate enough anger to pull me through the homestretch. But that idea didn't last five seconds past my feet hitting the asphalt.

"Dinah!"

I knew the voice without turning around, and honestly, that was my first impulse. I wanted to spin right there in the middle of the parking lot and smile at Dex when he called my name.

(And for a girl who usually has to make a conscious decision to turn her lips up, that's a weird feeling.) I wanted to walk to the building with him the same way we'd covered most of the school my first day, but I couldn't. I had to be upset with him for not sticking around to defend his best friend at the mall. Which meant that at the same moment I was reminding myself to loathe Brooks' very existence, I had to pretend to be completely on his side.

If this lasted much longer, I was going to have to ask Brucey if Dr. Useless would give us a group discount; I'd be needing the couch next to his.

"You're mad at me," Dex said. His tone turned my stomach. I couldn't face him; I could picture the puppy eyes just fine while looking at my feet. Full frontal exposure would have melted me on the spot.

"And here I thought psychic powers only existed in comic books," I said, gritting my teeth in an attempt at sincere sarcasm.

I sped up, but his legs were long enough to catch me before I got out of range.

"I didn't mean—"

"To run away and leave Brooks to rot?" My face felt exactly the way it does when my mother accuses me of being inhospitable, so I hoped that was how it looked. "People don't do that—not to their friends."

Instead of taking the hint that I didn't want to speak to him, Dex dug his heels in.

"How long did it take them to let him go?"

"That's not the point."

"How long?"

"We left the mall ten minutes later," I said, and I'll admit it stung when he flinched on the "we."

"I told you—Teflon."

"His dad didn't do it, *I did*. All Mr. Nonstick did for his son was not believe he was innocent."

"You gave them our real names?"

Dex stopped walking, so I did the same. "I didn't have to, but I should have. What you did was practically identity theft."

The anger was coming back, stoked by an argument that was turning more real than I'd intended. For some reason, the topic shift from Brooks' involvement to Dex's was making me mad. It was like he didn't even understand that what he'd done could have gotten someone innocent into real trouble, or he knew but didn't care.

"It's not that big a deal. Brooks understands."

"Well, I don't."

There should have been a brilliant, scathing remark attached to that, but I couldn't come up with one. Instead, I settled for my best Claire-flounce, flipped my hair in his direction when I turned away, and stalked toward the building alone. Halfway across the lot, I stomped down hard on a rock that nearly punctured the bottom of my shoe and had to limp the rest of the way.

I'd always heard revenge was simple and came with its own built-in clarity so long as you maintained focus, but how was I supposed to do that? I was in pain, and physically ill from the mental stress of keeping all the different versions of myself in their proper places. My neatly ordered world was turning into a muddy Rorschach blot. Everything was a mess, and I couldn't do anything to clean it up while I was living the lie of Lowry

Dinah. I also couldn't stop being her without abandoning the whole reason I was at Lowry in the first place.

"Look, I'm sorry, okay?" Dex made up the space between us in two quick strides. He didn't even ask me about the limp. "Maybe I shouldn't have run out like I did, but I can't afford to have any spots on my record. Not if I'm going to make it into a real school after graduation."

"There was no reason to lie," I said, shaking my shoe to dislodge the rock. "And from what I hear, you're smart enough to get into any school you want."

"You really think it matters?" I was no longer the angry one in the argument. Dex's words came out bitter and sharp, as though he were spitting them out so he didn't have to taste them. "Anything, even a shadow of a doubt, can torpedo a scholarship when you're competing against a few thousand others for the same four handouts. I can't risk it—and the girl I met last Friday would have understood why. I don't have someone waiting to hand me shiny new cars or fancy phones to make up the gap."

He jerked his head toward my parking space.

"You expect me to apologize for getting a late birthday present from my aunt and uncle?"

Annoyance was no longer an act. This was real, itchy-wool-on-a-sunburn irritation.

"I don't have aunts or uncles to bail me out like that. Or to make phone calls when I can't get in somewhere on my own."

"So I call *you* on *your* being an ass, and that means *I* don't deserve to be here? I guess you aren't the guy you were last Friday, either."

This Dex, who acted like my having family with means was

betrayal incarnate, wasn't the same Dex I'd met before. This Dex I kind of hated. And if this was the Dex Abigail-not-Abby knew, then it was no wonder she said to avoid him.

He slipped directly into my path, blocking me from the front steps and forcing everyone else who was trying to climb them to split around us. I could hear them whispering, taking quick looks over their shoulders as they passed. Even though I knew this wasn't my fault, embarrassment made me want to end it, just to stop them. I was beginning to understand how Claire's fears of humiliation started, and I didn't even care that much about this place.

No one likes to be stared at; the longer it goes on, the smaller and weaker you feel. You'd rather vanish completely than endure it a second longer.

"No! I didn't mean that," Dex faltered. "I didn't mean . . . I'm really blowing this, aren't I?"

The puppy-dog look was less cute, and a lot less effective, the second time. He was no longer "Dex, the guy I find interesting," but rather an unpleasant intrusion I couldn't abide.

"Not 'are blowing.' 'Have blown.' Get out of my way."

I stepped sideways and into the flow of others headed into the building, but he blocked me again.

"I said move, Dex."

"I didn't mean to start a fight or anything. The car threw me. You look—"

"What? Like one of *them* instead of one of *us*? You should really talk to someone about this whole persecution complex you've got going. Someone other than me."

"I'm serious, Dinah!" He grabbed my arm hard enough that I actually yelped, causing my opposite hand to curl into a reflexive fist. I still don't know if it was the fist or knowing that he'd hurt me that made him let go. "And I'm trying to apologize. For real."

"You need to practice your technique." I rotated my arm, wondering if I'd have bruises under my blazer later in the day.

"I know. I suck at this, but maybe I can make it up to you?"

"Not interested."

I managed to back him up far enough that it bought me a step.

"Just hear me out. You know the fairgrounds, right?"

"Bleaching my hair had no effect on my mental capacity, thank you very much. I was raised here—yes, I know the fairgrounds."

More by reputation than experience. We'd only gone once, when I was in fourth grade and I won a set of tickets. Even then it was an all-out fight to get Mom to okay the trip; she swore that going out to a place with so many people was an invitation to be mugged or have our car vandalized. Dad said we'd go without her if she was so scared. When she realized he was serious and that we were leaving, she changed her mind. My prize became four hours of her complaints streaming over everything that would have made the place enjoyable.

"I got a seasonal job there for the run of the carnival, and I thought maybe you'd drop by."

"And I thought you'd take the hint when I didn't show up Saturday. Carnivals aren't high on my to-do list." I forced him backward, up another step. "Between here and the hospital, I don't have lot of time, and what I do have is—"

"Just one night, you have to have that much time, right? Not even the whole night—two hours. One. I'd even—"

"She said no, Dexter." Jordan-from-homeroom came up the stairs behind me, with Chandi right behind her. Tiny as she was, Jordan's temper made up for the lack of body mass. When she was close enough, she shoved Dex backward by the shoulder, spinning him just enough that I could squeeze around and get past him. "It's a small word, it shouldn't be that difficult for you to understand."

He scowled.

"I wasn't talking to you."

"So you aren't entirely stupid," Chandi said. "But you *are* hard of hearing. You asked, she answered. That's the point where you shut your mouth and walk away."

"Aren't you more into playing damsel in distress than rescuing one?"

The two of them faced off while the last arrivals of the morning craned their necks to watch. Jordan stood with her arms crossed and her feet planted in the stance of someone used to bracing for a fight, and while Dex didn't alter his usual laidback posture, there was a strain on his face I'd never seen there before. Being outnumbered wasn't his position of choice.

"I think you need a stronger bottle of Nair, Cookie," he said, leaning in close, as though he'd noticed something on her face. "Looks like you've got a bit of a beard coming through."

The corner of his mouth rose, baiting with a taunt that only made sense to the two of them. Chandi lunged and probably would have tackled him straight to the ground if Jordan and I hadn't grabbed her.

"Get out of the way, Dexter. You're blocking traffic," Jordan ordered.

"Whatever," Dex scoffed. He caught my eye over his shoulder and called "Think about it, okay?" Then he disappeared into the crowd and let them jostle him inside.

Chandi growled and tried to break loose; she almost succeeded.

"Are you okay?" I asked.

"I'm fine," she spat, reclaiming her arms from me and Jordan. The blond hair that had been so perfect the week before was out of place and stuck to her cheeks, which were bright red to match her eyes.

"He's not worth it," Jordan said. "You know that. And you know he's only trying to get a rise out of you."

"It's working," Chandi said, scrunching her face to fight the tears.

"Then make him stop."

"I can't, and *you* know *that*."

Just like Dex, Chandi darted through the main doors, leaving me with a lot of new questions and no idea how to answer them. I didn't even get to thank her for stepping in for me.

"How about you?" Jordan asked me. She bent down to pick up the book bag Chandi had dropped on the stairs and slung it over her shoulder next to her own. "You okay? We saw him grab you."

"I'm fine . . . thanks. He just caught me off guard."

"He's good at that."

"Is she going to be all right?"

"At some point." Jordan glanced back to where Chandi had disappeared through the closing doors.

"It's not really Dex's fault," I said. "If I hadn't been trying to brush him off, he wouldn't have acted like that."

"It's never Dex's fault. Ask Chandi."

"Don't tell me those two—"

"Ancient, and exceptionally short, history."

That one I definitely did not expect.

"Brooks doesn't mind dating his best friend's ex-girlfriend?"

Jordan laughed.

"Chandi and Dex didn't date; it was a very fast crash and burn that he's still fuming over. And she and Brooks, well, that's their business, but I wouldn't call it dating, either."

The ten-minute warning sounded; I was startled to realize we were the only two students left outside. Jordan started for the doors and I trailed her into the building, trying to process the new information into what I already knew. It wasn't an easy fit.

"Typical," she snorted under her breath.

I followed Jordan's sight line across the entry hall to where Dex and Brooks were talking. Dex threw us a nervous glance as we got closer. I reached them just in time to hear the end of what he was saying: "We're good, right?"

"Forget it," Brooks said. "It never happened."

"Thanks, man. I knew you'd understand."

Dex slapped him on the shoulder and hurried off before Jordan or I could challenge the no-doubt rosier version of what he'd told Brooks about the parking lot. And the mall.

"Hey," Brooks said when he noticed us. Because of him, I'd chased off the only guy at Lowry I had wanted to spend time with, and Brooks had the nerve to smile at me. . . . The morning was not improving. "How's your arm? Dex is sorry, by the way. He only wanted to get your attention."

"He wasn't trying to get her attention," Jordan said before I could. "She told him to get lost, and he decided to be an idiot and not do it. He nearly wrenched her shoulder off. Then he sent Chandi running."

"Not again," Brooks groaned. "What is it with those two?"

"Ask the waste of free oxygen."

"Jordan—"

"For once, would you open your eyes and listen to something other than what he spins in your ear? Everything he tells you, he's the only common denominator. Poor little Dexter, always getting picked on, always being tramped down, always being misunderstood."

"You know it's not easy for him."

"That's crap, Brooks. You *make* it easy for him. The ones it's not easy for are the people your pet project decides to make miserable." Jordan took a breath and looked my way on that. "You've known Chandi since you were in primary, and she's never been the kind of wreck she turned into over the summer. I'm warning you. Put your puppy on a shorter leash or someone's going to neuter him while you're not looking."

"What are you talking about?" Brooks asked.

"Figure it out. Unlike some people, I keep the secrets I've been asked to. I have to go find Chandi before your stupid friend gets her written up for ditching class."

Jordan bumped him as she stalked past, heading down the hall toward the bathrooms—the official sulk site of teen girls everywhere.

"She's always been a hothead," Brooks said. The look of confusion that popped up when Jordan started her tirade hadn't faded. "I wish one of them would just tell me what happened so I could fix it and then this wouldn't keep happening."

"Some things you can't fix."

Like putting someone in a coma. At that point, all you can do is make amends. If I kept reminding myself of that, then it would be harder for Brooks to breach my defenses.

"You're okay, aren't you?" he asked, letting his eyes linger near the top of my arm where Dex had grabbed me, as though he could see through my sleeve. "He didn't hurt you or anything. I mean, if he did, I don't think he meant to, but I'll tell him to lay off if he's bothering you."

"It was nothing," I said. No way did I want Claire's personal demon acting like he was my guardian angel. Pity was making this hard enough; gratitude would have ruined it completely. "Jordan and Chandi came in on the end and jumped to their own conclusions. I couldn't get a word in to tell them it wasn't as bad as they thought."

Brooks nodded, accepting my version without hesitation. If there was nothing wrong, then he had nothing to fix.

Excuses make everything easier on everyone. They cover up faults and erase guilt. They split the blame between the person who did wrong and the one they hurt. And they maintain the illusion; that's the most important thing when you're in the enemy's camp. Appearance is everything, and I needed to appear to be the girl who didn't care that she'd been manhandled in public and almost no one noticed.

It's all appearance, even my embarrassment. . . .

I hoped repeating that to myself enough would make it close to the truth; that way I could believe it, too. Then I wouldn't have to hate myself for acting like a victim in the making.

The two of us stood there, not discussing Dex or the growing number of complaints against him until the second warning bell rang and reminded me that bumping into Brooks was more than an unhappy accident.

"I brought you something," I said, locating Tabs' cupcake in my bag. "To say thanks for helping me and all."

"I'm the one who should be thanking you." Brooks set the cupcake on top of his books. He took the position Dex had claimed the Friday before, escorting me toward the stairs and Mr. Tarrelton's class. "If you hadn't come home with me, I'm not sure Dad would have given me the chance to explain anything. Besides, you haven't been back to class yet. You still don't know if it did you any good."

"It did." Just like Brucey's improv act at the mall.

We'd almost reached the stairs when the sound of several dozen cell phones going off filled the halls. The stragglers who were waiting until the last possible second to go into their homerooms answered them quickly, lest the sound draw teachers who would confiscate every device in sight.

Two seconds later, the snickers started, followed by whispers and pointed looks in our direction. Down the hall, one boy I hadn't met nudged his buddy with his elbow so he could point Brooks out.

"What's going on?" Brooks whispered to me.

Dex's idea that nothing could impact Brooks or his mood crumbled. His posture was beginning to take on the signs I'd seen when he was anticipating his dad's temper after the mall, and it was very close to the way I'd felt in the parking lot.

I shrugged, waiting for the second wave, which came directly after the first. Brucey had arranged things by grade level,

Seniors first, and then us. This time when the phones went off, both mine and Brooks were included. (Brucey later claimed this was to make sure I didn't stand out by omission; I think he got lazy and didn't want to do the numbers one at a time.)

Our phones, like those of every other student in the school, showed an incoming message that, when clicked, opened to Brucey's phone-vid of Brooks' brush with arrest at the mall.

Brooks turned white, giving his skin a sick sheen that nearly blended with the wall. Frantically, he tried to find the sender's information, but Brucey had sent the videos from an anonymous account through the library's terminal. There was nothing to find.

"Who would do this?" I asked, proud of myself that I managed a note or two of real concern.

"I don't know." Brooks shook his head and said it again, quieter, repeating those three words over and over while he tried to force information out of his phone it didn't contain. He even shook it like an Etch A Sketch, as though he could knock a name out of it.

A commotion built from the far end of the hall, opposite the stairs, where swells of accusation and silence filtered through as people moved out of the way of someone walking quickly past them. I recognized Ms. Kuykendall when she was about twenty feet off. (Before that, I thought she was a tall student—seriously, the woman needed to consider not dressing to match the kids in her school. It was creepy in an "I want to be a teenager forever" kind of way.) She made another of those Botox-impossible scowls and stopped beside the bannister.

"Mr. Walden, there you are," she said. "I was just on my way to Mr. Tarrelton's class to fetch you."

"Am I in trouble?" Brooks asked. He stepped in closer to me, almost leaning, like he couldn't support his own weight.

"In my office" was the only answer she gave. "Now, please."

Ms. Kuykendall executed a runway-perfect pivot and left the way she'd come. Stunned students closed the gap they'd made for her.

"This is not good," Brooks whispered. "If whoever sent that out sent it to her, too . . ."

"Just tell her what happened. She'll believe you," I said, adding a generic promise to talk to him later.

It was likely true. Once Brooks told her what happened, and assuming she even bothered to confirm it, she'd dismiss him to class. She might even apologize for wasting his time, because he was the kind of guy everyone wanted to believe the best of. This wasn't about lasting trouble—not yet.

This was the seed—the moment of first doubt to knock the shine off the white knight's armor. Once the truth came out, everyone would forget about the video. Oh, they might play it a few times and use it to make Brooks the butt of a joke here and there, but it would all be in fun. But the next time . . . the next time something happened with his name or face attached to it, belief would come that much easier, and accusation would come that much faster, because, thanks to ten seconds of digital comeuppance, there was precedent for them to assume the worst.

One misunderstanding people shrug off. Two can be called coincidence or bad luck. Pile three, or four, or more of these little moments on top of each other, and it won't matter how many times someone claims they're innocent—it won't even matter that they can prove it. People aren't wired to accept that much circumstance. That tiny seed of doubt will grow, and even friends will begin to wonder if they don't need to reevaluate how well they really know someone.

I could afford to be reassuring, and I accept that all would be forgotten by lunch, because it was only temporary. Retribution would come, carrying Justice on her shoulders. Until then I'd wait and pretend I'd be there to catch Brooks if he really did need someone to lean on. He wouldn't know it was a lie until he hit the floor.

Later turned into much later.

Brooks was twenty minutes late to class, slinking in after we'd endured one of those "famous" pop quizzes Dex had warned me about the week before. Whatever else Brooks was, Abigail-not-Abby had been right about his trig skills. He was an excellent tutor; the time I'd spent with him and his math book back in his room had bought me at least one passing grade.

Dex had morphed back into his old, and very apologetic, self, only speaking to me once to ask if I knew where Brooks was. I whispered a quick rundown about Ms. Kuykendall just before Brooks appeared at the door, tardy slip in hand, and hurried to his seat without a word.

I tried to catch his eye, hoping to get an idea of what had happened in the headmistress's office or why it had lasted so long, but he stayed hunched over his paper, taking notes with his nose nearly touching the desktop and his arm guarding his face from anyone who might be trying to get a look at him.

By lunch, whispers were everywhere. I'd seen people replay the video of Brooks on their phones and heard them fantasize about what it meant and what he'd done. All that planning between me and Tabs and Brucey, and it was nothing compared to the efficiency of a good old-fashioned rumor mill.

I meant to sit with Brooks at lunch, even if it meant dealing with Dex, to score a ringside seat (and maybe some inside information), but by the time I got into the lunchroom, Brooks and Chandi were in the middle of a three-way argument with Jordan, while their table mates pretended nothing unusual was going on.

It lasted until Chandi cut the other two off with a very loud and annoyed "I'm fine!" Then she crumbled, terror evident in her eyes, her face turning red as she scanned the room to see how many people were watching her.

Dex laughed it off, giving her a thumbs-up and an attempted pat on the back, which she jerked away from.

Abigail-not-Abby was practically doing handsprings over the apparent end of Brooks and Chandi's romance, but her joyful chatter became little more than background noise, blending with the rest of the room. Another one of those nagging questions was creating a toehold in the back of my mind. Somehow, in the span of time between dealing with Dex and our shared history class, Chandi's shirt had shrunk again. I hadn't been paying too much attention to her clothes before, but the details were easier to pick out when she was having a meltdown that guaranteed people would be watching. The shirt was too short to tuck in; it was too tight across her midsection, and just like last Friday, it required two open buttons at the top because it wouldn't close all the way.

Eventually, she realized she was the center-ring attraction and shut her mouth. Her shoulders stooped, causing her blazer to drape farther over her shirt, but there was no using Brooks for an anchor this time. Chandi leapt up and ran for the door, with Jordan chasing after her the same way she had that morning. I assumed they were headed to the bathroom again.

The fight, or whatever it was that happened in the lunchroom, must have been serious, because the layer of ice between Chandi and Brooks hadn't thawed by the time we all hit the theater for last period.

Abigail-not-Abby had her usual seat. Chandi was snarling something at Jordan in the front row, and Dex was pouting. Brooks looked very alone in the center of the room, something I rectified by taking the seat next to him.

"You okay?" I asked.

"I'm here," he said.

"Not what I asked."

"No, I'm not okay. And I'm not okay because I still can't figure out who would send that video. I don't even know who could have done it. Who was there besides you and me and Dex?"

"It's a mall." I shrugged. "There were hundreds of people there."

"Yeah, but who would have access to the school's call list? And why me? Why would someone hate me that much?"

"They probably thought it was funny. You know, a prank."

"Some prank. Ms. Kuykendall made me sit in her office for a fifteen-minute lecture where she didn't give me a chance to explain it wasn't what it looked like. She dragged out the honor code I signed at the first of the year, and ticked it off point by point to tell me how my behavior 'reflected badly on the school.' And on top of that, because it was a 'disciplinary matter,' the quiz I missed in Tarrelton's class ends up a big fat zero."

My inner self was getting that urge to do embarrassing victory dance moves again.

"So your grade drops to ninety-nine and a half?"

"I'm serious, Dinah. *This* is serious."

"Can't you tell Mr. Tarrelton what happened and ask if you can make it up? Surely with everything you've done for him, tutoring and all, he'll give you one do-over."

"I hope so. Otherwise, it'll mean a call to my father."

Inner me stopped the rah-rah routine and gave me a dirty look for that one. I didn't even want to imagine how a full-blown rage by his dad would go; the censored version had been enough to make me revert to roughly the same place I'd been in when I was in second grade and my own dad caught me with a bald cat and a pair of clippers. Only, I was never actually afraid of my dad.

"And Chandi still won't tell me what's wrong with her. All I did was ask, and she came unglued. I just want to do this presentation, find a place to hide until I have to go home, and pretend today was a bad dream," he said.

"Presentation?"

"The monologue for Cavanaugh. You didn't forget, did you?"

Crap. Crap. Crappity, crap, crap, crap.

"I'll take the look of abject horror as a yes. Think of something, quick. Most of his grades are participation, so if you do anything and hit the time limit, you're good."

"I can do that."

I could, so long as Mr. Cavanaugh didn't . . .

"Miss Powell, you're up."

. . . call on me first.

The horror of hearing my name put my body on pause. I didn't move, other than to blink in his general direction.

"In front of everyone?" I said. Maybe if I bought a few seconds with my mouth, then my brain could figure out what came next.

"Right up here." Mr. Cavanaugh stepped to the side, yielding the mark at center stage. "We know you excel at getting people's attention, so let's see if you can channel your enthusiasm into something more controlled. Preferably without removing clothes this time."

So this was my punishment for Friday's peep show. Everyone except Chandi laughed.

"Go on." Brooks nudged my shoulder. "He'll only make it worse if you wait. He's got face paint and costumes stashed backstage."

I stood up and stuffed my bag in my chair, smoothed imaginary wrinkles out of my skirt, and tugged on my blazer. I'd just have to wing it. If the universe thought hitting one little bump was going to shake me off my game, it was dead wrong.

Walking up the stage steps spurred a flashback of me, four years old, wearing a blue tutu and a bow bigger than my head. Even then, I'd hated having people look at me. I could do choreography fine in the studio, but the stage floor felt different under my feet; there were no mirrors and no barre. The light was different. All those variables threw me, and I spent the whole routine stuck in one place while the rest of the pageant girls did their turns and positions.

Maybe I *couldn't* do this.

I looked down (which, for the record, is even less advisable onstage than on a tightrope) and the first face I saw was Chandi's. She smirked as though she could smell the fear and doubt.

Abigail-not-Abby nodded to make me move toward the mark, while Dex was trying to sneak a look down Jordan's shirt from the seat behind her.

Everyone else just waited.

"Whenever you're ready, Miss Powell," Mr. Cavanaugh said. I may have nodded at him; I'm not sure. I was too busy trying not to let my eardrums explode from rising blood pressure.

I had nothing—no words, no ideas, just a silver pen in my hand that I'd forgotten to set down.

"Dinah?" Mr. Cavanaugh asked. "You okay?"

I'm sure I nodded that time.

I risked another look out at the audience and tried to focus on the fact that most of the chairs were empty; one class wasn't enough to fill even a tenth of them. The others were still there, though Dex had given up on Jordan (who was now sitting with her arms crossed over her chest and scowling). Chandi's smirk was in transition to a full-blown smile of triumph. And Brooks . . .

Something clicked.

I glanced at Brooks, then back at the pen in my hand. It was no longer just the thing I'd brought with me as an extension of my own nerves. It had weight and heft. The lights caught the silver barrel when I turned it.

"Maybe you should sit back down, Dinah," Mr. Cavanaugh said.

"No." My voice was back. "I'm okay, Mr. Cavanaugh. I just get nervous onstage, but I can do it."

I closed my eyes and imagined myself at fourteen, heart-broken and terrified that my new school, the one that was supposed to be full of new people and new promise, was now a place that I dreaded. The voices of should-have-been friends were mocking, and their fingers all pointed at me because they knew what had happened.

I became Claire.

"They call it a safety razor," I said, and held up my pen. "You think that means it can't hurt you, but like everything else, it's a lie. Anything can hurt if it's used right."

I had to stop and try to get enough spit in my mouth to swallow so I could keep talking.

"The plastic isn't even very hard to break. You sort of hoped it would be. And then you're standing there, at the moment before it's not a choice anymore. You could throw it away, claim the razor got stepped on or that you dropped something on top of it, if anyone saw it in the trash. But who would bother looking in the trash?"

I laid the pen flat across my palm and started playing with the golden bird on the end of its chain while I spoke.

"It doesn't weigh much. Less than the thought it took to get you this far. It's so small, you figure: why not? It's not like you've never cut yourself before. You've had bumps and bruises and skinned knees . . . and this time you'll know it's coming. How bad could it be?"

My fingers closed around the pen and propped it, hovering, above my opposite wrist.

"The first cut isn't deep. You're not sure what you're doing, or how to do it, or when you decided it's what needs to be done. The steps don't matter. What matters is the cold tile under your feet, uneven and biting into your skin where you dig your toes against it. What matters is the flat face staring back at you from the mirror as blank and lifeless as you've become yourself. And what matters is that you don't want to be that person anymore. People are supposed to feel things beyond cold and flat. Is it so wrong to want that back?"

Heat rose in my face, bringing tears with it. My eyes blurred so I couldn't see anyone clearly. I ignored both and mimed slashing across my wrist.

"There's a moment of hesitation before blade meets flesh that makes you question whether you're doing the right thing after all, but satisfaction overrides reason. You feel the sting, and it's all worth it. It's not instant, but close enough that you can call it that and not be a liar. Lying's bad, you see; it's one of the rules."

The rules. Those unofficial and unspoken things we're meant to conform to if we don't want to be considered "odd" or "out of place." The tricky thing about the rules is that no one tells you what they are; you have to figure that part out for yourself. They aren't the same for everyone, and not everyone adheres to them. Some will expect you to follow their rules, but there's no sense in asking for details, because they won't give you any.

"Somewhere between the doubt and the pain comes release, a moment where everything breaks and all the pent-up anger or misery or fear—whatever you've tried to pretend doesn't exist—cuts loose. There's an odd comfort in the warm trickle, and an impossible fascination as you watch your blood speed down your wrist where your layers of bracelets should be and across your palm that's never supposed to be a fist, through your fingers that hate playing the piano, and into the sink."

My stomach clenched there, and I had to stop for a beat.

The image was too clear. I grabbed my fake-slashed wrist to stop the flow of blood that wasn't there.

"It's almost poetic, and absolutely hypnotic. You revel in the macabre familiarity of your own life running away from you in a downward spiral . . . the universe's dark sense of irony."

At the time, I didn't realize the whole auditorium had gone quiet. I'd forgotten they were there.

"No two drops hit the water below in the same place, and in that instant, you think it's worked. No, you *know* it's worked. What came out of you is so heavy that it can't float. Everything you hate sinks to the bottom and drowns."

Claire was drowning and no one noticed.

"It's out of you, so you think you're fine. After a few seconds, the relief kicks in with an endorphin rush, and it seems like it should be over. The water's turned off, your skin's clean, and your crashing blood pressure fights with your adrenaline for dominance in a vessel that can't go both ways at once. If you're really good at it, no one knows what you've done."

Of all the things for my Cuckoo to keep to herself, she had to pick this one. I guess she knew I'd have told her parents (fooling around with a guy was one thing, but dumping her circulatory system down the bathroom sink . . . yeah, that I'd have spilled).

"But it's a lie . . . *it's a lie.* You didn't get the poison out, because there's a canker inside you that you can't see. When you cut, you let off the pressure so it won't explode, but it just keeps festering and spitting out more bile, and more acid, and it keeps eating you alive from the inside out. And the next time, the release doesn't come the way it did before, the euphoric rush isn't there, and you're left to wonder when the pain started to hurt."

I could hear Claire's voice inside my head even as I spoke the words she never had, and it finally started to make sense. She'd lost her constant. The thing that was in her control crumbled through her fingers. It was confusing, and that made her mad. She felt broken and dirty and didn't know how to fix it.

"That's the point when all the shadows you've tried to hide in fill up the hole you made for yourself, and now they're all anyone can see. You're pale and the smiles don't come so easy anymore, but you can convince yourself it doesn't matter because your mind's drifting out beyond your sight. The whispers of disapproval you imagine fall away like the slowing beat of your heart in your ears. Peace is so close you could wrap it around your cold arms like a comforter, but that's a lie, too. Even Death turns his back on you and leaves you alone. He doesn't want you, either."

I have no idea how long I stood there on that stage, zoned into my own world. It very possibly could have been seconds, with me speaking so fast my voice hit a pitch only mosquitoes could hear. The heaviness in my arms and legs and heart made hours more likely. I dropped my hands to my sides, felt my fingers go slack, so the pen slipped free and pinged on the stage floor.

Mr. Cavanaugh watched from his seat on the piano bench at the far side with a sickening, genuine concern in his eyes. In the audience, they all stared. Abigail-not-Abby wiped her cheek, like she'd been crying. I caught Dex's eye, but he looked away quickly. Brooks had leaned forward, almost out of his seat, and Chandi . . . Chandi I couldn't figure out. She wasn't glaring at me anymore; the spiteful grin had left her face. It would have been easy to assume she was shocked or upset that I finished my presentation, but that wasn't it at all. She chewed nervously on the eraser end of her pencil, then tugged on her sleeves when she realized I was looking her way.

Her shoulders slumped; she ducked her head with a fearful pale creeping into her cheeks. That was all it took for my own body to respond in kind.

One hand tried to hold my lunch in my stomach, while the other clapped over my mouth in case the first one failed. I rushed off the stage, into the wings, and headed toward the closest dressing room, where I promptly threw up in the sink.

What had I done?

How could I have put myself—*Claire*—out there like that?

I looked at myself, wearing Claire's clothes, with my hair that was blond like Claire's and the hideous pastel tragedy of the makeup that stopped matching my face the instant red splotches erupted across my cheeks and forehead. I couldn't do this; I'd been an idiot to think I could. No matter what I did, it made things worse. Exposing Claire's secrets to the world wasn't going to help her. At best, I'd humiliate her. It was time to cut my losses and go home, assuming I could figure out where that was.

The water turned on in the sink next to the one I'd made into a vomitorium and someone stuck a damp paper towel under my nose. You'd think a school like Lowry wouldn't use the same cheap brown towels as your average public school, but there was no mistaking that wet cardboard scent. I glanced up, expecting to see Dex or Abigail-not-Abby—but I was in hell; I should have known I'd see the devil there.

"You realize this is the guys' dressing room?" Brooks said. He just stood there with that wet paper towel dangling from his fingers, waiting for me to take it, but I couldn't let go of the sink. After all that, after letting him hear what he'd done to Claire and after letting him see it break me, if I let go, I'd fall.

"You realize that standing there means I throw up on you if it happens again?" I asked.

"That's why God invented dry cleaners."

He put the paper towel in my hand, then soaked another and laid it on the back of my neck while I leaned over the sink and let him.

"I'm sure Chandi will love riding home in a car that smells like puke."

"Chandi has her own car."

Brooks went to a cabinet on the wall and rummaged a bit before coming back with two paper cups and a bottle of Scope.

"One for water," he said. "One for the mouthwash." He set the cups and bottle out on the counter. "Cavanaugh won't care if you want to stay in here the rest of class. You'll be able to hear the bell when it rings."

He nodded toward the speaker over the door.

"Thanks," I said. I took the mouthwash and started playing with the cap.

"I can stay in here if you want—"

"No," I said, cutting him off. "I think one round of public humiliation more than makes my quota for the day."

"Dinah, that was amazing," he said. "I don't know where it came from, but I can promise you no one's laughing out there."

"I can't do this." I put my back to the wall and slid down to sit on the floor between the sinks. "I didn't think it would be this hard."

Revenge was supposed to be cold and hard and completely detached. There weren't supposed to be any emotions involved. I wasn't supposed to let Lowry, or the people in it, get to me. But the further I got from the instant surge that had come when I'd first learned what happened to Claire, the more the fury cooled, and it wasn't so easy to keep up the constant desire for vengeance. Then I'd do or see or say something, like what had happened on the stage, and it would all roar back with that same intensity. I'd hate myself for doubting the course I'd set, all the while wondering if I hadn't made some massive mistake.

Brooks sat down on the floor, too, facing me with one arm propped across his knee.

"Do you know why there's a diamond on the school's crest?" he asked.

"Because rich people like diamonds?"

"Because Eleanor Lowry's family owned a diamond mine—*accidentally*. Her father won it in a game of cards. That's how they made their money."

"Nice work if you can get it."

"Not really. Most people think of mining as something glamorous, like in the movies. Guys go underground with lanterns and a canary in a cage to let them know if they hit a gas pocket. But it's not like that at all. It's dirty, and dangerous, and hard work, and in the end, the miners don't even get to keep what they find. The people who put in the most effort aren't always the ones who get the biggest payoffs—and it's a lot more like this school than the Lowrys probably realized."

The hard-work part was obvious, and Claire was evidence of

the danger; Dex and Abigail-not-Abby spoke to how little someone got out of the deal when they worked harder than anyone else. I wasn't so sure about the dirty part of it, but the rest was spot-on.

"People get all excited about the classes and the campus, or what putting Lowry on an application can do for their chances of getting into a university, but this place can eat you alive. That's the part they don't put in the brochure: the amount of pressure it takes to make a diamond will destroy anything else. All it takes is one flaw."

"I've got a lot more than one," I said.

"We all do, but around here, you're supposed to pretend you don't. That's all you have to remember. We don't just act in drama class."

It was happening again. Whatever magic Brooks could work on people without their notice was dulling my aversion to his presence. My self-loathing for what I'd just done, and the fear of being a public spectacle, began to lift, venting out the room as a dissipating fog.

It was so tempting, with only the two of us there in that room, in the relative safety of the school, to confront him. To tell him the truth and demand to know why he'd used Claire the way he had. I just couldn't shake the fear that he'd have something to say that might make sense.

Brooks stood up. The water turned on again, and when it stopped, he handed me a small stack of damp paper towels.

"I'll put your stuff back in your bag and leave it on the stage," he said. "You can wait to leave until the room clears."

That was the point I realized that Claire must have been an anomaly. Summer had truncated his act, and he'd had to work faster to get what he wanted, because he hadn't known she'd be there when school started. During the school year, he could go slower and really make someone twist. There's a reason "con" is short for "confidence," and this was all one masterfully crafted step in a long-term con game.

It had to be, because if it wasn't, the only other explanation was sincerity. And I couldn't believe that; I wouldn't let myself.

I sat there on the floor, holding those smelly paper towels as the water dripped through my fingers and onto my legs, and watched Brooks leave. If Brucey had been there, he would have supplied an appropriate movie line for the occasion, and I knew exactly where it would have come from. I couldn't remember the name, but the movie was older than my parents. It all centered on this knight playing chess with Death, trying to stall long enough to lengthen his life.

The running joke was that it all happened in front of people, but no one could see Death other than his opponent. It was the same with Brooks. I was the only one who could see who and what he really was, and I had to make sure I remembered that. The smiling face and kind words were nothing but the cloak Death used to hide himself from the rest of the world. Under the cloak, he hid a sickle sharp enough to cut me in two if I allowed him to distract me.

The moment I started to question whether Brooks was what I knew him to be would be the moment I failed Claire, and I couldn't let her down again.

I gave it until twelve minutes past the bell before I risked poking my head out of the dressing room. All the seats were empty;

the only people left in the auditorium were Brooks, who was sitting on the stage beside my bag, and Mr. Cavanaugh, who was packing up his own. I moved as quietly as I could, holding a finger to my lips to shush the required "Are you okay?" I knew Brooks was going to ask, but it wasn't enough to get us out of there unseen.

"Miss Powell, a moment." Mr. Cavanaugh must have been watching for me, because there's no way he heard me.

"You want a witness?" Brooks asked. "I can wait at the door."

"Don't bother. It's fine."

The last thing I needed was to have the guy who put Claire in the hospital hovering around while I got chewed out for recounting the story of her life.

Brooks shouldered his bag and left. I slung my own crosswise over my body, an accidental layer of protection between me and the rest of the world. I wiped my eyes, then walked slowly across the room. Mr. Cavanaugh leaned back to prop himself against the piano bench that sat near the wings. It was a relief; this way I wouldn't have to look up at him while he talked.

"That was quite the presentation you gave," he said.

"Thanks." I gripped the strap of my book bag with both hands, twisting the leather.

"Did you write it yourself, or was it something you'd heard before? Something you'd read, maybe?"

"I didn't cheat."

"I'm sorry, that's not what I was implying, Dinah. It was just . . . very convincing. One doesn't usually get that level of commitment or emotional depth with a high school home-work assignment."

"Mr. Cavanaugh, I swear I didn't copy it from anywhere."

"You didn't read it off cards, either."

"I thought we were supposed to memorize it."

"Is that what you did?"

I shifted my weight from one foot to the other. I couldn't look him in the eye.

"I'd like to see the original you wrote."

"I didn't bring it," I said quickly. "I mean . . . I didn't need it, so I left it at home."

"I see." Mr. Cavanaugh sighed, as though he were very tired. "Should I stop asking questions now, or do you want to keep lying to me?"

"I'm not ly—"

"I know it has to be hard being the new kid in any school, and it's worse at one like this. Especially when it's not the sort of place you're used to and you've got a rough situation at home. And I know that sometimes the easiest way to handle things is to pretend you're someone you're not. But that kind of stress can really get to a person after a while."

"It was weird here—at first. But I've got friends now. Abigail and Brooks—"

Did I just count Claire's personal demon as my friend? Going undercover sucks.

"Did you know acting used to be thought of as the career of thieves and reprobates?" he asked. It seemed like a random question, but I shook my head and answered it anyway. "The goal of this class is to give people the skills to convince strangers that they are other than their true selves. I've done this for fifteen years, and I'm pretty good at spotting those who like to play, those with talent, and those who are the real deal. What you did on that stage today, the words you said, those were not lies. What I want to know is if they were your truth or someone else's."

"It's complicated."

"If you need to talk to someone, we have counselors here."

"I have friends to talk to," I said. There wasn't a counselor alive I'd tell half the things Tabs knew about me.

"Sometimes friends aren't enough," he said. "And if I think something's wrong with one of my students, I have to take my suspicions to the headmistress, and she'll have to inform your guardians."

"Mr. Cavanaugh, I don't hurt myself." I tugged both my uniform sleeves up to the elbows to expose the skin underneath— including the tiny cluster of black stars tattooed on one wrist. "No scars, see?"

He looked genuinely shocked.

"I guess I'll have to add a 'plus' to the A you earned," he said. "It was an exceptional recitation."

"Thanks." I pushed my sleeves back down. "So you won't say anything?"

"I might mention that we have a gifted student in class, should the occasion arise, but so long as any mentions of bloodletting remain fictional, I don't see any reason to bring them up."

"I actually meant the ink."

"Tattoos are only against the rules if they're visible. Yours aren't. Though I wasn't aware that Oregon allowed sixteen-year-olds to obtain them."

"Isn't Oregon out of your jurisdiction?"

"Yes, I believe it is," he said with a laugh. He shoved the last of his books into his portable classroom crate and locked the lid. "Good afternoon, Dinah. I hope you realize that if things stay . . . *complicated* . . . there are people willing to help you sort out the hard stuff."

"Thanks, Mr. Cavanaugh," I said, but it didn't matter how well-meaning he was. There was no teacher or counselor equipped to handle what I was going through. Some things are too hard, even for a school founded on diamonds and a girl whose crazy mother wanted to name her after them.

It wasn't difficult to convince Brooks to come to my house after school. He really didn't want to go home, and between the video he was afraid someone would mention and the fight with Chandi, he didn't want to see any of his friends. I was also fairly certain he was trying to keep an eye on me. (Of course, that could have been the paranoia talking. When you start stalking someone, you get this nasty side effect of feeling imaginary eyes on your back everywhere you go.)

I let us in the gate, raided the fridge for drinks and more of Tabs' masterpieces, and we were set—so long as I didn't let him look around the house, where he might notice the photos of Claire or see Tabs lurking about to put the next phase of Brooks' downfall into action. He didn't even blink when I led him out back.

"You have a tree house," he said.

"More like a tree floor with two walls you shouldn't lean on unless you feel like base jumping without a parachute."

"I'll be sure to remember that."

I bypassed the wooden planks nailed into the tree and headed to the other side.

"We're not using the ladder?"

"No."

"If your uncle had an elevator installed in his tree, then I may have to start hating him a little."

"Ladders and elevators are for mere mortals. If you want to get into my clubhouse, you have to know how to fly."

"Is this going to involve broomsticks? Because then I'll have to hate you, too." He grinned, adding something about owing Chandi twenty bucks in a voice I'm sure he thought was too quiet for me to hear.

"Careful there," I warned. "People who imply I'm a witch are more than twice as likely to end up in a biology lab dissection tray with a tack pin through their liver."

Brooks laughed. I was finally getting to the point where I could anticipate his reactions and control where things went from step to step. The trust bought by Brucey's moment of klepto-brilliance at the mall was paying off in the form of Brooks' dropping the walls that had surrounded him during our first few conversations (not to mention the lockdown that came when his dad was nearby).

I showed him how to use my "elevator"—nothing more than a long rope—to pull himself into the tree by looping the end around his shoe and hoisting upward through the pulley at the top.

"This is seriously cool." He stepped onto the tree house's floor and unhooked the loop from his shoe, wearing the kind of smile on his face that I'd forgotten how to put on my own. My muscles couldn't make the gesture anymore.

"Dad rigged it up to move boards and supplies up here while he and Uncle Paul were building it. We never took it down."

"I always wanted a tree house when I was a kid, but my dad didn't think up a tree was an appropriate place for me to spend my time."

He settled into a green bean bag chair Claire had thrown in the corner.

"I wanted one, too, but our yard didn't have any branches wide enough to support one. When my uncle bought this place and it looked like I might actually get to stay, Dad got it into his head that he needed to make good on the promise he'd made me when I was little, so he started building what he called 'The Tree Palace.' Sort of a stamp he could leave behind while he was across the country."

"Why didn't he finish it?"

"Mom saw it before he was done, which clued her in to the fact that I might not be going with them into her state of delusion." That, and she couldn't stand the fact that I was getting the playhouse she never had. . . . "She started screaming about how I was going to fall off and break my neck, which led to an all-out fight with her accusing him of not loving me or her or anything else. . . . It kind of killed the momentum."

It was also the first fight I can ever remember hearing my dad shout in. I found Dad under the tree the next day, just standing there with his neck craned up, staring at it. He'd been so happy the day before, talking about what color I wanted him to paint it and making jokes about having a dish put on top so we could have a TV up there, or adding a tower so I could grow my hair long like Rapunzel until it reached the ground. After the fight, it was all gone. Joy had become a chore, and real happiness a distant memory.

I told Dad not to worry about it, that it didn't matter. I was too old for a tree house, really, and that knowing he'd wanted to build it was enough.

It didn't help like I'd hoped it would. Dad didn't say anything to me, but he went back in the tree, braced up the walls he'd set, and packed his tools away, mumbling about letting Claire use it since she was younger. He never mentioned it again.

"Claire and I tried to finish it ourselves, but—"

"You're more ground squirrel than tree squirrel?"

"We hoisted the bean bags up here and found some old rug scraps to make the patchwork carpet. She dragged the rails off her toddler bed out of storage so we could fix a third and fourth wall to keep anyone who came up from falling out, but it wasn't the same. I don't even know if she ever used it."

He reached for the tub of cupcakes I'd brought with us and peeled the wrapper off one.

"Your friend is a great cook. Not what I expected from a girl with a nose ring and pierced eyebrows."

"You noticed that, huh?"

"She's kind of hard to miss. So's the sticky-fingered string bean."

"Brucey," I corrected. I was allowed to make jokes about his habits and appearance; Tabs was allowed. Brooks definitely wasn't.

"Right—the overprotective not-brother," he said. "You don't exactly match."

"We used to."

In what felt like a lifetime and another reality ago.

"You mean when you looked like your old profile pic?"

"I felt like making a few changes," I said.

"You don't owe anyone an explanation. I was just curious."

I picked at the wrapper around my uneaten cupcake so I had something to focus on.

"You don't like yours?" Brooks asked—I wasn't the only one getting better at directing the conversation.

"I don't really like chocolate," I said. "I only eat them so it won't hurt her feelings."

"More for me." He grinned. Brooks snatched up another one and shoved the whole thing in his mouth. Getting him to eat enough of Tabs' special recipe for it to show on a drug test wasn't going to be hard at all. I tossed him a bottle of water so he could wash the frosting off his teeth. He climbed out of his bean bag and took a peek over the nearest edge.

"You know, if I had something like this, I think I'd live in it, even without the roof. There's no chance of suffocating up here."

I nodded and joined him at the edge.

"Climb out of real life and get above all the problems on the ground," I said.

School tomorrow? How could I go to school if I was in a tree?

Parent drama? They'd have to climb high enough to make me care, and Mom wouldn't go that far. Her voice would simply blend with the rest of the noise down below.

Hospitals? No hospitals in a tree.

If I was in a tree, then I couldn't possibly get on a plane back to Oregon.

"Let me live in the clouds, eating nothing but chocolate cupcakes," Brooks said.

"Until you eat so many you weigh four hundred pounds and break the branch."

He scowled. "You've found the flaw in my brilliant scheme to escape reality forever. For that, you get frosted."

He plucked the last cupcake out of the tub and took a swipe

at my nose, leaving a blob of goo on the end. My eyes crossed in, focused on the smudge, so he grew blurry in the background, and when I let them relax again, he was smiling, holding the cupcake like he was considering a second strike.

"You're out of ammo," he baited. I turned my attention to the tub, but it was, of course, empty.

"Not really," I said, snatching up a can of soda.

"You wouldn't. . . ."

I shook the can and poised my finger on the pull tab.

"Now, Dinah . . . you wouldn't really spray me, would you?"

"I'm not hearing any convincing reasons not to."

"Um . . . this is my school uniform?"

Brooks backed as far away as the cramped floor plan of the tree house would allow.

"That's why God invented dry cleaners," I said, shaking the can again. "If they can handle puke, soda's no problem."

He raised his hands protectively.

"I'm too cute to drench?"

"Your negotiation skills need some serious improvements."

"Can I play on your sympathies and claim it might get in my eyes, therefore blinding me for life or at least two minutes?"

"There's more water; I can dump it on your head after and rinse them out."

"Nice girls don't attack people with soft drinks?"

"Sorry, I'm not that nice."

"Hey . . . what's that?"

He tried the lamest trick possible, and I'm the idiot who fell for it. True, I had my reasons—number one being that I was afraid he'd seen Tabs; it didn't even occur to me that he was creating a diversion.

I turned my head and he made a run for the rope elevator.

With my nemesis escaping, I pulled the tab and the can lurched in my hand, leaving Brooks dripping cherry soda onto the floor.

"Now you've done it," he said.

I had to dodge the cupcake when he pitched it toward me—another diversion, which he used to reach my soda stash and start shaking a can of his own.

"Don't you—"

The "dare" was drowned by an explosion of soda hitting me square in the face. We both dove for the last unopened can and chased it when it rolled off toward the ledge and finally over, denying anyone the last shot.

"I guess that makes us even," Brooks said. "Can we declare a cease fire?"

During the scramble, we ended up on the floor. I rolled off my stomach, pushing away from the edge of the tree house where I'd landed. Brooks did the same, at almost the same time, and we stopped, facing each other.

Impossible or not, the air between and around us grew thick and heavy, hovering over our heads and pressing down. We were too close to each other, so close I wanted to believe it was only some kind of static from his clothes or mine that made my arms and legs prickle. I wanted to believe it was the rush of adrenaline from laughter and fighting over soda cans that made my breathing hitch. I wanted to believe no other explanation was possible.

Brooks became the bottle labeled "Drink Me," altering the reality I accepted as true.

Gravity or inertia or any scientific phenomena other than

the impossibility of attraction took over. I'd have taken the easy out of a small earthquake or a heavy wind if it meant explaining how his mouth ended up on mine. But there was no explanation and no excuse. Everything from time to the rotation of the earth itself stopped dead, and the shock made my arms and legs useless. The only thing moving was my stomach as it somersaulted through my abdomen.

He tasted like sugar frosting, sweet and sticky, the kind of thing you know you shouldn't enjoy but can't help yourself. That taste mixed with the cherry soda still on my own face, creating a permanent paradox in my brain. Better sense told me Brooks was evil, but my senses—taste and smell, even the feel of his damp hair in my hands, redefined things to make me think he was something I wanted more of. I was a diabetic, and Brooks was the super-sweet thing that was going to kill me someday.

If his phone hadn't picked that exact moment to signal an incoming call, someday would have been right then and there. We pulled apart awkwardly while Brooks attempted (and failed) to retrieve his phone from its pocket without moving.

"I got it," I said. I used the back of my other hand to wipe my mouth, excusing it with a mumbled "frosting" as I pulled myself up to sit.

"Sorry."

Brooks actually blushed when he took the phone from me. Our hands touched, causing another spark that put my stomach back to its original place. My heart was going so fast and loud, I was expecting to stroke out any second.

I had kissed him.

No . . .

He had kissed me.

No . . .

What difference did it make? We'd kissed. My lips had touched the lips of the guy who had put Claire in the hospital. Lips that had kissed Claire, and told her things to make her giggle and dream; lips that had shut tight, refusing to acknowledge her existence.

The cherry soda I had no choice but to smell with every breath turned rancid. All that heat and electricity I'd felt before settled in my face until I could imagine it blistering from the inside, disfiguring me so everyone would know what I'd done. I deserved to wear my shame in public.

My hands, now fists, had clenched so tight I'd forced all the blood out of them. I wanted to put them around Brooks' neck and squeeze until his skin turned just as white and lifeless; then I'd do the same to myself. I'd betrayed Claire; traitors were supposed to be executed.

An angry rant came from Brooks' phone, muffled, as it was on the other side of his head, but there was no question the person calling was shouting.

"What are you talking about?" Brooks asked. "Slow down. Dad, no. Calm down. Someone's made a mistake, my interview wasn't scheduled for today. Neither of them were. No! I have them on my calendar. Wednesday and Friday. No, I didn't email them. No! Dad, I swear, I wouldn't do that. Dad. Dad. Dad!" Brooks dropped the hand with his phone into his lap. "He hung up."

The choke hold he'd put on my thoughts broke, and I allowed myself to breathe again. It didn't matter that I'd slipped off my goal—Brucey's emails to the college recruiters had done their job. There was another black mark on Brooks' spotless record, and my mistake (aka the kiss) hadn't ruined anything other than my desire to eat cupcakes or drink cherry soda for the foreseeable future.

"I have to go." Brooks' voice turned as hollow as the empty glaze in his eyes. "My dad . . ."

"Don't tell me someone emailed him the video, too." Miraculously, my voice still worked.

He shook his head, still staring at the phone in his lap. He hadn't even stood up.

"College recruiters . . ."

"Someone sent it to college recruiters?"

I kicked myself for not thinking of that one.

"No. I had interviews this week on Wednesday and Friday, but the recruiters called the house upset because I wasn't in either of their offices today. Dad heard the message, so he called them back, saying there'd been some kind of mistake. But someone had emailed them and changed my interview schedule at the last minute. I have to go. I'm sorry. I just . . . I have to go now."

Just like that, the kiss was forgotten. Brooks didn't use the pulley to get down; he chose to climb—anything to extend the trip home, I guess. He walked around the house instead of cutting through, and got in his car and left, chanting "He's going to kill me" the whole way.

Knowing what little I did of his dad, I couldn't even say it was out of the question.

"You were brilliant!"

Tabs burst out of the house, where she'd hidden after she'd finished her part in the next phase of our plan. Since there was no way to get to Brooks' car when it was at his house, and no way for Tabs or Brucey to get into the Lowry lot to reach it during school, we settled on luring him to my house, where the car would be in the open. His dad's phone call was a bonus.

In five minutes, Brucey would report an erratic driver to the police, who would pull Brooks over and find the minibar Tabs had just stashed behind his seat. As out of it as he was, they'd probably give him a Breathalyzer on the spot.

"Did you do it?" I asked, horrified that someone had actually seen the kiss.

"Yeah. There's a half-empty bottle of vodka, minus fingerprints, under the seat with a couple of empty beer cans I found beside the Dumpster at the bodega. I threw in Mom's expired pain pills from the dentist, too. Don't worry, I didn't leave the bottle, just the pills in a Baggie. No names."

Vicodin and vodka would definitely get some attention.

"The way he tore out of here, we might not need Brucey's call," she said. "I bet he was doing ninety-five by the time he hit the main road. Why are you not celebrating? This is a good thing, isn't it?"

"What?" I asked, barely listening. "Yeah, of course it's a good thing. Why wouldn't it be?"

"If I didn't know better, I'd think you were flirting for real. Dinah, please tell me I know better."

I didn't answer her. Tabs is one of the only people in the world who can tell when I'm lying, and even though I wanted to say "Yes, it was all an act, none of that was real," I couldn't. I was terrified she'd see a truth I wasn't entirely sure of myself.

I didn't sleep well that night, so it was a good thing that neither Uncle Paul nor Aunt Helen dropped by the house where they could see me pacing the downstairs. I couldn't get Brooks' face out of my head.

That look of hopelessness and horror he'd worn—*I'd put it there*.

The way he had to force himself to hold his breath and run to make it to his car before he changed his mind—*I'd done that*.

The feeling of hopeless claustrophobia as his world began to collapse in on him for no apparent reason—*I'd caused it*.

Me.

It *should* have been a moment of triumph. I was *supposed* to be the good guy in all this, Claire's avenger in the real world while Mitch was on duty guarding the angel room. I wasn't the one who'd hurt someone who didn't deserve it, so why was I the one with the malfunctioning conscience that insisted on screaming at me at two in the morning?

And I couldn't stop thinking about that kiss, either. I was still trying my best to push it out of my sleep-deprived mind when I dragged myself into Lowry's main hall the next morning. Sure, going moon-eyed and tripping over my own tongue would have sold the idea that I was falling for Brooks, but I was hoping to find a way to pull off a fake fall while maintaining a healthy distance. Preferably one that didn't involve references to anyone's tongue renting space in the wrong mouth.

"You look awful." Dex fell into step beside me at the base of the staircase. "Actually, you look hungover. I thought you'd sworn off partying in favor of hospital duty."

"I'm sleepwalking," I said. "Which means I'm not legally liable for my actions—something you should keep in mind."

"Have you thought about it?"

"Pushing you over the bannister to stop your voice from echoing in my head? Yes. I'm thinking about it right now. Would you rather hit the marble, or do you want me to aim for a fish to break your fall?"

I've been drunk exactly once in my life (Brucey tried to make sangria punch out of Kool-Aid, wine coolers, and canned fruit cocktail—long story, bad ending), and the headache I had the morning after was nothing compared to the elephant tap-line currently prancing behind my eyes.

"Have you thought about the carnival," he clarified. "You aren't still mad at me, are you?"

"Maybe."

"Maybe you're mad or maybe you'll go with me?"

"Pick one."

It felt like one of those tap-dancing elephants was twirling a fire baton. When I closed my eyes, there were actual sparks.

"The season's closing at the end of the week, and I'm not afraid of begging in public. I'll get on my knees right here on the stairs and everyone will think it's charming and romantic."

"Try desperate and pathetic."

I pulled him back up by the arm, dragging him with me as I continued to climb.

"There, now we're even for the arm thing. You have no excuse to say no."

"Fine! Stop bugging me and I'll upgrade you to a definite maybe."

"I'll take it."

The idiot kissed me on the cheek and ran the rest of the stairs two at a time. I lugged myself to trig at half his pace, relying on the hope that Brooks would look worse than I felt to get me there, but Brooks wasn't in his seat.

Class started and he never came in.

He wasn't in the hall before history, and my attempted inquiry to Chandi about where he'd gone was cut off by Dex's arrival and her quick escape into the room.

By lunch, curiosity was turning into worry. I'd been betting on Brooks' mood to get him pulled over, but it could just have easily distracted him into crashing his car. Instead of walking a straight line for the highway patrol, he could have ended up in the hospital, or put someone else there if he hit another car instead of a tree or guardrail. Surely, I thought, if Brooks was in trouble, one of his friends would know, and then the whole school would.

I hadn't heard so much as a whisper, and didn't until last period, when he showed up in class.

"Where have you been?" I slid into the seat next to him.

"At the hospital annex, in their blood lab," he said.

"Are you sick?"

"Sick would be an improvement. A brain tumor would be an improvement. Right now, *dead* would be an improvement. Sorry. I shouldn't have said that."

He straightened in his seat long enough to answer the roll call, then ducked back down.

"If you're not sick, then why were you at the hospital?"

"For a drug test."

The picture in his lap was stuck in a holding pattern. Brooks traced and retraced the same lines, making them darker and wider until he scratched through the paper. He ripped it out and started over.

"I got stopped two blocks from home after I left your place. I wasn't thinking about speed limits, just trying to defuse my dad. The cop said I was doing ninety-seven."

"You didn't argue with him, did you? That only makes it worse."

"No, I didn't argue. I told him I had an emergency at home and that I hadn't been paying attention. But whoever's got it in for me must have gotten bored with taking shots from behind their computer."

"I don't get it. What happened?" I hoped I sounded more curious than eager.

"He was going to let me off with a warning, until a quarter-full bottle of vodka rolled out from under my seat."

Another sheet of paper died a horrible, inky death.

"Someone stashed the bottle in my car, along with empty beer cans and enough pills that the cop dragged me down to the police station. They towed my car. They called my dad. This isn't funny anymore, Dinah."

I thought I was going to faint straight out of my seat when he looked up and our eyes met; I think my heart stopped for a beat or two before it sank in that he wasn't calling me out for the traffic stop.

"W-was it ever funny?" I asked, praying the hitch in my throat didn't actually make it into my voice.

"No, but until now, I thought this was some idiot trying to show off. I thought they'd get bored and move on to someone else if I didn't retaliate or give them any attention. My own father thinks I'm an addict . . . how is that a joke?"

It wasn't, but it was coming very close to justice. I even let myself hope that Brooks would be leaving Lowry before me, and I'd have however many days between his expulsion and Claire's return to actually enjoy myself with Abigail-not-Abby at lunch or hang out with Dex.

"Who does something like this?" Brooks' rant had continued while I zoned out. "Both of my top college picks have probably blackballed me. Headmistress Kuykendall informed me that I'm on strike two and one short step from being kicked out of here, which means I'm half that far from being kicked out of my house, as Dad says I'm a disgrace to my mother's memory. I have a police report with my name on it. I have an arrest record. They ask that when you get a job, don't they?"

He groaned, grabbing the sides of his head with his hands.

"Why is this happening to me?"

"Psycho ex-girlfriend?" I suggested.

"I don't date psychos. I don't even know any psychos."

That was an interesting thought. I'd heard Brucey talk about his sessions with Dr. Useless and all the things he'd learned snooping through her office when she had to leave to take calls or other quick emergencies. She had a patient who would black out and wake up hours later with no memory of what he'd done, even horrible or dangerous things. Maybe that was what was wrong with Brooks. Multiple personalities would go a long way toward explaining why the Brooks I'd seen and spoken to was nothing like the one in Claire's letters. And if that was it, at least his dad had the cash to get him serious help.

"You believe me, don't you?" he asked as Mr. Cavanaugh called time on the last presentation and made us start class for real.

"Yeah, I do."

"I think you're about the only one."

Our conversation ended there, replaced by Mr. Cavanaugh's insistence that everyone line up on either side of the stage for what he called "drama drills" (charades for a grade). The rest of last period ticked by sixty seconds at a time while we pulled every identity from space cowboy to beached mermaid out of a hat in an attempt to get our character across. (No, it wasn't funny when Jordan drew "the Venus de Milo," pulled her arms in her sleeves, and Dex yelled out "Dinah's first day" as his guess.)

I was anxious to get home and fill Tabs and Brucey in on how well things were going. We'd finally made progress, and Brooks was becoming acquainted with that suffocating crush that had plagued my every moment since I'd first found his name on Claire's computer. When the bell finally released us for the day, I was ready to skip the stage steps and jump into the pit just to shorten the wait that much more, but I forced myself to stay inconspicuous.

Brooks beat me back to our seats, and by the time I got there he had my bag in his hand stuffing something under the front flap.

"What are you doing?"

He froze with his back to me, and I watched his ears turn red the way my dad's do when he's embarrassed. A folded piece of blue paper was in his hand.

"I wanted to give you something, but now it feels stupid," he said, facing me. "I was trying to sneak it into your bag so you wouldn't see me with it."

"What is it?"

"Probably me losing whatever shred of sanity I had left before today. I had a lot of wait time at the hospital this morning; I couldn't think of anything else to do with it that didn't involve self-mutilation and a longer stay in the hospital."

He shoved the page into my hand.

"Don't open that until I'm out of here. And I'm sorry I can't draw people."

Brooks snatched up his stuff and bolted without bothering to put the strap from his bag over his shoulder.

The folded page stayed clutched in my hand, slightly rumpled from the way he'd crushed it trying to fit it into my bag. I opened it, dreading whatever poisonous viper inside would explain the sudden change in Brooks' skin tone. After all, there wasn't much chance of this being a signed confession.

It was my tree house.

Brooks had drawn the tree house from Uncle Paul's backyard, finished it and made into the kind of palace Dad had dreamed of building, complete with a tower. There was an arrow pointing to the rear, labeled "Broom Parking in Back," and where we'd taken the pulley up, it read "Flight Pad: No Mortals Allowed." Instead of a rope, the pulley had been threaded with the braid coming off the head of a stick-figure princess leaning out the window. He'd even remembered the dish for the TV.

Tabs was going to kill me.

24

Three days was a record for me keeping a secret from Tabs, and I think the only reason I lasted that long was because I forgot I'd stuck Brooks' drawing in my bag after the first one.

For those three days, I went to class, failed most of them miserably, pretended to listen to Abigail-not-Abby at lunch, and consider meeting Dex when he got off his shift at the fairgrounds, all between running to the hospital, only to be told there'd been no change with Claire, and waiting for word of Brooks' drug test failure.

The short version on that one is: TV lies. Drug tests take days, not hours. This was not a pleasant discovery. Waiting made me sloppy and forgetful.

"You'll be lucky if they get results in under a week," Tabs said as we headed back to Uncle Paul's house from one of those pointless hospital treks. "If his dad's like you say, he probably wanted the detailed kind that only like two labs in the country can do."

She followed that with a request for gum, which I told her to get out of my bag. Tabs dumped it out in the seat between us, and that forgotten piece of blue paper fell out with everything else.

"What's this?" she asked.

"Nothing." I tried to grab it, but the car swerved and I had to put both hands back on the wheel.

"*He* did this, didn't he? Because of the lip lock in the tree."

"What difference does it make?" I asked, and made another grab. She held it out of reach. "Give it back."

Instead, she unfolded it to let it flap over the side of the car, where the wind tattered the top. I made a grab for it again, not really sure why I cared what she was going to do with my picture.

"You have to destroy it, Dinah."

"Why?"

"Because you don't hang on to things created by your sworn enemy," she said.

"He doesn't know we're enemies. He thought he was being nice."

"And I'm getting the feeling that *you* think it's nice, too. He's sucking you in. It's like those movies where a bunch of kids stumble on an evil artifact and one sneaks it home without telling the others. They start acting all weird because it connects them to thing trying to kill them. Destroy it."

"I don't care who made it—I like it."

It was what Dad would have made me if Mom hadn't got in the way. My appreciation of the image had nothing to do with the person who had created it. Maybe.

"I care," she said, crushing the page, and the dream it held, into a ball.

"Tabs!"

"I care because this is not helpful. This is a distraction. This is him baiting the hook and you falling for it."

"It's a piece of paper with pencil scratches on it, not GHB in a Coke."

"No, this is a problem, and the only way to handle problems is to get rid of them."

217

She let it drop. In a matter of seconds, my tree palace was flying through the air behind us, to land somewhere on the side of the road in an overgrown ditch full of stagnant rainwater. There was no chance of saving it, but that doesn't mean I didn't try. I coasted the car onto the shoulder and jumped out, hoping there was something left, but it was floating out of reach.

I tried snapping off a stick to draw it closer, because I couldn't tell how deep the ditch was or if there was anything alive in it.

"Look at yourself," Tabs ordered. She pried my hand out of the muck and held it in front of my face, shaking it so that grimy bits of water hit me in the nose. "You're fried, D. You need a break."

"I'll take a break once I'm done with Brooks. Once he's gone, I'll stop going to class until Lowry calls Uncle Paul to tell him they've removed me from the roster for truancy. Satisfied?"

"No. You're coming with me and we're going to do something crazy like normal teenage girls with a car, cash, and no adult supervision."

"The only place I'm going is home." I threw my stick down and pulled my feet out of the slosh, shaking them to get the mud off.

"Are you seriously pouting because of this?"

"I am not pouting!"

Does anyone not say, or at least not think, that when they're accused of pouting? Especially if it's true.

I trudged back to my car and slammed the door. Tabs slammed hers a second later, so we were both sitting in my front seat, arms crossed, scowling at the road like the next exit sign was to blame for all of this. Arguments we weren't actually having grew in my head (I won all of them—home court advantage). I glared at Tabs, Tabs glared at me, and we got absolutely nowhere.

She was right. I was fried.

"I'm sorry," she spat, finally breaking our mutual ignore-a-thon.

"Shhh."

"You don't shush someone who's apologizing!"

"Shhh!"

"Fine! I'll walk home!" She opened her door and got out.

"Shut up and listen." I cocked my head to the side toward the faint sound of something familiar.

"Is that—" Tabs got quiet.

"Uncle Paul's ringtone! Where's my phone? Do you see it?"

The argument was forgotten on the spot. We shoveled through everything that had spilled out of my bag, checking between the seats and under them, searching for the phone, which was already on its third ring. When it hit four, it would go to voice mail, and if Uncle Paul had left Claire's room to call me again, I didn't want to get whatever news he had to share by checking messages that would no doubt include a dozen or more angry rants from my mother.

"Got it!" Tabs wriggled the phone out from where it had wedged between her seat and the console and tossed it to me. She started clicking her fingernails against her teeth.

"Hello?" I said carefully. "Are you there?"

Uncle Paul's voice came through, speaking quickly, and probably all in one breath. When he was done, I didn't even remember to press End to hang up.

25

"She woke up!" I screamed it so loud into the phone that I probably busted my dad's eardrum.

When Uncle Paul called to say Claire had opened her eyes—actually focused her eyes and looked at him and Aunt Helen—my voice went up two octaves and got three times louder. I must have taken my hands off the wheel at some point, too, because Tabs had sretched across the center line and grabbed it.

"Dinah!" she shouted as she leaned out of her seat belt. "Can you maybe find a way to tell your dad about Claire that doesn't land us in the room next to hers?"

She squeaked as the Mustang drifted a little too close to the next lane. In my ear, Dad was firing questions about Claire and traffic at the same time.

"I've got the wheel, Dad," I said. "Both hands, I swear. I was just excited."

"Then pull over and be excited on the shoulder," he scolded.

"Sorry, Dad—I've switched it to hands-free." Hands-free meaning I shoved the phone at Tabs and she held it against my ear while I steered the car. "We can talk now."

"Tabitha, are her hands on the wheel?" he shouted. I'm not sure if he was afraid Tabs couldn't hear him or if his own hearing was still off from my announcement.

"Yes, Mr. Powell," Tabs said.

"Are you lying?"

"No, Mr. Powell."

"Good," Dad said, satisfied. "Are you girls headed to the hospital?"

"We were, but the doctors won't let more than two people in at a time, so I can't see her yet. Claire only opened her eyes for a minute or so, and she's really confused about what's going on and where she is, but she knew her name and recognized Aunt Helen. They said things are—and I quote—'cautiously optimistic.' Aunt Helen and Uncle Paul want to be there when she wakes up again to see if she can tell them anything about what happened the night she fell. Unless they call, I'm not going over there until tomorrow."

"Let me know how things go, D. I'll look into getting a flight back there as soon as she's up and around."

"Dad . . . does this mean I have to come back to Oregon now? Mom said I could only stay until Claire got better, and she's already bugging me about coming home, but I don't want to leave yet. I haven't even gotten to talk to Claire, and I don't know how long she'll be in the hospital."

If the doctors really did decide to move Claire up to the psych ward, then she wouldn't get visitors for at least a couple of days while the counselors tried to get her to talk to them. They might let one of her parents in, but not me. After all the time I'd spent waiting to see Claire and hear her actually say something beyond the words I assigned her voice in my head, I couldn't leave before I got to see her.

"I wish you'd told me your mother was giving you a hard time, D," Dad said.

"She always gives me a hard time."

221

"But this time, I know why—I've been talking to Helen. She said having you around was her life preserver. It reminded her there was some light in the world."

"When did you talk to Aunt Helen?"

She never left the hospital, and Dad hadn't been alone with her while he was there.

"There's not a lot for her to do while she sits in that room with Claire, so she's been trying to work out a way for you to stay there."

Tabs cleared her throat, the way she does when she thinks she's hearing something she shouldn't. I took the phone from her and switched it to the ear nearest the door.

"Aunt Helen didn't say anything," I said.

That was very nearly a literal statement. I hadn't heard my aunt say a single word since the first night I went to the hospital.

"She didn't want to get your hopes up if things didn't go well."

"Did they? Go well, I mean?"

"Dinah, you're sixteen. I think you're old enough to decide where you want to live, and if that's back there with your friends, then so be it. You have my permission."

"But, Mom—"

"You're old enough to be emancipated, and if your mother wants to push it, Helen said she and Paul would get it done, then rent you a room in their house for a dollar a year until you graduate to satisfy the court conditions."

I tried very hard not to bounce up and down in my seat—which would have done nothing for an image that had already disintegrated by degrees since I bleached my hair out. I was getting to stay with Aunt Helen and Uncle Paul and Claire; I wasn't a placeholder anymore.

Tabs smacked me on the arm and mouthed "What?" Apparently I wasn't doing that great a job of not bouncing.

"I don't have to go back to Oregon—ever," I said, for Tabs' benefit, before she made me do something that would have Dad asking if both my hands were on the wheel again.

Now I had a bouncing buddy.

"Helen said she'd speak to the school as soon as I spoke to you. You're welcome to stay at Lowry if you like."

Do I like Lowry?

That was a question I never thought I'd have to ask myself. The answer should have been a simple, slam-dunk no. Lowry was just supposed to be the backdrop for my personal tragedy— not real beyond the context. But Dad's words that first day of school had become closer to reality than I was comfortable with. The people at Lowry weren't strangers anymore.

Abigail-not-Abby and Dex were a couple of people I was going to miss. But it still wasn't me. Not really.

"I don't think you need to go that far," I told Dad. "Claire's welcome to keep Private School Land all to herself when she's back home."

I wanted to go back where I belonged—Ninth Street, where sleep was an elective, Tabs and Brucey wouldn't be weekend faces, and trig was actually trig. Besides, Dex lived in the same neighborhood, so going to Ninth Street wouldn't cost me everything.

"We'll work it out when I come back to town, okay?" Dad

said. "You don't have to make any decisions tonight. Go do something fun—consider that my last parental order before you become a legal adult. I'm sure you can use the break."

"Thanks, Dad. I'll call you when I know something."

I clicked the phone off and threw it onto the dashboard.

"So?" Tabs asked.

"So, I don't have to go back to Oregon."

"And you don't have to stay in the kingdom of knee socks and headbands?"

"I don't think so."

"Yes!" Tabs pulled her elbows in close to her stomach and beat her feet against the floor mats. "You realize what this means."

"The world is going back on its axis and I may actually graduate before I'm twenty-five?"

"Bzzt. I'm sorry, the answer we're looking for is: 'The Cuckoo bird's on the mend and you're staying here for good—so there's no reason to go back to Paul's house and mope.'"

"I do not mope!"

She made the buzzer sound again.

"You are in desperate need of reality augmentation."

"Sounds painful."

"Only if you argue with us."

"Us? Who's us?"

"Us," she said, pointing her finger at my chest and then back at her own. "Me and you, that makes 'us,' which is a short hop from 'we.' And *we* need to celebrate."

"Who else is included in this 'us' that you're trying far too hard not to name?"

"Come on, Dinah—come with me. I haven't been to a real

carnival since we were in elementary school. Mom was always afraid I'd touch something dirty and catch Ebola or the plague."

"Carnival?"

"Yes. I want to go and I want you to come with me. Ride something, eat everything in sight, walk around in a daze—I don't care, so long as there's no mention of psycho-boys or the Cuckoo bird."

She was whining. Tabs *never* whines without a reason, but there was no point in asking her what the reason was until she was ready to share. All I needed to know was that she was up to something and it involved getting me to the fairgrounds.

"Wouldn't you rather help me burn my Lowry uniform? Uncle Paul can buy Claire a new one before she comes home."

"Come with me, distract yourself, and maybe by the time we're done, Claire will be conversational and they'll let you and your uncle switch out visitation so you can see her."

Whining backed up by dirty tricks and playing on my weaknesses. Whatever this was, it was big, and when Tabs dealt in big secrets, strange and unforeseen disasters usually lurked nearby. But with the promise of a new dawn to destroy what had been a very long and dark night, I wasn't all that worried about it. Maybe we'd gorge on junk food and I'd throw up purple cotton candy for two days, or maybe I'd get stuck at the top of the zero-gravity drop for an hour.

Right then, I could have handled anything.

26

I had expected to hate the carnival. It was noisy and dirty and full of too many people, but my mood was indestructible. Tabs and I hit the midway hard and fast, stuffing ourselves and downing enough soda to power a small country with the sugar rush.

For once, I wasn't putting everything into terms of "this should be Claire and not me." Pretty soon, it could be Claire, and it would be.

There were still the therapy sessions to deal with what she'd been through, but that was a good thing. Claire awake and talking meant she could tell her own story. All I had to do was convince her to talk to her parents—and the police—and things would work themselves out. If she didn't want to talk, she could at least print out all those letters she'd never sent me; they'd do it for her. All of the edges of my soul that grief had worn sharp were softening.

"Where to now?" I asked. I had been following Tabs around the midway, happy to let her decide the whats and wheres for a while. It never occurred to me that she might have been herding me somewhere without my notice.

"How about there?" she asked, pointing to a large red and yellow stand painted to look like a popcorn bag.

"How are you hungry?" I asked. "You've eaten three hot dogs and more of my nachos than me."

"We're not going there for me, we're going there for you."

She tugged me in the direction she thought we needed to go. When we were about ten yards off, I recognized a familiar dark-haired boy sitting at one of the picnic tables out front.

"Oh . . . gee . . . would you look at that. What are the odds we'd run into him here?" Tabs asked as Dex stood up and walked toward us.

"You set me up," I said, and stopped walking.

"I do not know what you are speaking about, silly friend of mine. This is not at all a setup, nor did I text this person to let him know when and where to expect you. This is a totally random occurrence of me randomly bringing you to a specific location, where a specific guy, who is gorgeous, happens to be waiting for you, *specifically*."

She got behind me and shoved.

"You planned this, traitor."

"I am not understanding your distrustful tone, dear BFF. It's nigh onto mocking, in fact."

"Tabs, I'm serious."

"Yeah, and that's the problem." She stopped pushing, and dropped the kung fu movie dub-in voice. "You're always serious lately. You need to have fun. There's a cute guy—now go have fun."

"You all right?" Dex asked.

"Here," Tabs said. "The package is delivered. Now I must go in search of lemonade and maybe escape through the front gate before clowns are involved and I'm forced to resort to self-protective violence."

"You can't leave me here," I said. "You don't even have your car."

"I'm taking yours." She jingled the keys that ten seconds earlier had been in my pocket. "You can thank Brucey for the pickpocket lessons tomorrow."

Tabs ran off, leaving me once again contemplating bodily harm against another human being.

"Should I say hi or run for my life?" Dex asked. "Because the look on your face right now is making me think it's the second one, and I want a head start."

"You did this on purpose."

"Is that a bad thing?"

"Not really," I sighed.

I couldn't be mad at him for plotting against me with Tabs—he was pathetically cute in his carnie costume; the vest looked like a piece of peppermint candy. I was a bit confused as to when Tabs had had time to squeeze another conspiracy into her schedule, though.

"Being yourself today?" I asked. The electric blue piece of plastic pinned to his vest read "Jackson."

He shrugged.

"Sometimes there's no benefit to being someone else."

"I don't know. I think you'd look great with a few of Abigail's curls. . . ."

He frowned.

"I haven't had curls since I was three, and we're all better off not revisiting that dark period in history."

"Nope, sorry. It's in my head now. Nothing you can do about it, Curly Top. Ohh, were they blond, too? I bet you were one of those boys with little blond ringlets around your face like a baby angel."

"Better than being born with a pointed tail," he said. "Did you get the pitchfork afterward, or was it part of the package?"

"Ha. Ha. Ha," I deadpanned. Even with Claire on the mend, I was in no mood to be called a little devil. Someone else already had that category locked up. "I'm faster than I look. I can still catch Tabs before she makes it to the exit if you don't want me around."

"Truce?"

"Terms?"

"You cease discussing my preschool appearance and I stop comparing you to creatures with cloven hooves."

"Deal," I said.

"Come on. You've never really seen this place until you see it with someone who has backstage access."

Carnivals are made for cheese—the kind you can drown your nachos in, and the kind that says the midway is that weird combination of lame and fun that's only acceptable at a fair or circus when things aren't supposed to be exactly normal. While Dex dragged me through the crowd, we passed kids pigging out on ice cream and grannies waiting to ride things that couldn't possibly have been compatible with their heart medications. One little girl with a glittered butterfly painted on her face had a firm grip on the fingers of a thirty-something-year-old man in an expensive suit who was sporting a butterfly of his own across both eyes like a mask.

Everything evened out at a place like this; classes dissolved. Everyone was subject to the rule of priority by order of appearance . . . except us. There was an unwritten understanding among those who worked at the carnival grounds that they took care of their own, and part of that meant their own never waited in line.

Over the groans and protests of those waiting in the queue with tickets clutched in their hands, Dex and I were allowed to enter through the exits and bypass the lines completely. Even with all the things Uncle Paul had been able to buy since his business took off, none of it was quite the same as being ushered through and around scores of people as though "special" were branded on our backs. It was its own kind of power rush, and just plain cool.

Dex gave the man we ousted from his spot as "next" an unapologetic grin as we took the open seat offered by the zero-gravity drop's operator. The safety bar came down and we were off, rocketing into the air and watching the crowds shrink to the size of ants below us. At the top, a brief jolt of panic shot into my stomach when I remembered my earlier worries of getting stuck at the top, but it was quickly replaced by the sensation of free-fall. The ride worked flawlessly, bobbing up and down to pause at different heights while our legs hung free over the edge of the seat.

"You okay?" Dex asked after we landed.

"That was . . . interesting," I said. All the junk food I'd eaten earlier was reassigning itself space in my digestive system, but thankfully nothing decided to make another appearance.

"I love this thing," he said. "Want to go again?"

"I think once is enough."

Those waiting in line visibly relaxed with the knowledge that we weren't going to make their wait even longer.

"It's not *that* scary," he said.

"No, but nachos only taste good going down—coming back up, they're a nightmare."

"Okay, so we'll come back later," he said, then opened the gate to let us out of the ride's fence. "I was afraid you were one of those people with an irrational fear of carnival rides or something."

"Nah. My dad used to work at one of these places when he was in high school. He said to watch how the tracks move and how the arms balance; that'll tell you if the ride's sound enough to risk a turn."

My mother, on the other hand, simply forbade me to go to them, period. *Oops . . .*

We left the rides and drifted into the part of the carnival that housed the games and walk-through attractions like the fun house and the house of horrors.

"Your friend said you were in need of cheering up, but you seem to be in a pretty good mood to me," Dex said.

"My cousin woke up today. Only for a few minutes, but it's the first time she's done it."

"Then this is a celebration," Dex said, brightening. "Wait here. I'll be right back."

"Where are you going?"

"It's a surprise!"

He left me with no chance to demand more details and jogged off toward the "employees only" section of the grounds, blocked by a tall redwood fence. I closed my eyes and just listened. The air was alive with positive energy, ringing with the sound of laughing kids and everything that said life was good and still would be tomorrow.

The world was kaleidoscope bright when I took another look; smiles were everywhere. Being in the middle of so much excitement, it soaks into your skin, making it impossible to believe that reality is anything else. You start putting even the worst things into a happier perspective.

Even the guy you might have spent the last several days trying to destroy.

I knew there was a chance of seeing people from Lowry there—the fairgrounds draw tens of thousands of people when they're open each year—but it was still a surprise to see Brooks standing beside one of the gaming kiosks. He was spending half his fortune, one tossed quarter at a time, to win an overdyed blue doggish creature. Rather than wait where I was, I decided on a last conversation before I checked out of Lowry and never had to see him again. If nothing else, it gave me an excuse to get out of the middle of the walkway and stop looking like a human speed bump.

"It's a little morbid, don't you think?" I asked.

Brooks turned at the sound of my voice, completely blowing his toss. He had a blank look in his eyes, like he'd been focused on nothing other than hitting that glass plate for way too long.

"What is?" he asked.

"Hangman's Row."

I pitched my head sideways and pretended to hang myself with an invisible rope, adding popped eyes and a lolled out tongue to match the appearance of the stuffed animals over our heads.

"Now that you mention it . . . maybe those aren't happy faces at all," Brooks said.

232

"You have a little sister stashed away somewhere that I've yet to see?"

"Chandi's having a rough day. I didn't know what else to do, so I promised her I'd win something for her. . . . This stupid thing's about to make me a liar."

I choked on the instant urge to tell him the game couldn't make him into something he already was before he entered the midway.

"No luck?" I asked instead.

"I'm forty bucks in."

"I could get you one for half that."

"With or without losing your clothes?"

"Very funny," I said. "I *was* going to explain that these things are rigged and that you can stand there all night pitching coins at the glass and never win. But if you don't want my help . . ."

"I saw a six-year-old dragging a giraffe twice as tall as he was. If he can figure it out, so can I."

He flicked another quarter off the end of his fingers. It hit a plate in the sixth row, bounced to one in the seventh, then rolled right off the edge onto the ground.

"Maybe if you bite your tongue and stand on one foot. I think the left is probably your best bet."

"Go ahead, mock my pain. The plates are inverted or something. It's impossible."

"Watch and learn, rookie." I leaned across the barrier and tapped the shoulder of the guy supervising the stand. "'Scuse me."

He turned around with a delayed smile that said it had already been a long night and it wasn't even ten o'clock yet. From the back, I would have thought the guy was close to my age, maybe someone in college at the most, but despite being nothing but pimples and teeth, he had to be over thirty. He was a walking warning sign for why you shouldn't eat a steady diet of carnival food. It looked, and smelled, like he'd styled his hair with french fry grease.

"You wanna try, cutie?" he asked.

The universe was determined to ruin my good mood; it was the only explanation. Another, more satisfying, response went unspoken while I picked another part to play.

"My boyfriend bet me I couldn't win a thing tonight," I whispered, then glanced back at Brooks.

"He's probably right," French Fry said.

"See, that's my problem. He thinks he's always right, and I'd really like for him to be wrong this time."

"Maybe you'll get lucky." French Fry reached under the counter for a scoop of coins as I dipped my hand into my pocket. "Girls like you draw business. I'll spot you a round for free advertising."

"Luck's for those who don't plan ahead." I held a folded twenty out between my fingers. "You drop this?"

"Maybe . . ."

"Because I'd swear it fell out of your pocket when you bent down to pick my quarter up off that platform. . . ."

"Lucky and honest." French Fry snatched the bill, checking to make sure it had the right president on it, and crammed it into his back pocket. "You want a pink one?"

"Blue."

"Blue it is." He pulled one of the doggish things down with a loop and handed it over the counter. The shabby fur was stiff and dyed darker in places. Missed stitches allowed the stuffing to poke out here and there, and whoever had glued the tongue into its mouth had let the adhesive spread too far, causing a hard ridge.

Cheap, and oh-so-less-than-perfect. I named it Chandi, Jr.

"You have to sign the list," French Fry said. "Only one big prize per customer per night. We can't have ringers going around robbing the games."

I took the clipboard he offered and scribbled "Bite Me, Esq." in tiny, cramped script that could have said anything.

"Thanks, mister." I winked.

"Any time, sugar. It's always a pleasure to meet someone who understands how to play the game."

I tucked my prize under my arm and headed back to where I'd left Brooks at the other end of the kiosk.

"Like I said, nothing to it."

"That's just not fair," he said. "How could I not have thought of that forty dollars ago?"

"It's not even worth four."

"I know, but it's what Chandi wanted."

"Here. The cheap dog is officially your problem." I slapped the doggish thing into his chest.

"I'll pretend you mean the toy," he said. "You're not here alone, are you?"

"My best friend sort of dumped me on yours, and now he's run off after some sort of 'surprise' and I have no idea how long it'll be before he comes back."

"You're here with Dex?"

"So?" I asked.

A strange tone had crept into his words that brought out the colder edge in my own. He had no right to ask who I was with or what I was doing or anything else.

"So, you haven't talked to me in a while."

"I talked to you yesterday morning," I said.

"A wave hello isn't a conversation. I was beginning to think you'd switched sides on me."

Nope. I was on the same side I'd always been on—Claire's.

"I've been preoccupied," I said. "Too much time in the hospital."

"Your cousin?"

"Yeah." That cold edge flamed white hot. I was not discussing Claire with him. Not while he was holding the prize I'd just won for the girl who was I-don't-know-how-many notches down the line from her on his conquest list, and not when there was finally a chance that all my worrying was about to be past tense.

"Should I assume your being here means she's okay?" he asked.

"She woke up today."

"That's great," he said; I almost bought it. I don't care how good an actress Chandi was, she had nothing on her boy toy. Brooks' eyes actually lit up as though he were capable of sharing in someone else's good fortune.

"It'll be great when she's home," I said shortly. "What about you? You said that's for Chandi."

He shifted the dog-thing to his hip like it was an overlarge baby.

"Jordan dragged her off to the fun house, I think. They should be back any minute."

And they were. The fun house exit opened, releasing a small cluster of people into the night. Chandi and Jordan were the first two out. Jordan pointed an angry finger at our bench and stalked off.

"Speak of the bi—"

"Dinah!"

"What? I was going to say 'big dog lover.'"

"Sure you were."

Well, I was. At least, I was going to say something dog-related. Technically it was a female of the species, and the queen "b" herself was headed straight for our bench with a scowl hard enough to crack the porcelain coat she called makeup.

"You owe me twenty bucks." I stood from the bench and headed back to the center of the midway, where Dex had left me.

A glance back didn't give me the angry girlfriend scene I expected. Chandi had the blue dog-thing in one arm; her other one was around Brooks, and her face was buried in his shoulder. The way she shook while he rubbed a hand up and down her back made me sure she was crying.

He reached for one of her hands, but she jerked it back, hugging it around the stuffed monstrosity as a shield.

People walked past them, as though they didn't notice the teenage girl in the middle of a breakdown. Others obviously did notice but were trying not to. A minute or so later, Jordan appeared with two soda cups, sat on Chandi's other side, and the dynamic shifted along with Chandi's posture. Brooks and Jordan locked eyes over her head; he twisted his wrist in the air like it was some sort of prearranged signal, then gave Chandi a kiss on the head and walked off with his hands in his pockets.

I began to feel a niggling prick of something suspiciously remorse-like for the things I'd said. From the look of it, this was more than the usual "bad day" I'd been picturing when Brooks said he was trying to cheer her up.

He looked in my direction, if not directly at me; the naked concern on his face made me want to go back over and find out what was going on. Brooks turned, like maybe he'd come my way and spare me the need to go his, but he changed his mind. He ducked his head and retreated.

I was confused until I realized Dex had come back. Whatever had been in Brooks' head, he didn't want to share while his buddy was nearby.

"Come on," Dex said, oblivious to the entire scene. He took my hand.

"Do you know what's wrong with Chandi?" I asked.

He hardly bothered to look her way before puffing out a scoff.

"She probably passed a mirror and realized one eye's higher than the other one or something. Let's go."

He shook a set of keys at me and yanked my hand hard enough to pull me away.

27

There wasn't much toward the back of the carnival grounds besides the walk-through attractions. The fun house, with its awful, ear-bleed-inducing music that sounded like a carousel on crack, had a winding line that snaked through three rounds of crowd control ropes. There was a boat ride with a shorter line made entirely of couples—most of which had decided not to wait for the darkened space inside to start making out. The third structure, and our apparent destination, was the house of horrors.

A plywood cutout of a creepy Gothic mansion with blacked-out windows served as the entry point for the house, but it was chained shut. There was no music coming from inside like with the other two, and a large wooden sign read "Closed for Maintenance" in tall orange letters. A couple of kids seemed to be testing the lock, but other than that, it was deserted.

"Where are we going?" I asked as he steered me toward another of the red-painted employee access fences. "It's closed."

"Only for the plebeians who must use the front door, *chérie*." He stuck his nose in the air and put on this horrible fake French accent that made him sound like a waiter in a really bad movie. It was a habit I assumed he'd picked up from Brooks, because he was acting a lot like Brooks had when he'd showed me around his house. "Those of us with higher connections get the gold star treatment."

Dex was the only person I knew who could make me giggle like an idiot at will; he was a human lithium shot. All the irritation dealing with Brooks had brought back and all the worry I'd felt for Chandi dissolved as easy as someone pouring cold water on a pile of soap bubbles.

"If it wasn't so cold, I'd sneak us into the lakeside. It's shut down for the run of the carnival, and we'd have the whole place to ourselves, but this is almost as good—trust me."

On the other side of the employee fence, we stopped at a metal door on the back of a cement wall; Dex used his key to open the padlock. He reached for a light switch inside, finding it with enough ease that I was sure he'd come through that way several times. I wondered if this was one of the places he had to clean.

The first exhibit was the torture chamber, with a skeleton chained to a rack and another in a giant cage that hung from the ceiling, only with all the lights on, there wasn't much to be afraid of. The shaded plastic bones didn't have the right effect.

Dex led me from room to room, showing all the carnival's tricks and where the different monsters would pop out along the track. He was the giant goofball version of himself I'd met my first day at Lowry, swinging from chains and switching the hats (and occasionally the heads) of the dummies to fit his own vision of how the place should look. Every room came with a story or a song; one even came with a dance. By the time we got to what he referred to as the finale, I was composing apologies— and thank-yous—to Tabs in my head. She was right; this wasn't a night I needed to miss.

The last scene was a posh banquet table with dead roses and

brown ivy for a centerpiece. A pair of skeletal ghoul dummies sat in the center, one wearing a tux and the other a wedding dress. Melted-down candles were in candelabras spaced every few feet along the surface, and the set dresser had even gone to the trouble of making a rotten wedding cake for the display in the background. It was mostly green, with one side collapsed in, but instead of smelling like mildew, the whole space reeked of resin and latex.

"I have a confession," Dex said. "This is where I used to bring my old girlfriend, but things didn't work out." He circled around behind the corpse bride and laid his chin on her shoulder.

"Couldn't compete with someone prettier than you?" I asked.

"We all have our faults," he said. "Sit down."

"You want me to sit in the corpse chair?" I asked.

"It's not contagious."

He lifted the dead mannequin up by her arms and set her aside. Strangely enough, neither she nor the groom had legs; tablecloth and cobwebs ran all the way from the tabletop to the floor, making it impossible to see behind them. Once the groom was out of the way, Dex took his seat.

"Why are we sitting at the dead people's table?"

"Because we're celebrating, remember? This place may not sparkle, but you can't argue that it's not built for a special occasion."

If you define "special" as attending your own wake . . .

I wasn't sure why he thought hanging out with the Crypt-keeper's family was in any way something I'd consider worthwhile when I'd just come too close to attending a real funeral, but somehow this had become a good idea in Dex's head. I figured a few minutes of playing along couldn't hurt.

He reached down for something below the hidden part of the table and set it next to his gold plate of rotten roast beef.

"You keep a cooler stashed with the dead-heads?"

"Why not?" he asked. "No one bothers anything in here."

That I could believe.

"I grabbed these out of the fridge. Mom never misses a few."

Dex pulled a wine cooler from the ice and twisted off the top before pouring it into the plastic goblets beside our place settings. Tiny bits of gold paint flaked off to float on top, but it didn't seem to faze him at all.

"Cheers," he said, and tipped his glass, expecting me to clink mine against it.

"No thanks," I said.

"Don't tell me you're some kind of drinking prude."

No, but I was officially annoyed.

"I don't like the taste," I said.

Or the smell—especially after Tabs puked for fifteen minutes from drinking too many of those things. Every time I smell cheap alcohol, it makes me green. I pushed the glass a little farther away, just to make myself feel better.

"What are you doing with a liquor stash in the freak house, anyway?"

"I like to hang out here," he said, then drained his glass. "No one bothers me. The only way in when the front's locked down is with a key, so it's a good way to get away from interruptions and eavesdroppers. Just because it's a celebration doesn't mean we need an audience."

He ducked his head, stretching over the space between us, and kissed me. No lead-in, no moment of mutual attraction where we got closer by degrees and sealed the deal because we had the same idea at the same time. He just kissed me.

I'm not stupid. I don't expect kisses to be like the over-practiced, stylized lip locks in the movies where the chemistry's as fake as the spray tans, but it would have been nice if there had been one thing even halfway decent about the experience. Even locking lips with Brooks in Claire's tree wasn't as clumsy.

This was squishy and wet, and Dex tasted like the wine cooler mixed with popcorn (which is worse than wine cooler on its own). With him that close, I realized that French Fry wasn't the only one who smelled like a grease trap. The warm, sticky scent weighed down the others into a stomach-turning glob of stink that stuck in my nose and my mouth, and I was pretty sure it was on my hands when I tried to push him back.

I gave him a gentle tap, to cue him that he needed to back up, but instead, our awkward moment turned worse. Dex leaned in harder, with one hand against my back, pulling me toward him.

"Dex . . . wait." I turned my head so his lips had nowhere to go other than my jawline. "Hold off a minute."

When that still didn't get the point across, I shoved him hard enough that I felt the resistance when he didn't want to move. He stopped, but he wasn't happy about it.

"What are you doing?" I asked.

"Celebrating," he said again, as though it were his personal buzzword. "Your cousin's feeling better, so you should, too."

Talk about your mood killers. I didn't want to think about Claire anywhere near a guy's lips. All that did was make me think about Claire and the lips of the guy who'd started her downward spiral in the first place. It didn't help at all that the second time he kissed me, the only thing I could focus on was the greasy smell stuck to his clothes.

Despite the popular opinion of a few nameless drones from my old school, I am not, in fact, a slut. I don't go around attaching my face to anything with a Y chromosome. I had kissed a grand total of four guys when Dex's better judgment jacked into his hormones—including Brooks and Brucey, which is the sort of subject for which brain bleach was invented—but even with only four reference points, I knew it was a bad sign when the number one thought in my head was that he was making me think of French Fry from the coin toss.

"Stop it, Dex," I said.

His hand dropped from my back, so at first I thought he was listening, but instead of letting go, he stuck it inside the back of my shirt, inching his fingers up. They got as far as the back clasp on my bra before my patience ran out. If he couldn't hear me at a normal volume, I had no problem with yelling.

"Stop!"

He bypassed the clasp and tried to work his hand around to the front. I flattened both of my palms against his chest and shoved, using the momentum to push myself back and duck out of his grip. The chair fell over when I stood up.

"What was that for?" He sat there, his hands out wide as he asked the question. The first hints of anger hardened his eyes and mouth.

"I said stop!" I backed up just to prove to myself I was on level ground. "I'm not doing this."

"I told you, no one's going to bother us in here. There aren't even any cameras; the owner's too cheap to install security. No one's going to see anything, if that's what you're worried about."

"I am *not* worried."

"Are you a virgin or something?"

"That's none of your business. I said no—I'm not in the mood to make out while stuffed dead people stare at us with their eyes hanging out of their sockets. I'm leaving."

"Then why'd you come in here?"

"Because you brought me?"

"Yeah, and you should have known why. Why else would I bring someone into a closed ride with a locked door?"

"Because until two seconds ago, you weren't an ego-inflated ass like the rest of the boys in burgundy and blue."

Dex was out of his chair almost as soon as I'd said it, and like mine, his crashed to the floor. Unlike me, however, he showed absolutely no signs of nerves or being uncomfortable. He was pissed.

"I am nothing like them!"

He grabbed for me, and I honestly don't know what he had in mind when he did it. Maybe he was going to shake me or drag me back out of the house of horrors physically to salvage his pride—maybe he was tired of hearing no and had decided it didn't matter anymore. I didn't care. All I saw was a guy with half a foot and sixty pounds on me coming my way like a raging bull, and this time there wasn't much chance of Chandi or Jordan showing up as backup.

"Don't touch me."

Strange as it sounds, I didn't scream it or shriek. An intense calm had settled on me. I wrapped my hand around the closest thing I could reach and swung it at him. One of the prop candelabras collided with his arm and crumpled. The stupid thing wasn't metal, or even plastic. It was some sort of molded papier-mâché painted to look like lead. Dex knocked it out of my hand.

The alien serenity that had allowed me to stand my ground shattered; I walked backward as fast I could. I was afraid turning around would take longer, and there wasn't that much space between us. As it was, Dex could have caught me with one short lunge, if he hadn't been so out of it.

"You think you're better than me, too?" he growled.

I didn't know what to think. I had convinced myself that the scene in the parking lot at school was a misunderstanding, or the fluke of a bad morning, but this wasn't the same guy I'd sat with in class. Some enraged creature wearing Dex's face had replaced one of the few sure friends I'd made at Lowry, and I was torn between retreat for self-preservation and wanting to break down and beg for details about what had happened to flip his personality.

"Dex, calm down."

"You think just because you've got an uncle who's some kind of big shot with a nice house, who can afford to buy you a car, that gets you off the servants' floor and into the inner circle?"

"What's wrong with you?" I asked. "Why are you acting like this?"

"I'm not the one acting, Dinah; you are. You pretend to be like me, but you're not. I've seen a dozen girls like you who trade up as soon as they get the chance, and then they never look back. You're all alike—dangle something shiny and you'll roll over for a few tricks. Channing did it. Even that pug-faced slag Abigail, who likes to pretend her brain could keep her grades a point higher than mine without her being on her back."

My stomach dropped when I felt something solid behind me. Without watching where I was going, I hadn't walked a straight line the way I had hoped. I was still inside the banquet exhibit, and up against a wall. Dex closed the last few feet between us, using his extra height to make me feel as small as possible.

"You only give it up for someone who can get you what you want—so here—" He stuck his hand in his pocket and pulled out a quarter, flicking it at me as if the space between my eyes were one of the platforms from the game kiosk. "I expect change," he said, and dipped his head down toward my face while his hands stretched the neck of my shirt until I thought it would rip.

It was in that moment that Kyle Smith became my hero. During that fight when Tabs and I were pummeling him with toy horses, Kyle was awarded the honor of being the first (and until Dex, only) guy I'd ever kneed in the crotch. With Kyle, it had been an accident, and Tabs and I had leapt off as soon as his face turned red and he rolled up in a ball. With Dex, I anchored my hands against his shoulders, which were now conveniently placed as a brace, and did my best to turn one hundred and ten pounds of me into three hundred pounds of upward thrust.

There are perks to being a mechanic's kid; I just never expected Dad's lessons on piston movement to be quite so relevant to life in general.

"Actually, I flunked charm school."

While he was doubled over, I gave him a punch to the jaw, to ensure he toppled, grabbed the bright orange key placard hanging out of his pocket, and sprinted out of the exhibit area, back toward the maintenance hall we'd used to get there. All it took was the open, hot-dog-scented air of the carnival grounds and the sound of a few hundred strangers laughing and screaming to make the tears start.

They were oblivious. All of them. I'd been mauled, right there in the middle of at least five hundred people, and not one had a clue.

Was that what Claire had felt?

So many people flooded Freeman's Point every weekend, especially in the middle of summer. To think that they could have been walking over her head while she was afraid to scream would have made the helpless feeling worse.

Even now, and even knowing that I'd fought back, I caught myself adjusting my clothes, trying to smooth the stretched wrinkles out of my collar, rubbing my arms because I could feel his fingers on my skin no matter how much distance I put between us. My knee throbbed from the force of impact, and I was fairly certain I'd broken my knuckles punching his jaw. There was pain even in escape; I couldn't imagine what it was like for someone who hadn't been able to.

I couldn't keep the panic back. Tabs was long gone by now, and Dex was surrounded by friends here. There was no guarantee that even if I found a security guard they'd believe me; Dex was one of them, and they'd seen us together for the last hour. If I could make it to the front gate, there was a security hub with a real cop, but that was a long walk, and Dex knew the layout a lot better than I did. If he didn't come to his senses, I'd never beat him there.

And I really did hope he'd come to his senses. It was impossible to wipe away the Dex I'd known and replace him with the version from the house of horrors. Evil Dex had as much substance to him as the legless stuffed corpses from the banquet table. I couldn't rationalize it. That quick less-than-a-minute stretch played over and over and over in my head, but no matter how I looked at it, nothing changed. There were no signals to miss or cues to misinterpret. He simply flipped out.

A second wave of nauseous dread came behind the first, putting Chandi's behavior around him in a different light and calling back Abigail-not-Abby's first reaction when she thought I'd been ogling Dex at lunch instead of Brooks. Chandi folded anytime he was close to her, turning into a smoldering mess; she only worked up the nerve to speak back to him when someone else was nearby. And Abigail-not-Abby . . . unless there was a file drawer nearby to slam his hand in, I couldn't imagine her doing anything to defend herself.

I felt the terrain shift under my feet from the loose gravel of the behind-the-scenes areas to the paved sections of asphalt and looked up to find I'd reached the outer edge of the midway, where Dex had left me before. For a desperate moment, I searched for the bench where Chandi and Jordan had been, but four kids sharing a boat full of cheese fries had replaced them. None of the cominations of blond hair and black were anywhere close to either of the girls I knew from school, but I did find one I recognized.

What's that saying about it's better to stick with the devil you know?

Well, that's what I chose. I glanced back at the red-painted fence around the house of horrors and saw the gate open slowly.

Dex limped out at a careful pace, but the damage I'd done had zero effect on his ability to find me in a crowd. And there was no question that Evil Dex had stuck around. He started straight for me.

"Brooks!" I called out toward the dark-haired boy with his back to me. It's ironic that I'd thought Brooks' description to be so generic that first day at Lowry, because there was no way to mistake him for anyone else, even from behind. The way he carried himself was completely unique, and probably a lot more representative of that aristocratic bloodline he loathed than he realized. "Brooks!"

He turned at the sound of his name, scanning the crowd to see who'd called him; there was surprise on his face when he figured out it was me. I started running his way, no longer calm enough to simply walk.

"Dinah? Are you okay?" he asked.

"No. I'm not." I cut my eyes sideways, vindicated by the sudden stop in Dex's advance. He wiped his mouth of what I could only hope was blood and stalked off.

"Are you crying?" Brooks asked.

"Was crying," I snapped. "Past tense. Now I'm not."

For the moment, I'd let him help. Later, he could share a jail cell with Dex. Even if Dex could talk his way out of what happened with me and whatever he'd done to Chandi, Abigail-not-Abby was younger, and as she'd been avoiding him all year, whatever history they shared had occurred well before she was legal.

"What happened?" Brooks' tone hardened as he shifted his focus from my face to my arm and clothes. His attention paused at my collar, then dropped to just below my shoulder.

It was a reflex to throw a hand up to block his when he tried to use his hands for a closer inspection. "Your hand, it's—"

"Don't touch me," I ordered, shifting my weight onto my back foot to lean away. "Sorry . . . just give me a minute to get my bearings."

"Where's Dex?"

"Gone."

Hopefully.

"Did he say something to you?"

"Say? No."

"What's that supposed to mean?" he asked.

"That saying things wasn't the problem."

"Dinah, what happened to your shirt?"

"It got stretched."

Brick walls and iron bars rose up around the humiliation I felt standing there with my arms crossed over my chest while he tried to read the expression on my face. I had the sudden urge to go home and burn everything I was wearing, right down to my underwear, then find the bra I'd shown off that first day of school and torch it, too. Maybe then my clothes wouldn't feel so heavy or clammy against my skin.

"Stretched how?" he asked. "I don't know what's going on, but about five minutes ago, Jordan unloaded on me. The things she said . . . I came looking for you and Dex. Now you're shaking, and it's not that cold. Tell me what happened and where he went."

"I don't—"

The ringtone belonging to Uncle Paul and Aunt Helen bought Brooks a reprieve from my temper. I couldn't believe I'd forgotten I had it in my pocket, but the whole time I'd been trying to think of a way to avoid Dex, I hadn't even given a thought to that nearly weightless piece of plastic. I didn't need Tabs, and I didn't need Brooks—Dex was sunk.

"Uncle Paul," I said, not bothering to hide the relief in my voice. "I'm at the fairgrounds. I really need . . . What? . . . . When? . . . How?"

New tears stung my eyes as my legs forgot how to function; suddenly the ground was much closer than the five and a half feet away it should have been. Uncle Paul's voice faded to black; all thoughts of asking for help vanished.

Someone was beside me, shouting and calling my name. A familiar voice asked for help from others I didn't recognize as cold water dropped onto my face.

The whole time, my eyes were open; I was staring straight up, confused by the way the world looked from my place on the ground. A vast canopy of stars, interrupted by vague, human-colored shapes, filled my field of vision from one edge to the other. It was as if a screen had been pulled between me and reality and I'd realized how very small I was in the scope of the universe. All the plans and all the power I thought I'd had was nothing in the grand scheme. One moment of hope was a dim Christmas light compared to the blazing dots out there beyond my reach.

I was pointless—just like all the effort I'd put into trying to make things right for Claire.

"Dinah." The familiar someone called again. He shook my shoulder, and when I tried to sit up, he helped me the extra few inches I couldn't manage on my own. "Somebody get security."

Brooks.

It was Brooks talking to me.

I was sitting here at a carnival with Brooks while Claire was back on life support.

"What happened?" he asked. "Your call log said 'Uncle

Paul,' but he'd already hung up when you fainted. He wouldn't answer when I called back."

"He had to go back into the hospital," my voice said, but I don't remember my mouth moving.

"Dinah, you're scaring me. What's wrong? Does this have something to do with Dex?"

I heard him asking, but the words didn't register as a question until much later. At that moment, nothing was getting through as coherent, other than what had come from the other end of my phone.

"I need to get to the hospital," I said. "I d-don't h-have my c-c-car. My fr-friend t-took it."

The stutter was new. I'd never gone far enough into a hole that I couldn't remember how to speak in whole words without tripping over them. Not only could I not form real sentences, I couldn't get my legs to cooperate with me and get my body off the ground. Either I worked it out on my own or Brooks pulled me up, because at some point I was able to look down and see my own feet. Everything was gray except a puddle of teal syrup sticking out from under my shoe.

Brooks had ceased to exist as a real person, even though he was close enough to put a hand on my arm to draw my attention. He was more like a shadow or a stray thought on the edge of my mind. Not quite solid, until he spoke.

"I can take you," he said. He could have said other things, and I have no reason to think he didn't, but those four words were all I registered. It didn't matter who he was; I latched on to the lifeline he offered and let him pull me out of my scattered haze.

"Do you know where Trinity is?"

"My phone's got GPS; I can figure it out," he said. "Come on."

He walked me to the car, I guess. It's the only way I could have made it, because I wasn't in any shape to get there on my own. One second, I was testing the tensile strength of whatever cotton-candy and bubble-gum mishmash had glued my shoe to the asphalt, and the next Brooks was opening the door to his Beemer so I could climb in. He even buckled the seat belt for me.

Time shifted. The world passed like a stop-motion camera with a sluggish shutter. The next time I blinked, we were on the highway.

"Is it your cousin?" Brooks asked.

There's not much room in the front seat of a car like the one he drove, and rationally, I knew he was close, but his voice sounded miles away, like I was listening through deep water.

I was drowning.

"What?" I asked.

"It's your cousin, right?" he asked. "The phone call?"

"Y-yeah. Uncle Paul said to get there quick. W-we're almost there, aren't w-we?"

"Maybe five miles," he said.

"Is it cold in here?"

I was freezing. My legs shook so bad they were bouncing up and down off my toes against the floorboard.

"I think you're in shock," Brooks said. "Keep talking."

"She woke up." A fire started in my cheeks, making a stark and unpleasant contrast to the chill everywhere else. "She was fine. . . . They said she was getting better."

"Something changed?"

We'd hit that point where one person realizes the other is going to pieces so they try and keeping them talking to stay conscious and sane. I just let it happen. Words spilled out of my mouth in a newly formed nervous tic that required me to answer any question asked.

"He said her heart stopped. They shocked her, but she's fifteen. A heart's supposed to last for like seventy or eighty years."

Unless it's broken . . .

I turned to look at Brooks, as though he should have been able to answer me, but he didn't. He kept his eyes on the road, except for an occasional darting glance in my direction.

"Do you want me to roll the window down?" he asked.

"What?"

Yes, it was a simple question, and I should have been able to comprehend the basic mechanics of operating a window, but windows didn't have anything to do with Claire or her sudden lack of fight; therefore, windows made no sense in my world.

"Should I call my dad?" My phone was still in my hands, which were now in my lap. I kept turning it over and over. "I should, right? That's what you do, isn't it?"

"You're really pale," he said. "Do you need some air? I can roll the window down."

He went ahead and did it without waiting for my answer. The tiny motor buzzed in my door and the draft sucked my hair out the window to fly wild. It slashed right across my face, and I barely noticed the change in scenery.

I navigated the hospital by memory. All those tiny details I'd found comforting before turned mocking in the dark, when there was no one to sit in the chairs or watch the TVs or read the magazines. Everything was turned off except the auxiliary lights. The green rugs looked cheap, and the art had all the appeal of a ten-cent garage sale bargain. In the elevator, I started to push the button for the fourth floor before a random burst of clarity told me Claire would be back in the ICU. They'd taken her out of the angel room and away from Mitch. How was he supposed to watch over her if she was on a different floor?

It took five seconds for the car to lift us to the second floor; I squeezed out of the elevator before the doors had even opened all the way.

I didn't have to ask which room Claire was in, because I could already see Aunt Helen through the glass partition where they hadn't pulled the curtain completely shut. . . . She'd lost it. Uncle Paul was trying to hold her still, but she was screaming. She beat against his arms with her fists and tried to pry them away from her waist. Her feet were pulled up off the ground, but that didn't help, either; she looked like she'd lost her mind.

The nurses waved me over as I rounded their station, having recognized me from before. They all had the same somber mask in place, the kind people use to hide deep emotion. I'd never seen anything so terrifying. I couldn't get a decent grasp of what was happening in Claire's room—every space not filled with a curtain was blocked by the back of someone in maroon scrubs or a white doctor's coat. The second they stopped trying to block Aunt Helen from the part of the room where Claire's bed was hidden, Uncle Paul let go of her and she charged into the knot of people there.

Most of the time, when you hear that someone's fighting for

their life in the hospital, it doesn't look as impressive as it sounds. They're lying in a bed while nurses either man the station in the hall or answer call buttons. Doctors do their rounds, and very little changes. But right then, fighting was an understatement. Everyone in that room was playing tug-of-war with death, using Claire as the rope.

The closer I came, I started picking out specific sounds. I had expected to hear Aunt Helen saying actual words, even cursing, the way she was flailing about, but it was just noise. Choked sobs and muffled gurgles. I raised my hand and knocked on the glass; I still don't know how Uncle Paul heard me over everything else that was happening. He slipped out of the room, and I knew it was bad, because he didn't even try to hug me.

"Dinah—"

"Have they fixed it yet?" I asked. "They're fixing it, right?"

Of course they were; they had to be. Doctors fixed things. That was their job.

"Dinah," Uncle Paul said.

"I want to talk to Claire."

"Dinah, honey, Claire's—"

"No . . . she's better."

He was not calling me "honey." Honey was the name reserved for bad news and dogs that got hit by cars while playing in the street.

"She opened her eyes because she was getting better," I insisted. "She's going to see a counselor and tell him what upset her, and then she'll come home and laugh at me because I look so different from the last time she saw me. I'll still be here . . . Dad said I can stay."

"The doctors call it an end-of-life rally—"

"No."

Nothing qualified by "end-of-life" was supposed to be anywhere near my Cuckoo. Not anymore.

"It happens sometimes. She gave it all she had, but it was more than she could—"

"No! She's just tired from being in the hospital. Uncle Paul, let me talk to Claire. I'll tell her to listen to the doctors, to not stress herself out so bad and take it slower. She'll listen to me. She always listens to me."

"She's gone, honey. Her body hasn't shut off yet, but Claire's gone. There's nothing on the brain scan. As soon as they finish the last test to make sure and turn off the machines—"

"No! You're wrong."

I dodged around Uncle Paul, into the room, just in time to catch Aunt Helen being pulled back from kissing Claire's forehead. The doctor nodded to a nurse who had her hand poised over the control panel of a piece of clunky equipment, and for the first time all the noises stopped. The pings went silent and the LEDs quit blinking. I held it together until the doctor tugged the sheet up toward the top of Claire's head.

"Time of death—"

"What are you doing?" I demanded, grabbing his arm. "Don't. She won't be able to breathe under there."

Aunt Helen wrapped her arms around my whole body with more strength than a woman her size who had barely eaten or slept in days should have possessed. My arm ended up pinned under hers while she cried into the top of my head, allowing the doctor to finish his declaration for the official record.

Your brain goes strange places at times like that. Aunt Helen was nearly snapping me in half, and I was overcome with the need to call my dad, because as far as I knew, he was still researching flights from Oregon so he could see Claire when she came home. But she wasn't going to come home. She was never going to sleep in the bed she hadn't made; she wasn't going to get to see me with my blond hair, or make me give her a picture of myself in her Lowry uniform. She was going into the basement—into the freezer.

Claire hated the cold, and she hated the dark, and they were going to take her out of the ICU's bright lights and shove her into a drawer without her clothes. She'd hate that.

And the whole time I was thinking about it, Aunt Helen was still hugging me like I was the only thing that existed in the room anymore, and if she let go I'd disappear, too.

It was too much. There wasn't enough air in the room for all of us; it was too hot and too quiet without the machines. Aunt Helen's heart beat close to my ear with a rabbit-quick pulse, and every shaking breath wheezed down through her chest as though she were suffocating in slow motion.

I twisted loose and ran for the open space of the hall, then kept going past the nurses' desk, back toward the elevators. I even punched the call button, but I couldn't make myself get inside. Sliding metal doors closing me into a box were too much like the freezer drawers in the morgue.

The only other way outside was to use the stairs, so I turned to see if I could find the access door to the stairwell, and ended up crashing straight into the guy I'd forgotten was even there.

"I'm sorry," Brooks said.

"What?" This was not the time for him to choose to apologize.

"About your cousin . . . I'm sorry. I know it doesn't help, but it's what people say, and I didn't want to stand here and not say something."

"Who are you?"

Uncle Paul had followed my retreat, probably to make sure I didn't go off and do something stupid. Considering his daughter had just died because of a delayed reaction to slashing her wrists, it wasn't a ridiculous precaution.

"Brooks Walden," he said. "I go to school with Dinah. We were at the carnival when she got the call, and her friend had sort of left her stranded, so I drove her over. I'm sorry about your daughter, sir."

"Thank you," Uncle Paul said automatically. Brooks nodded in return, out of words and apologies.

"Excuse me, Mr. Reed?" A woman with a clipboard and an understanding face appeared behind Uncle Paul. "I'm sorry, but I need to know who to call to handle the preparations for Claire."

Preparations. They had to prepare her body for a funeral. I was going to have to go to Claire's funeral.

"I don't know," Uncle Paul said, more lost now than numb. "We have a parish priest, but I don't know anything about funeral homes or—"

His voice cracked; he coughed a sob into his fist.

"If you come with me, I can put you in touch with someone."

She'd likely given this speech a hundred times to strangers in deserted hallways who were going home with one fewer member of their family than they'd arrived with. Every word she said was precise and polished, but she seemed genuine enough. Uncle Paul nodded and she walked away, leaving him to come whenever he was ready.

"Would you stay with her, please?" Uncle Paul asked Brooks. How could he know he was leaving me to Claire's killer?

"Sure."

They were talking about me like I wasn't there or had gone deaf. My ears worked fine; it was the rest of me that wasn't behaving the way it should.

"Do you want to sit down?" Brooks asked. "There's a lounge at the end of the hall if—"

"I know," I snapped. "I've spent enough time there already— and I *don't* need your help."

"I could get some coffee or something. The caffeine might take the edge off. When my—"

"No." I cut him off. I was in no mood to hear about his losses and his mourning. Crying over a parent was nothing compared to having a fifteen-year-old girl's killer offer to get me coffee while her body cooled off down the hall. "I'm going outside for some air."

I found the exit door, shoved my weight against the release bar, and rode my own momentum into the stairwell, hoping Brooks wasn't stupid enough to follow me.

He was, of course. I heard his feet on the stairs behind me, knew they'd be right there all the way to the parking lot or however far I chose to go. The only thing that kept me from ignoring the exit to go into the basement was knowing the morgue was down there.

Outside, there was no more air than there had been in that

cramped ICU cubicle; I exited in a vacuum of my own misery. It pulled harder against my self-control the longer I stayed within reach of Brooks without lashing out.

"Do you want me to take you home?" he asked. I wanted to beat him to death with his own words; the false compassion grated against my temper like sandpaper until it was raw and bleeding.

"Leave," I said. Losing it in the parking lot would only make things worse for Aunt Helen and Uncle Paul. I couldn't deal with Brooks there.

"What?"

"Leave! Go away! Leave me alone!"

"Dinah, I know how—"

"Finish that sentence and I will shove it back down your throat one word at a time. Get in your car and drive away before I decide to do it anyway."

"Look, it sucks. I know that. You're going to be stuck in the middle of a crowd of people, and you may not even know half of them, but they'll act like they've known you for years. They'll say meaningless words so often you won't be able to remember what face goes with what voice when the swirl stops because they're all alike. I've been there—with my mom."

I dodged the hand he tried to lay on my arm.

"Don't touch me."

"You've been building up to this moment from the day you got here. I don't know if this was the end you expected, or if you thought she'd come home, but your whole life has revolved around the girl in that hospital bed . . . I get it. But Claire—"

"Don't you dare say her name," I snarled.

"It doesn't work, you know," he said.

"What?"

"Pretending you can put it off. As lame as it sounds, sometimes it really does help to talk about it, and now or later you're going to want to. If you find yourself without an ear on the other side of the conversation, my number's still in your phone."

"Don't lose sleep waiting for my ringtone," I said. "You've already done enough."

"Fine," he said. Brooks unlocked his car and climbed in. "But I'm here if you change your mind."

The Beemer's engine fired up, humming loud in the otherwise still lot. He pulled out onto the main road and vanished.

Experience told me I had maybe three days before Claire's funeral. That meant I had less than two to bury Brooks first.

30

It was after midnight when Uncle Paul finally forced me and Aunt Helen into the Land Rover and drove us home. No one spoke, and luckily for me no one had enough spare brain cells to dedicate to things like asking why I looked like such a mess. We got out of the car in the dark and still didn't speak. We went into the house and split apart, everyone going somewhere different.

Uncle Paul headed for his office; Aunt Helen made for the stairs. I know she wanted to go to Claire's room, but she couldn't raise her foot high enough to climb; I sat in the kitchen until she gave up. She ran toward the master bedroom with her head in her hands. That meant I had the whole top floor to myself, so there was plenty of room to pace. I needed it. I had to burn off some anger before I started breaking things like my mom would have.

The clock was striking one when I caught my reflection in some sort of decorative wall hanging Aunt Helen had in the upstairs hall. It wasn't as smooth as a regular mirror, and most of my features were smudged, but what I could see were tearstained cheeks, running makeup, and blond hair that fell past the mangled collar of my shirt. I'd completely forgotten about Dex and what had happened at the carnival.

I wiped my hand across my face to stop the tears, and the bruises on my knuckles glared back at me.

My mind filled with the sudden image of Brooks' face at the other end of my fist, but no matter how much I knew I wanted to hurt him like that, I couldn't. All I'd done from the moment I began planning was prove how much of a coward I really was. If I'd been brave enough, I would have marched into the head-mistress's office that first day, shut the door, and told her everything. If I hadn't been a completely useless lump, I'd have told Brooks' father that day in his office and let him handle his son. I'd have told my dad or Uncle Paul, given them Claire's diary, and let them call the police.

I wasn't some vigilante out to make Brooks sorry for murdering my cousin; I was a stupid little girl playing princess in a mansion with nice clothes and my very own dream car. It was no wonder someone like Dex thought I was a doll he could play with.

But I could fix it.

I could, the real me, not the reflection of Claire stuck in that mirror.

I flew down the hall to my room, dragged the bag I'd never unpacked from under the bed, and hauled it to Claire's bathroom. I rummaged her desk for a pair of scissors and stood in front of the sink where she'd made her last stand. Holding my breath, I said goodbye to the girl in the mirror. No one would ever see her again.

After Tabs abandoned me at the fairgrounds, she'd brought the Mustang home and left it so she could pick up Grimace; the keys were still in the ignition. And despite the total absence of sleep, and the insistences from Uncle Paul and Aunt Helen that

I not go to school the next day, I was out of the house before they were awake. All the Lowry guards looked at was the car; they never even noticed me.

I walked up the steps as though nothing had changed, and ignored every look and whisper as I made my way to class. For the first time, Dex wasn't glued to Brooks' side. I saw him with Hayden Leung just inside the room, watched the shock register on their faces and everyone else's, and didn't react when Dex leaned over and said: "Careful, man. This is the part where she locks the doors and makes the walls bleed."

Hayden didn't laugh or respond. He acted like Dex was contagious, heading for his seat rather than lurking at the door.

I took my own seat, not bothering to look for Brooks at the back of the room. I'd see him well enough later.

The morning ticked down to a cadence only I could hear; my pulse realigned itself to match, falling into the lockstep of a military march. The steady rhythm was the only thing keeping me calm in the last moments before I planned to make my final move.

I was going to do it.

As soon as class started and everyone was listening, I was going to walk up to the front of the room, introduce them to my real self, and tell them all the reason I was there. Then I'd leave Claire's books and papers where I dropped them, along with her blazer on the back of my chair, walk out of the building, and drive home, forgetting all about Lowry and everyone in it.

But nothing ever went the way it did in my head.

As if I needed further proof that I'd been elected Fate's whipping child, Mr. Tarrelton entered class as the last bell rang and the first person he noticed was me. It wasn't a surprise—I looked so different, with the short black hair and my newly replaced piercings, but I was hoping for at least a couple seconds' worth of shock value to buy me my opening. Instead, I got the angry teacher face.

"Miss Powell, I suppose there's some sort of explanation for your appearance? You're a month early for Halloween."

"There is," I said. "And I'm happy to explain—"

"Then I suggest you do so—to the headmistress."

"But, sir—"

"Now, Miss Powell."

"It's not her fault, Mr. Tarrelton." When Brooks came to my defense, I snapped my head toward him so fast my neck popped. All it would have taken was hearing him speak Claire's name again and they'd have had to call the cops to haul me away, because there wasn't a force in that room strong or fast enough to save him from the firestorm that had replaced my self-control. But I forgot who I was dealing with—the devil's a smart one, and he knows how to paint himself as one of the good guys.

He looked straight at me.

"What are you even doing here? You should have had your uncle call you in."

"Sit down, Mr. Walden. I don't think you can afford any more time in Ms. Kuykendall's office."

My courage failed; it was never really courage to begin with. It was anger, and now that I was being denied my chance to purge, all I could think was how unfair it was. I didn't even wait for Mr. Tarrelton to write me out a slip. I left everything other than the clothes I was wearing and rushed for the door, desperate to escape before the tears started.

31

Movement was all that mattered. If I kept moving, I could stay ahead of all the grief and pain, and I could get my heart pounding hard enough to drown out my own voice chanting how big a failure I was. I wasn't expecting anyone to try to stop me, and I definitely wasn't expecting to get tackled as I fled down the hall.

One second I was alone, and the next Channing Pepperidge was dragging me toward the girls' bathroom. I didn't even hear her follow me out of the room.

"You, me, talk, now," she ordered.

"Get off me!" I swatted at her, trying to dislodge myself from her grip.

The expression on her face was one I couldn't figure out; it was as though her facial muscles were trying to decide how to best interpret the cues from her emotions and coming up blank. A toilet flushed in one of the stalls and a girl who was probably a freshman stepped out toward the sink. She froze at the sight of Chandi squaring off with me.

"Out," Chandi ordered. "Big-girl talk, no toddlers allowed."

The friend who'd obviously been waiting on the poor little fishstick took her by the hand and slipped between us, out of the bathroom. Chandi shut the door behind them and propped it shut with the doorstop.

"I see those etiquette classes are really paying off. With people skills like that, you should run for office."

"I don't like you," she said.

"Shocking."

She crossed her arms over her chest and looked me straight in the eye. Her own were storms in a bottle, dark and dramatic. The usual fake posture had melted off her body and taken the pandering ditz with it. Whoever this girl was, she was the real Channing Pepperidge, and it was the first time we'd met.

"Aside from Brooks, I have a rule about avoiding people who hang around Jackson Dexter by choice."

"I'm going to assume you think you're being subtle," I said. "Maybe you should buy a dictionary."

This Chandi wasn't throwing tantrums or going for the diva histrionics. She stood her ground and didn't react to insults.

"And I don't like you because there's something about you I can't quite put my finger on," she said.

"Yeah . . . I wouldn't suggest putting your finger on anything concerning me right now, Cookie Cutter."

Maybe hitting her sore spot would get her to back off.

Instead, she laughed at me. Not like I'd told a joke, but more the way you do when you mean "Is that all you've got?"

"I also don't hate you."

"Great. Glad we cleared that up. Now if you don't mind, I'm late for never going to class again."

Chandi didn't play any sports, so far as I knew, and she certainly didn't act like the athletic type, but she beat me to the door and slammed her hand against it hard enough to close it again, then flipped the lock.

"I'm not done."

"Get out of my way."

She just stared at me. Barbie/Twiggy hybrid or not, she was bigger than me by at least four inches.

"I'll move when I'm finished," she said. "Until then, I'll stay here, and if you want to try and hit me, you can, but you'll only get one shot. I could pretty much beat you unconscious with my shoe right now, call it self-defense, and no one would question it."

"Get that line from a script?"

"Just thought of it, actually."

"Nice."

"Thank you."

Who thanks someone for complimenting them on a threat?

Against my better judgment, and fighting the urge to make her prove she could make good on her promise, I backed away and propped my hip against the sink row behind us. Chandi stayed leaned against the door. So she was at least smart enough to realize I'd make a run for it if she gave me the chance.

"What do you want?" I asked.

"To talk."

"Yeah, we covered that. It's the topic of this alleged conversation I'm fuzzy on."

"You aren't as hard to figure out as you want people to think," she said. "And I'm starting to get why."

"You don't know *anything* about me." Certainly not enough to psychoanalyze me in the girls' bathroom.

"You'd be surprised," she said. She took off her blazer, hung it on the door handle, and unbuttoned her shirtsleeves so she could roll them up. This time her shirt fit, I noticed. "When you did that presentation in drama, I almost came out of my skin. The words you used and the feelings you described, it felt like you'd been eavesdropping on my inner monologue."

When her sleeves were at her elbows, Chandi turned her wrists toward me, inside up. A row of parallel scars notched her skin every inch or so in horizontal lines. Half of them were completely healed, and most of the others were on their way, but two on each arm were red enough that I could tell they'd been open cuts within the last week. One looked like it had fresh scabs on it, maybe from earlier that morning.

"You cut yourself?"

Her eyes had turned red. She wrinkled her nose like someone trying to force their tears back, and spots of color burst across her cheeks. Reaching for the pocket of her blazer, she put her hand inside and pulled out a fist. It took several deep breaths for her to get up the nerve to open her fingers.

A long silver pin sat flat across her palm. Three or four inches long, with a butterfly and fancy metal swirls on the top. The pointed end was too thick to be a straight pin or a needle but too thin to be a knitting needle.

Chandi picked it up and pricked along the freshest scar on her arm until she'd worked one of the scabs loose and it started bleeding again. I didn't even think; I yanked one of those smelly cardboard paper towels from the dispenser and wet it before holding it out to her. She covered the new wound and held her other hand on top of it.

"I stopped for a while, but lately, things have piled on, and it was too easy to take the out. That's the part you forgot to mention. Scars heal, but they don't go away. They're always there, taunting you. Tempting. I've bled through three shirts since school started; Jordan's started bringing extras in her bag, just in case, so I don't have to explain the bloodstains."

A cold shiver of remorse dripped down my back, thinking of that day in the cafeteria with Abigail-not-Abby and what I'd said about Chandi looking like a stripper. No wonder she'd been so introverted in the pictures I took.

"Chandi . . ." I faltered over what to say to her. Getting out of the bathroom dropped off my priorities list as soon as she stuck her arms out. This was . . .

I didn't know what this was.

She didn't like me. She had no reason to trust me, and here she was with her biggest secret open to the air.

"You aren't the only one who had a rough night. No one died, but things aren't going so good for me, either."

"Chandi, it wasn't me. In class, I mean. What I said onstage, those were my words, but not my experiences."

She kept going like she hadn't heard me.

"I won't pretend to get the small stuff—that's private—but the big picture I understand." She wiped her eyes with the edge of her hand, trying not to smudge her eyeliner. The bloody paper towel went in the trash. "I get how things spin so far out of control that you want to find anything that's just you. Something you can choose to do or not to do. It keeps you from losing your mind."

Chandi smoothed her sleeves into place and buttoned them back up.

"I don't cut myself."

"You don't have to," she said. "The process is the same no matter what. I use my Grammy's antique hatpin with the pink pearl topper and enamel butterfly. You used a box of dye and a pair of scissors. You made a choice to change something, and that's more than most people do."

"Why are you telling me this?"

"I know what people say about me, and I know what they think of me." I must have been doing a lousy job of hiding my thoughts, because she added, "Don't look so surprised. You've been here less than a month and you probably know most of it. For the record, I never said having a cookie name made me sound like a hooker. I don't like my last name because it's not mine. My dad's last name was Taylor, but my mother remarried when I was little. She thought it would be easier on everyone if she changed my name at the same time she changed hers. I didn't even know until I was twelve a person has a right to know their own name."

"Chandi Taylor does sound better than Chandi Pepperidge," I said.

"Doesn't it?"

She actually smiled.

A bitter trail of mistaken assumptions wound its way into my stomach. If I'd met this Chandi my first day, the ones that came after would have been a lot different. I thought about her name in my phone, listed as an enemy right behind Brooks, and decided to move it when we were done with whatever this was. She might not be a friend, but she wasn't really an enemy other than the one I'd made of her.

How much of what I thought I knew had been shaped by the order in which I'd met the people who had told it to me? I had to wonder if I would have despised Chandi so much if I'd spoken to her or Jordan before Abigail-not-Abby's opinions determined my own.

"Just so you know, last night . . . it wasn't on purpose. I was there with a friend. Brooks didn't ask me to meet him there, and I didn't go looking for him. That's actually the opposite of what I intended last night."

"I know," she said. "Brooks told me."

"You talked to him?"

"He told me about the hospital."

Low self-esteem or self-delusion or whatever is normal for someone who takes the same piece of trash back over and over and over. This was more than that.

"He's worried about you," Chandi said.

"Sure he is."

"He is. And I'm sure it only got worse today when you showed up like this. He just can't decide if it was because of your cousin, Dex, or a combination of the two."

"Dex is nothing."

"Dex is slime, but he's not nothing, and pretending he is has caused at least a quarter of these."

She twisted her wrists in the air.

"No one noticed when things went bad for me. I pasted on a smile and pretended the world hadn't changed. Considering the makeover, I'm guessing you weren't planning on doing the same."

"That had nothing to do with Dex."

"Really? How'd you bruise your knuckles?" she asked, with the smug half-smile I was getting used to seeing when she thought she'd scored a point.

"What did he do to you?" I asked, instead of answering. I stashed my hands behind my back so she couldn't keep staring at them.

"Made the same assumption everyone does—only last summer, he tried to act on it. I told him I wasn't interested, but he didn't believe me. So I thought if I told him the truth he'd make one of his usual jokes and forget it. I thought he was the guy Brooks said he was. I even tried to laugh it off, I told him I wasn't worth the trouble because, small as she is, Jordan's the jealous type. But it only made things worse."

Okay, so I apparently knew all of *nothing* about Channing Pepperidge. Even less about Chandi Taylor.

"You and J—"

"Yeah," she said.

"You're . . . I mean, Jordan is . . . You and Jordan are . . ."

"Wow. I don't think I've ever induced stammering before. Interesting effect."

"Sorry, I just thought—"

"That I was straight?"

"Dating Brooks," I said.

"That's the general idea."

"It's an act?"

If it was, then every assumption I made about the way he treated his girlfriend, which was based on his interaction with Chandi, was wrong. Some of Brucey's insights about Jordan's responses to Dex also made a lot more sense.

"One that's had many repeat performances and multiple curtain calls." She raised her hand like we used to in Girl Scouts to recite the oath. "Brooks Walden is not now, nor will he ever be, my boyfriend."

"But . . ."

"Brooks and I have known each other since we were kids; our families are old money. A century ago, we'd probably have been engaged from birth, but best friends is as far as it's ever gone. We've got a lot in common, including the fact that we both like girls."

"He knows?"

"Since I was fourteen. Brooks is my social armor. We have a sort of unofficial deal. So long as it looked like we're paired off, my parents don't know anything different, and no one whispers. Dex did his best to ruin that as soon as he found out."

"Brooks is pretending to be your boyfriend?"

I don't know why I kept asking that. It wasn't really a difficult concept to grasp, aside from admitting that if he'd run interference for Chandi, he had to be a decent guy who actually cared about his friend and wanted to help her for that reason alone. My brain kept kicking the assumption out as bad data.

"Was." She nodded. "Until yesterday. Jordan's been after me to tell my mom and stepdad for months. She thinks it'll muzzle Dex if he doesn't have leverage."

"They didn't take it well?"

She picked at the button on her shirt cuff.

"I . . . I actually never got that far."

She backed against the sink and pulled her weight onto the counter so her feet could swing off the floor. My exit was clear, but I'd lost the desire to run.

"You're new here," she said. "And you're new money—don't take that as an insult; it's just context. You don't know what it's like living in a world where the rules of behavior are five decades behind the curve. I was going to tell my mom . . . I really was . . . but then I was there in the house, and she was chattering on the phone to one of her friends about some upcoming charity thing and how I'd be bringing this 'lovely young man' as my escort, and I panicked. I was stupid. I thought I could beg some sense into Dex. When that didn't work, I offered to bribe him."

Knowing how Dex responded to mentions of his net worth, that couldn't have gone over well.

Chandi wiped her nose with the back of her hand, which only made the open slice run faster. I fixed her another paper towel, took a seat beside her on the sink, and put enough pressure on her arm to stop the bleeding.

"Thanks," she said sheepishly, and took the towel from me. "Until then, Dex and I were on even ground. He couldn't out me without falling off Brooks' friend list for the betrayal, and I couldn't tell Brooks what a worthless parasite Dex was without him airbrushing my orientation onto T-shirts and handing them out for souvenirs. So long as there was threat of mutual social annihilation, we hovered."

"But then you tried to bribe him . . ."

She nodded, scrubbing the wet towel over her arm.

"The power balance shifted. Dex said he'd agree not to tell anyone I was a lesbian, but first I had to prove it so he wouldn't be lying if someone asked. Prove it once a week for three months."

"You didn't—"

"I ran," she said, lobbing the wadded-up towel into the trash can. "And gave myself a set of new lines. That was yesterday."

"Is that why you were crying when you came out of the fun house?"

"You saw that?"

She froze but forced herself to breathe.

"I went to Brooks, like I always do when things are too hard for me, but I couldn't say it out loud. He took me out there to cheer me up, not realizing we were entering enemy territory. I tried to keep the act up, but those stupid fun house lights did me in. You can wash blood out of fabric, but let it hit a black light and the stain still shows. Jordan saw them and refused to let up until I told her why I'd cut again. When I finally told her, she said that no matter what she'd promised, it was time to do something about Dex, so she told Brooks everything she knew."

"I'm sorry," I said.

"Useless words, aren't they?"

"But they help, in a weird way."

"Yeah, they do. Don't worry about me, I've got my credits; I only have to last the rest of the year, then I'm off to whichever school is farthest from here to start my own life. Brooks has sheltered me long enough."

No wonder she was so loyal to him.

Chandi stood up and started replacing her blazer to regulation, making sure she'd removed all traces of blood.

"Chandi . . . there's something I have to tell you about Brooks."

"Whatever it is, it doesn't matter. You need to go home. Take it from someone who knows exactly how well running doesn't work—go home. That's where you should be. Don't worry about trig or school or anything else that will still be here to deal with when you've got a clear head."

She unlocked the door and pushed it open.

"And for what it's worth, you look better with the black hair."

She winked, and then she was gone, leaving me sitting on

the sink wearing Claire's uniform and the face I used to find familiar.

Maybe Chandi was right. I'd been beating myself up trying to control the uncontrollable and it hadn't gotten me anywhere. Life isn't like the movies; we don't get the hero speech at the end of the third act, or the rally of friends that forms to help us right the wrongs we've been forced to endure. Sometimes, instead of the dramatic exit and swelling music cue, the heroine has to walk out of a bathroom alone so she can go home to mourn the one she couldn't save.

32

Uncle Paul and Aunt Helen decided against the church and chose to use the stone pavilion at the cemetery instead. It's not like they suddenly turned atheist or railed at God for Claire dying, though they could have done that, I guess. . . . They weren't around a lot between the hospital and the funeral. I'm not really sure what they did. All I know is that they chose the pavilion because it was more Claire than being inside a building with four walls, dark wood, and the scent of candles left over from the last Mass.

Perpetual Hope, which is a horrible name for a cemetery, was the color green you usually see on a golf course. The pavilion with its white stone columns and carved angels sat in the center so that the graves fanned out in all directions. Death on all sides . . . Claire would've hated that.

They set her coffin on a pedestal up front and arranged all the flowers and wreaths around it; a huge stone cross was carved into the wall behind the dais. The churning sky matched my mood perfectly.

"Wait," I said as they prepared to seal the casket before the service. Uncle Paul told the men in charge to hold off. "Can you open it for a second?"

He nodded, and they opened the lid. I don't know why they wanted a closed casket; Claire liked sunshine and open air, grass and trees. She was happier outside. No, not true. She was happier alive, because dead she could never be happy again. She couldn't be sad or cry or scream or laugh, because she was gone.

I struggled with the latch on my necklace before finally tugging it off with a tiny snap. The charm didn't mean anything anymore. My Cuckoo was gone—a "was" instead of an "is." She was past tense, so I left the remainder of Cuckoo and Dodo with her, draping the broken chain over the hands I couldn't stand to touch because I knew they'd be cold.

"I'm sorry," I whispered. "I tried."

I slipped my hand into my pocket, grasping the memory card she'd poured her heart and soul into. I'd planned to bury that, too, hoping it would end things for good, but I couldn't let go of the last bit of clinging hope that said it still might come to some good if I kept it.

"Are you ready?" someone asked me. It had to have been Uncle Paul, because Aunt Helen hadn't spoken since the hospital.

"Go ahead."

The workmen set the pins with a drill so the casket couldn't be opened again, then arranged the flowers over the seam. Claire was already buried, and she wasn't even underground yet.

When I turned around, the seats behind me were full, except for the family row, and there were so many people standing that they had to line up outside the pavilion itself. I'd heard that young funerals were the most crowded, but I don't think it would have mattered how old she was. Claire would have created a mob.

My mom and dad were in their places, and the seat obviously meant for me—the one between them—was the last place I wanted to be. I sat there anyway and hoped things wouldn't get any worse.

Of course, I'd run out of good luck the day I started Lowry.

"Mom, stop picking at my hair."

She pulled at the strands while I anchored myself to my chair so I couldn't slap her hands away. That was what she wanted.

"I don't see why you couldn't have waited another day or two to dye it back," she said.

"Not now, Mom."

"But your father said you looked so pretty with the blond hair. . . . I didn't even get a picture. And now you've cut it short, too. This is because you knew I couldn't stop you, isn't it? You knew I'd be coming and—"

"Stop it!" I jerked my head away so she lost her grip on my hair. "Just stop. Everything, and especially today, is not about you."

"Dinah Rain Powell, don't you dare talk to me that way."

That was the point when she tried to cry tears of frustration, but she's a horrible actress.

"Please, Daddy, do something. Can't you make her go to the car?"

"Just because I may not dress as nice as your precious aunt and uncle who spoiled you rotten . . ."

People were throwing us uncomfortable glances, whispering things I'm sure my mom thought were sympathetic toward her.

"Listen to yourself, Mom," I begged. "Can you honestly not hear what you're saying? We're at Claire's funeral—she's dead, and you're still yammering on about how unfair it is that all you got out of life was a husband who loved you and a kid who gave up trying years ago. Unfair is Claire never graduating high school . . . never *starting* high school. If you really believe Uncle Paul and Aunt Helen have it better, then you're more delusional than I thought."

I knew my mother; this was only the beginning. If someone didn't shut her down soon, she'd keep going until the entire focus of Claire's memorial shifted to her.

"You little brat. If it weren't for me, you'd—"

"If it weren't for you throwing another temper tantrum, and Daddy letting you when he should have filed for divorce and left you in whatever world you live in, I'd have been close enough to Claire to stop this from happening, and we wouldn't be here."

She was starting to catch on that the situation had shifted out of her favor, so she made one last bid for sympathy.

"Just because you've spent a couple of weeks pretending to be better than the rest of us . . . wearing fancy clothes and driving that fancy car . . . and don't think I don't know about it—"

"Stacy, that's enough."

"Don't try to blame this on me. Do something about your daughter and her mouth."

"Dad," I said. "Switch seats with me before I lose it."

Anything I did because of a lost temper would only make things harder on Uncle Paul and Aunt Helen. They were doing a great job of ignoring my mother in favor of flower arrangements when Grimace roared into the cemetery, blessedly loud enough to drown out whatever my mother's complaint was.

"Go on, D," my dad said.

"She can't leave the family row," my mother snapped. "What will people say?"

"That at least one member of this family has enough respect for the dead to act like they're in mourning."

Mom had never been speechless before, but his words cut the bluster right out of her. She deflated into her seat and tried to make herself cry again.

"Go on," Dad said again. "Stay with Tabitha."

I was out of my seat as soon as he'd said it, but sadly not far enough to keep me from hearing my mother's last remarks.

"And I don't know why you let her associate with that cast-away freak. That girl . . . if that's what you want to call her . . . the way she dresses, no one could be sure one way or the other. And don't pretend it's not just to spite me, either. You let that . . . *thing* . . . corrupt my daughter, talk her into cutting her hair off. I wouldn't be surprised if they were dating behind your back."

"If Dinah wanted to date Tabitha, she'd tell me to my face. Then I'd give her forty dollars for dinner and a movie."

I thought Mom was going to choke on her own tongue. Funerals are the last place to break out pom-poms, but I wanted to cheer for my dad right then.

He got up and went to stand with Uncle Paul and Aunt Helen—the way Mom should have done. She should have been trying to comfort her sister, or even crying over her niece, not . . . whatever she was doing.

"I see your mother came," Tabs said.

"She thinks we're dating. Dad's all for it."

"There are many reasons I love your father."

"I don't know why she even bothered flying in."

Except to be a bother, which is pretty much her goal in life. Like some twisted addiction to chaos.

Tabs had stopped at the back of the crowd, between the pavilion and the paved road that snaked between the burial sections. Brucey, with a brushed ponytail and clothes that for once didn't make him look like he was on his way to a rave, had gone straight from Grimace's passenger seat to the dais, clutching a bundle of pink tulips.

There's a story behind that. . . .

I'd always suspected that Claire had a bit of a crush on Brucey (as did he, but Brucey's not the kind of guy who would rub it in). He wasn't the sort of person she hung out with in her own circle, and the things he'd learned from old movies made him just unusual enough to qualify as a then-preteen's brand of mysterious. What sealed the deal on her permanent fascination was when she'd been sick for four days straight with some kind of superflu when she was twelve. She was miserable; she couldn't even get out of bed.

Brucey came by the house to visit because that's what he does when people are sick—he never catches anything himself. Mr. Sleight-of-Hand put on a reverse pickpocketing act and snatched a handful of pink tulips out of thin air. Sure, he'd asked me ahead of time what kind of flowers the Cuckoo liked, but she never gave it that much thought. It was magic.

And if I thought about it, and how Brucey had been since he learned about Brooks' role in Claire's misery, maybe the crush hadn't only been on Claire's side of things.

I hadn't really cried that whole day, but seeing Brucey with that bouquet nearly did me in. He stood next to Claire's casket, arranging the tulips one at a time, so they'd mesh with the spray already on the box (he gets a bit OCD when he's upset). The last one he laid on top, right above where her hands would be.

It was the kind of scene that makes a great fairy-tale ending, only the princess was bolted in and the prince couldn't kiss her awake. Alice couldn't make it back from Wonderland.

Lines from the poem Mr. Tripp had made us read in class droned in my head like a broken music box.

> *Still she haunts me phantomwise,*
> *Alice moving under skies*
> *Never seen by waking eyes.*

I'd never see Claire again. I had to turn my attention back to Tabs before I ended up a puddle on the pavement.

"What happens now?" Tabs asked.

"After the funeral, I guess I go back into solitary. At least we can still talk online, assuming Mom doesn't trash my computer. Dad was going to let me stay before, but now . . ."

"I don't guess you'd want to stay here, huh?"

"I'd rather stay with Aunt Helen and Uncle Paul than Mom, but I'm not sure they're even going to stay after this. They may stay in the city, but they'll probably move houses or something."

Moving was a good idea. Aunt Helen couldn't climb the stairs to Claire's room without bursting into tears; if they stayed in that house, she'd probably end up one of those people who kept a shrine to their dead kid forever, never letting anyone move the furniture or wash the dirty clothes.

At least *her* mental issues developed for a good reason.

Brucey joined us. He had his head down, and his shoulders were bowed more than normal. He'd undone his hair so it would cover eyes I knew were red. He didn't say a word, just stepped up next to me and hugged me around the middle so I was hidden behind the curtain of his hair and his too-tall self.

It was an invitation to cry where no one could see, and I was ready to take him up on it, but the universe's dark side didn't take days off for funerals.

"Dinah, don't turn around," Tabs said, out of nowhere.

I did what most people would do, which was the exact opposite of listening. Brucey was smart enough not to let me go.

"I don't believe it. . . ."

Scratch that. I believed it; I just wished it weren't happening. As mourners' cars filled in along the road, there were a lot of faces I didn't recognize. But one . . . one young face with dark hair and brown eyes, wearing a black suit, was forever burned into my brain. I hadn't been near him since he'd tried to defend me in homeroom, but Brooks had been in my nightmares ever since the hospital, and now my nightmare was crossing the grounds, straight for me, with a bunch of flowers in his hand.

"D, don't." Tabs grabbed me by the shoulder before I even knew I was moving forward. Brucey's arms tightened around my waist.

I was already beyond the possibility of "don't." "Don't" had ceased to exist. First dealing with my mom, and now Claire's murderer showed up at her funeral with a bouquet of roses and violets. "Don't" didn't compute.

"Remember what you said about making things harder on your aunt and uncle."

Harder? No. The only thought in my mind was how *easy* it would be to end everything right here. I might not have been able to come through for Claire while she was alive, but I could get her some peace before she was buried. This time, there was no teacher to stop me.

Brooks walked past us toward the front of the pavilion, where the rest of the flowers had been placed. His weren't in a vase or arrangement so much as they were the sort you'd hand off, so he laid them on top of Claire's coffin, over Brucey's tulip and next to her photo. For one desperate second, I thought he'd finally decided to stop pretending. I thought he'd come to confess.

But he didn't. He just laid his flowers down, glanced at the photo like the face was one he didn't recognize, even though it was from her fifteenth birthday, and turned away.

"Hey," he said as he came back to where I was. Somehow "homicidal rage" must have translated into "grief" in his head, because I was not in the mood to have him say "hey" like we were friends and it was all right for him to be there. "I called your uncle; he told me when the service was . . . I just wanted to be here," Brooks said nervously. "I hope you don't mind."

"Finally decide to grow a conscience?" I could have counted the placement of Brucey's fingers against my abdomen, I was pulling so hard against him.

"Look, I know you're upset, and that you want someone to be mad at, but I don't know what I did to you. . . ."

"To me?" I scoffed. "You didn't do it to me. You did it to her!"

I pointed to the coffin and the photo of Claire he'd all but ignored.

"Dinah, people can hear you," Brucey whispered.

Let them. Wasn't that the point of this whole thing—to expose the truth and make people see it?

290

"Dinah, I've never met her. I don't know why you think I have," Brooks said.

"Because Claire told me, that's why."

"I'd never seen her before the other night in the hospital."

"Maybe you didn't recognize her with her clothes on."

"D? Everything okay?" Dad stepped up beside us, resting his hand on my shoulder, and Brucey let go. I'm sure he thought with my dad there things would get better, but when you're sharing air with a murderer, "better" requires a U-turn mood swing, and I hadn't hit bottom yet.

Uncle Paul and Aunt Helen were staring. Everyone was staring, including the priest. One thing was for sure: if Mom wanted to catch the crowd's attention, she was really going to have to work for it this time.

"Why don't we go sit down?" Dad asked.

"Good idea." Tabs tugged on my arm, pulling me back toward the seats. Brucey'd stuck his hands deep in his pockets and was already shuffling that direction.

"I'm not sitting down, not anymore. I'm not waiting anymore. I'm not stalling anymore. I'm not even trying anymore. And no, I'm not okay, Dad. I'm not okay because I will not stand here while the guy who killed my cousin brings her flowers and pretends it never happened."

There's a kind of silence and stillness that's only possible in the center of a cemetery when you're in the presence of the dead. You don't choose to stop talking; speech becomes impossible. That's what happened then. All the whispers and hushed conversations triggered by the scene with me and Brooks cut off at the same time. And while there was no communal shout of "What?" and no giant gasp, with the sort of melodramatic horror you see in bad movies, the scream of shocked outrage was implied by the length of time during which no one said anything.

"What are you talking about?" Brooks asked finally. He was the outsider, so he was the only one who could have broken the bubble.

"Dinah?" Uncle Paul filled in the space beside Dad so we were blocked from everyone's view.

"You want to know why Claire cut her wrists?" I asked. "There you go."

My self-control had reached critical mass; the explosion was coming, and I couldn't stop it. I stabbed the air in Brooks' direction.

"She did it because of him. Because he spun her around in so many directions that she didn't know which way she was going anymore. And then, when he got bored with riding the merry-go-round, he ditched her—two weeks before school started."

"I—I didn't," Brooks stammered.

"Claire spent the next week imagining how her new school was going to go when everyone knew that Prince Charming had made the maid feel like royalty for a while. She couldn't face them, and she was afraid to tell you and Aunt Helen why she didn't want to start Lowry. And now he shows up here with a ten-dollar bunch of flowers and can't even remember the face of the girl he ruined."

"Is this true?" Uncle Paul turned his attention to Brooks like he'd get an honest answer out of him.

"No! I swear, sir. I don't know what she's talking about. I never met Claire."

"No? Well maybe this will help you remember." I dug the memory card out of my pocket and slapped it into Brooks' hand.

"What is that?" Uncle Paul asked.

"Claire's month-long suicide note, starting the day she met him. The whole story's there. Go ahead and take it; I have copies."

"Have you lost your mind?" Brooks asked.

"No, I lost my cousin. Claire will never drive a car, she'll never go to college, she'll never have kids—she'll never live. *Because of you.*"

"I never touched her!"

"You may not have held the razor, but it was still because of you," I said. "Oh. And guess what. Your little skinny-dipping adventure with Claire, the one that ended up under the dock at Freeman's Point—that was the day before her fifteenth birthday."

"What?"

That time, someone did say it. I just wish it hadn't been Uncle Paul. My stomach clenched as I drove the point home.

"She was fourteen, Brooks. You're what, seventeen? I'm pretty sure that makes it a felony."

"Dinah!"

"Kind of knocks the luster off drug abuse, shoplifting, and joyriding in Daddy's car, doesn't it?"

"That was you?"

The betrayal on his face didn't faze me one bit. Nope, not at all. I absolutely didn't feel my heart drop into my feet.

"What happened to you?" he asked. Brooks reached toward me, but Uncle Paul and Dad stepped between us.

"Get away from me before they have to dig another grave."

Brucey was back—he and Tabs each had one of my arms.

"I think you should go," Dad told Brooks.

"Wait a minute, Wyatt," Uncle Paul said.

"We'll get things sorted, but this isn't the time. Focus on Claire for now. Everything else can wait. Dinah, stay here."

Dad took Brooks by the shoulder and escorted him away from the pavilion back toward his car. He was gone for a while, so I know they had to have talked, but he didn't give any hint as to what either of them had said to the other. He just came back and took his seat next to my furious mother while I stood in the back of the pavilion holding Tabs' hand so hard she probably lost feeling, and leaning against Brucey.

I kept waiting for it to feel like it was over, for reality to cross some kind of dividing line, but the world was no different after the truth came out. Claire was still bolted into a box with Brooks' flowers on it, and the big reveal hadn't lessened the crushing pressure around my chest. Every note of somber music leeched another bit of life out of me.

Nothing had changed. I'd accomplished nothing. I was nothing.

33

I felt like I'd left my soul in the cemetery, haunting Claire's grave. Only my body rode home in the backseat of Dad's truck, numb and apathetic, while my mother rattled off her endless list of complaints in the front. Most of them were directed at me, but the beauty of losing feeling is that even sharp things don't hurt so much anymore.

"Did you see how people were looking at us?" she rasped out. "They have to think we're the worst parents in the world, which of course they'll blame on me because it's always the mother's fault."

I wished I'd thought to bring my earbuds so I could have blocked her voice completely, but I had to make due with the distraction of my phone. No matter what file I intended to open, they all inevitably became photos of Claire, or copies of the words she'd sent me. I flipped back through her accounts of the month with Brooks, wondering if he'd have the nerve to read it himself. I couldn't stand reading about her daydreams and hopes for the future, or about sunshiny days at the Point when she was so caught up in her fantasy that au natural became her swimwear of choice. The Claire I left behind for Oregon never would have gone skinny-dipping with anyone— much less a guy she'd only known for a couple of weeks.

I couldn't stand it. I shut the phone off and let my mother's continuing complaints wipe everything else out of my mind.

"Honestly, who *does* something like that at a funeral? They're supposed to be quiet affairs, not full of screaming and screeching. I don't know where she gets it."

It went on like that for miles, with Dad's shoulders shrinking down tighter and tighter beneath his suit. His ears were turning red to match the bald spot he hadn't worn his cap to cover.

"And you were no better," Mom snapped. "Joining in like you did. You should have stopped it. You're her father—you should have ordered her to sit down and be quiet rather than indulging in whatever fantasy she's got playing out this time. At least there was a nice turnout. All those beautiful flowers. The colors were a bit gaudy, and hardly anything matched, but they were lovely. I wonder if Helen would mind my taking a few back to put around the house. She hates gardening, and they'd look just perfect under the windows."

That was the point my out-of-body experience ended.

"I'm sure Aunt Helen would love to have you plant reminders of Claire's death next to the roses, so long as they match, of course."

Mom's spine wrenched straight to its full length as her whole body went rigid. Strangely enough, Dad seemed to relax.

"I mean, Claire's dead, but so long as you get a few nice plants of it, that makes it better, right? It won't bother you at all to know the spring color in your flower box was bought with your niece's life; it's just one less trip to the nursery, and a few dollars you didn't have to pry out of Dad."

"How dare you speak to me that way after what you did today?"

"And what about what you did, Mom? Did you even hug

Aunt Helen or offer Uncle Paul a simple, useless 'I'm sorry'? Because if you did, no one saw you. You didn't even say good-bye to Claire."

"Claire was already gone by the time I knew she was that dire. You know I didn't get the chance—"

"At the funeral! You didn't even tell her goodbye at the funeral!"

Mom huffed in her seat, crossing her arms as though I were the one being difficult to understand.

"I don't know why you insist on throwing these tantrums, Dinah Rain, but I can promise you they're going to stop right here and now. Once we're home in Oregon—"

"There is no home in Oregon," I said. "I'm staying here."

We had reached the outer gates of Uncle Paul and Aunt Helen's house. Dad turned in behind their car to follow them up the long drive.

"You most certainly are not."

"Yes, she is." Dad said each word precisely, with a point on the end. "We've already discussed this, Stacy. If Dinah wants to stay here, even without Claire, then she's going to do it. This family's lost one child because of something terrible and beyond our control; I'm not having you lose the other one by design."

"Wyatt." Mom dropped her voice to what she thinks is a dramatic whisper, but it's actually loud enough for anyone to hear, even if they aren't listening. "You can't expect her to stay here after what happened back there. People will talk."

"If it doesn't bother Dinah, then it shouldn't bother you."

"I won't allow it. I'll get a lawyer and have the police fetch her home if I have to. I refuse to continue—"

I couldn't stand hearing her anymore, so I did something I hadn't done since I was a kid. Dad's old truck has a sliding window in the back where the cab attaches to the bed. It's short, but it's wide enough to squeeze through if you're determined. I flipped the latch and pulled myself into the back of the truck, still holding my phone.

"Dinah!" Dad yelled, slowing down exactly like I thought he would. I took the opportunity to climb over the tailgate and drop to the ground.

Then I ran. The direction didn't matter as much as the energy release; I ended up tracking the fence line around the house, kicking my funeral shoes off as I went when the heels stuck in the dirt. The cars went on to the front of the house and I kept running, even when the storm that had threatened to break during the funeral cut loose and soaked me to the skin.

Something had to make sense. There had to be a reason; I just wasn't seeing it. This was no different from one of those ridiculous math problems in not-trig with too many steps, or the cube puzzle I eventually gave up on and rearranged the stickers so it would look like I'd solved it.

I ran harder, because both of those things made me think of Brooks Walden, and I didn't want to think about Brooks, with his phony perfection and near-rapist friends. How someone like Chandi, who'd known him for a decade, had never noticed anything strange about him, or his stick-figure me hanging out of my tree house palace. His too-convincing sincere-face and the way my stomach cramped at the thought of his shattered eyes at the cemetery. But everything made me think of him, especially the rain as it hit my skin and filled my nose and reminded me how the two of us had hidden away in his garage because the big bad monster was afraid of water.

My feet ground to a dead halt as the rain poured down my back, dripping off my hair and nose with the scent of three-day-old hair dye, puddling around my ruined and soaked pantyhose.

It isn't possible.

My fingers flew across the screen of my phone, searching out the saved messages I'd been looking at in Dad's truck. I had read something wrong . . . I had to have. But Claire's words were still there, and still talking about going into the lake.

I changed direction and headed for the kitchen door, ignoring the groan in my calves from the pain of running so far barefoot.

It absolutely isn't possible.

I charged through the door, letting it slam and bypassing the people in the kitchen who were arguing at the table. I wiped out on the bottom step, but clawed my way up, taking the stairs on hands and feet until I could push myself upright again. Snatches of their conversation, mainly my name and Claire's, mixed with "Brooks," "Oregon," and "police," followed me up the stairs as my mother screamed about dripping on the floor.

"Dinah!"

Dad's voice barely made a dent in the mantra looping through my head.

It can't be. Not now. Not after all this.

I didn't stop running until I'd hit Claire's room and pounced on her stuffed animal stash, shaking and squeezing each one in hopes of finding another toy with a voice box, and hopefully hidden treasure. I had to have missed one before.

"Dinah!" Dad called again, closer this time. He was in the room's doorway, with a horrified expression I wouldn't have ever thought of seeing on his face. Uncle Paul and Aunt Helen came up behind him.

"Dinah, honey, stop it," Aunt Helen spoke directly to me for the first time in weeks. "It won't help, sweetie."

They thought I'd snapped.

She tried to get her arms around me, but I ducked.

"I'm looking for something," I said desperately, before I risked having them call the psych ward to haul me away.

"What?" Dad asked. "We'll help you look."

"I don't know. . . . I don't know where to look."

I sat on her bed with a sudden heavy, hopeless feeling. There weren't any other animals with voice boxes, so there was no telling where she would have hidden something. And then it hit me.

"Her phone." I jumped off the bed and grabbed Aunt Helen's hands. "Where's Claire's phone?"

"In my purse," she said. "I thought I'd keep it at the hospital in case one of her friends called, or if she woke up and wanted it. . . . Why do you need her phone?"

But I was already out the door, racing back down the stairs to where my mother was still at the kitchen table drinking a cup of coffee. She said something, but it didn't register. I spied Aunt Helen's purse on the counter and flipped it over, spilling everything into plain sight. A sparkly yellow phone landed on top of the pile, still turned off from being in the hospital.

So much time without use or charging had left it dead, but this time, I finally caught a break. Claire's phone was the previous incarnation of the one I carried—the megabucks beta model I smashed against the kitchen counter until the battery popped loose so I could snap it into Claire's phone.

Everyone gaped, too stunned to do anything that required thought or action.

"Don't be there . . . don't be there . . . don't be there . . . please don't be there," I pleaded, scrolling through the pictures she'd saved.

Claire might have had a hard time taking pictures of Brooks after he deleted the first one, but I knew her. She would have found a way to do it.

"Don't be there . . . don't be there . . . don't be—"

"Dinah!" Dad said, shaking me by the shoulders. "What's wrong, honey? Does this have anything to do with that boy you think hurt Claire?"

"Not think, Dad. I know he did."

"Is his picture in her phone?" he asked at the precise moment I hit pay dirt.

"I have to go."

I grabbed my keys off the peg by the door and ran out, soaked and shivering, into the storm with Claire's phone clenched in my hand. I didn't even stop for shoes; I just got in my car and peeled out, throwing gravel and mud. I shifted gears with one hand and dialed with the other, steadying the wheel with my knees.

Tabs picked up on the second ring.

"Hello?" she said cautiously. I should have thought about how she'd react to Claire's ringtone, but I'd left so fast I didn't even have my license, so I was praying there were no cops nearby to see me out driving like a maniac and dish out some poetic justice for the pills in Brooks' Beemer.

"It was Dex," I said.

"Dinah?"

"It was Dex, not Brooks."

"What?"

"The man of many names, remember? Dex hands out random names when he's afraid he's going to get in trouble, like at the mall. He told Claire his name was Brooks, and she never questioned it."

"Are you sure?"

"Trust me, Dex can turn into a real monster when he wants to."

"Dinah . . . did something happen after I left you with him?"

"It doesn't matter right now."

"Dinah! Of course it matters. I want details. . . . No, forget that. Stay where you are. I'm getting Brucey, and we'll—"

"Tabitha!" She stopped the angry babble. I hadn't called her by her full name in years. "I don't have time to wait. My dad called the cops, and I don't know how long it'll take for them to pick Brooks up."

"What are you going to do?"

"I have to fix this, Tabs. I've got Claire's phone. There's a half-dozen pictures of her and Dex together. . . . I guess I'll take them to his house and wing it from there."

Hopefully, this time, I wouldn't crash on landing.

34

Brooks was afraid of water; that was the missing piece poking at me the whole time. One stupid, simple fact that I'd shoved out of the way because it didn't fit with everything else I thought I knew. Just like I didn't really process any of the things I knew about Dex, because they interfered with the image I had created of him that first day.

I knew Dex was a liar, but I excused it.

I knew Dex had no problem being physically intimidating, but I ignored it.

I knew other girls couldn't stand him for reasons they didn't want to discuss, but I never asked why. And when I found out, I still chose to believe there were two predators prowling the halls at Lowry, rather than seeing the obvious.

I knew Brooks was terrified of water, but it didn't matter.

When he first said it, I'd thought he was exaggerating or making conversation that he thought made himself sound cute, but there was no way a guy who ran from half an inch of rain would have been able to take a girl skinny-dipping. *No way.*

And now I'd ruined an innocent guy's life because I didn't know half the things I thought I did.

The only solution I could think of was to try to undo as much of the damage I'd caused as possible, and for that, I had to see him. Not surprisingly, no one opened the door at his house when I rang, not even when I pounded on the door and shouted to be let in.

I went around the side of the house, took a guess at which window was Brooks' based on the time I'd spent there, and did my best to climb the nearest tree with something approaching purpose and dignity.

"Let me in," I called when I spotted Brooks through his window.

He glared at me, then went back to reading something on his computer screen.

"Brooks! It's important!"

He stuck a pair of earbuds in his ears.

I inched as far out on the branch as I felt would support my weight, stretching my foot toward the railing on his balcony. The motion made the branch dip down, which made me slide in turn. I ended up hanging off the railing with my knee hooked over the top and my hands holding on for dear life.

Two stories up may not sound very high. It may not even seem very high when you're standing on a balcony looking down. But when you're hanging off the outside of that same balcony, dangling three times as far from the ground as you are tall, it's high. Very, very high. The last few days had caught up with me, and this was my punishment. My life for destroying Brooks'—it seemed like a fair trade.

"Are you insane?"

Brooks tore the doors open and stepped out onto the balcony. He grabbed my upper arms as I took hold of his in turn.

"I'm surprised you have to ask me that," I said as he pulled me over the top rail.

"Is everyone in your family suicidal?" Brooks left me on the balcony and went back inside. "Most people take the door not opening as a reason to leave, not try breaking and entering."

"It's only breaking and entering if you have to break something to get in. You opened the window."

"Right. I forgot I was talking to a criminal mastermind."

He plopped into his chair and went back to clicking through whatever he was reading.

"That's Claire's diary," I said.

The familiar letters filled his screen, each in its own window.

"I didn't do any of this," he said. "*Any* of it. I never met a girl named Claire during break; I wasn't even in the state when this happened." He clicked over to that first letter, the one where Claire mentioned meeting him at the mall and highlighted the date. "I was in DC doing one of those stupid Junior Congress summits Dad forces me to endure. That's the *only* reason he's waiting until tomorrow to take me to the police. He's got Ryland petitioning for an attendance roster to prove it. Why are you here?"

"To apologize. I know it wasn't you now."

"You didn't have to make the trip to state the obvious. Take the stairs when you leave, I'd rather not have actual murder added to the list of things people think I've done because you decide to break your neck."

"I don't blame you for being mad, but I came here to try to fix this."

"You accused me of raping a fourteen-year-old girl at her funeral! How do you fix that?"

"I don't know, but I'll do anything. Brooks . . . it was Dex. The things in Claire's diary happened, even if you didn't do them. It was Dex; I can prove it. Look—this is at Freeman's Point. The time stamps should match the date on her diary entries."

Cell service at the Point is always lousy, but that wasn't why Claire never sent me the pictures when she finally got them. The more I thought about it, I was sure she didn't send them because she was too embarrassed. They'd been taken the same day she met Evil Dex, and as much as I'd like to believe she didn't delete them because she thought they'd come in handy as proof when she came to her senses, I knew they were still there because of that embarrassment. To delete them, she'd have had to look at them again, and Claire wouldn't have done that. She'd have left them in her past and gone on like they didn't exist.

I handed Brooks Claire's phone and watched the horror cycle across his face with each new photo.

"When did you get back from DC?" I asked.

"Two weeks before school started. Why?"

And there was the final piece of the puzzle. Claire was so wrapped up in Dex that his dropping her had made no sense. He could have kept using her—but not if there was a chance the real Brooks Walden might spoil his act.

"He was pretending to be you," I said. "When you came home, he had to stop."

"It has to be a mistake."

"You know better than that. Jordan told you. I hope Chandi told you, too."

"Yeah, but—"

"The night . . ." I choked trying to say it. "The night Claire died, when I was such a wreck at the carnival, your first thought was that Dex had done something, wasn't it?"

"I'd just talked to Jordan, but she was so angry, I hoped she was overreacting. Blowing things out of proportion or something. . . . You . . . you were okay, weren't you?"

"Only because I fought back. Others didn't."

"Others?"

"Like Claire. And Abigail. The only difference is, Abigail knew who Dex was. Claire only knew who he claimed to be. That was you."

"He wouldn't do that. We're friends."

"You heard him do it, Brooks. He told that guard at the mall his name was Courtney D'Avignon, because he didn't want anyone at his own door if something happened. Dex didn't know Claire was going to be a student at Lowry, so he gave her someone else's name, not realizing she'd learn the truth when she started school. He picked someone who was out of town, someone with dark hair and eyes like his own, and someone with a dad who had connections that he thought would protect them. It's his safety net."

In his own twisted way, he probably thinks the people whose names he takes deserve it. They get the reputation people expect a spoiled rich boy to have.

"I have to show this to my dad," Brooks said, flipping back and forth through the pictures, zooming in on Claire's face and then Dex's.

"I told you, I'll do anything to fix this. I'll tell your dad, his lawyer, the police. Whoever I have to."

He didn't answer. Brooks was still thumbing through the

photos on Claire's phone, wandering into the older ones that dated back before I'd moved out of state with my parents.

"So the black hair and tattoos, the piercings and boots, that's the real you?"

"I don't know," I said honestly. "I've pretty much lost track of who I am. I'm not sure I ever knew."

"I know the feeling," he said. "Dad's downstairs, in his office, most likely. He's been on the phone with Ryland since your dad called the cops and they called him to arrange a voluntary surrender. I'm sort of under house arrest."

I nodded and let him lead the way out of his room, back into that nearly pristine hallway and down the stairs.

"She was pretty," Brooks said as we walked. "Your cousin."

"She was beautiful," I amended.

She was sweet and kind, and never understood that others weren't. Claire flitted through the world without letting any of the darkness in it touch her. Nothing bad mattered, because she always thought there'd be another day, with a day's worth of chances for the bad to improve.

"I'm sure you know this, but I'll warn you anyway: he's not in a good mood."

We'd reached his father's office door, which was shut, exactly as it had been the last time I was there, without any noise to say there was anyone alive inside. Real fear bubbled up within me for knowing I'd have to face that scowl again, and this time for a reason. If the first time was how Brooks' dad looked while trying to be hospitable, I wasn't eager to find out how much that face could sour when he was angry.

"Ready?" Brooks asked.

"For this to be over? Definitely."

We entered the office together, Brooks in front, me behind, so hopefully all his dad could see of me was my hair poking up over the top of Brooks' head. The place looked abandoned, with the lights on their lowest setting and the office chair turned backward, toward the bookcase behind it.

"There's been no word, Brooks," his voice said from the chair. "Go back to bed. I told you I'd call you if anything new developed."

"That's why I'm here, Dad," Brooks said. "Something new sort of fell through my window."

"I'm in no mood for nonsense." The chair turned and I had the sudden flash of one of Brucey's cheesy old movies. The villain, who was the head of some secret group of super-baddies, sat in a chair just like the one in front of us. The only difference was that the guy in the movie had a fluffy cat in his lap, and I'm not sure there was an animal in existence that would have been willing to sit with Brooks' dad. "Nor am I in the mood for visitors. Who is this, and why is she here?"

"It's me, Mr. Walden," I said from the back of Brooks' shoulder. "Dinah Powell . . . I was here before. . . . You thought I was a scholarship case at Lowry."

"You don't look like the girl who was here."

"Bad haircut," I said.

"She came to help, Dad," Brooks said.

"Yet earlier this evening, you told me it was the girl who had been to the house who accused you this afternoon."

"I did," I said. "But I was wrong . . . and . . . and . . ." I had to swallow before I could finish. "And so were you."

"Explain."

Easier ordered than accomplished. Brooks' dad didn't get up

or unfold his hands from where he had them steepled under his chin, but his voice was toxic enough, even across the room.

"Brooks didn't do any of the things you think he did," I said, then quickly added a polite "sir" for good measure. "He didn't get himself in trouble with the mall cops. He didn't do anything to his car, other than speeding, but that was my fault, too, because I'm the one who messed up his interviews and he was afraid you'd blame him, which was sort of the point. It was all me."

"Take a breath before you pass out," Brooks whispered. Somehow he'd ended up behind me instead of in front, and I'd moved closer to his dad's desk without realizing it.

"All you?"

"Yessir." I swallowed again, trying to stop the nervous slurring. "And if the drug test you made him take came back . . . just know it's a false positive."

"You're not serious," Brooks said.

"Sorry." I cringed. "You really shouldn't eat things you don't cook yourself."

"Your friend tried to poison me?"

"No . . . maybe a little, but only because you ate so many."

His father cleared his throat to put our attention back on him.

"I'm sorry, Mr. Walden, and if you want to call the cops and have me arrested, I won't argue. I'll tell them the truth."

"Good, because that's exactly what I *should* do."

"Dad—" Brooks started, but his father held up his hand for silence.

"However, my first priority is to have you speak to my son's attorney, so that we can stop this unpleasantness before it goes any further. You have the time it takes Ryland to reach the house to explain your actions and your sudden change of heart; perhaps I'll have one as well."

He still hadn't moved, and I felt like I was being circled by the grim reaper.

I spilled my guts until that didn't feel like a figure of speech. I physically hurt from the admission of everything I'd done or had Brucey and Tabs do for me. (Their names stayed out of it.)

Ten minutes in, Brooks' dad made me stop and call my parents to let them know where I was; I think it took him that long to realize I was still barefoot and dripping wet. He had Brooks bring me some dry clothes so I wouldn't, as he said, catch pneumonia.

After I changed, I was headed back to the office from the downstairs bathroom when the bell rang. I assumed it was either my dad, Uncle Paul, or Brooks' lawyer, maybe even some combination of the three, but when Brooks opened the door, I discovered the night hadn't yet hit its lowest point.

"You have to help me." Dex tripped across the threshold in worse shape than I'd been before Brooks' dad had me dry off. If I had to guess, he'd made most of the trip from his neighborhood to Brooks' on foot. "You have to let me stay. There's no one else—"

"You can't be here," Brooks interrupted him. Dex still hadn't seen me.

"I know . . . but she's going to kill me."

"Who?"

"Too many girls to count, I'd bet," I said. Dex looked past Brooks and the foyer to me. He backpedaled a step or two, stopping short of going outside into the storm, where the mystery vigilante could be lurking. "Whoever she is, she's going to have to take a number. The first shot's mine."

I lunged for him, but Brooks, once again, got between Dex and danger. His arms wrapped around mine at the shoulder so he could spin me sideways until Dex was out of reach.

"Let me go, Brooks! He did this! He deserves to pay for it!"

"Calm down," he said in my ear.

"What's she doing here? It's her psycho friend who's trying to kill me! She tried to run me down!"

Apparently, since my plans had been a bust, Tabs had reverted to her original.

"She came to talk," Brooks said as I tried to kick loose. "About a lot of things."

"She's lying."

"You don't even know what she said."

"Look at her—she's as crazy as the other one."

"Which means I'm not responsible if I rip your black heart out through your chest. Put me down!"

Brooks had lifted me off the ground the same way Uncle Paul had with Aunt Helen at the hospital. There was no way to get traction. My arms were stuck under Brooks', so all I could do was flail my feet.

"Not a chance," Brooks said.

"Why are you still protecting him?"

"I'm not." He shoved me out to arm's length by the shoulders. "I'm protecting *you,* idiot. Most of what you've done can be explained away—assault, not so much."

"It's only assault if there are bruises. I don't have to leave a mark on him."

"Stop arguing with her and call the cops," Dex said.

"No need, when they are already on their way." Brooks' father, and his icy voice, had joined us in the hall.

I swear I still can't figure out where that man finds the extra inches to increase his height when he's mad, but Brooks' father had an instant growth spurt. He crossed his arms behind his back, holding on to his elbows with his hands.

"I took the precaution when I realized it was neither Ryland nor Miss Powell's guardians at the door. They should be here shortly. And we"—he glared at each of us in turn—"will wait for them in my office, as they will no doubt be requiring statements from you all."

"Brooks . . . you know me," Dex said desperately.

"I thought I did, but right now I'm trying to find a single reason not to let Dinah go and tell the cops it was self-defense."

"You can't believe anything she says."

"On the contrary, I've found Miss Powell to be a rather accurate source of information, when she's inclined to cooperate, of course," Brooks' father said. "You, however, I have never trusted. I suppose we're about to discover whether I had reason for my reservations or not. Once the police arrive, each of you will tell your respective stories to them, and this insanity will cease. Understood?"

Brooks shuffled me toward his dad's office, but Dex was eyeing the door, weighing his chances if he made a run for it.

"I have already alerted security, Mr. Dexter, and requested they detain you, if necessary, until the authorities arrive to sort this out. It's dark and they are armed. I wouldn't try my luck if I were you. It's time to show a bit of intelligence and prove you deserve that scholarship you've no doubt managed to squander."

There was no point in arguing with Brooks' father; there

wasn't even much of a chance anyone would try. He opened the door to his office and held it while Brooks hung on to me long enough to make sure I didn't take another shot at Dex when he crossed in front of us.

Dex had become another person, yet again. No arrogance or swagger in the trembling steps. No cocky tilt to the head that hung down toward the floor. No uncomfortable laughter in the silence he didn't have the voice to fill.

I felt it the instant a flashing red and blue light bounced through the windows and ignited the terror of impending justice in his face. Whatever came next didn't matter. I could handle the cleanup and consequences, because I'd finally stepped across the finish line.

This was it; things finally felt like they were over. Claire had her ending, and so did I.

35

I left Lowry after the disaster with Dex and Brooks, and everyone else whose lives I nearly ruined. It wasn't like I wanted to see any of them again anyway. Not Abigail-not-Abby with her limitless energy, who was so much like Claire I couldn't help liking her, or Chandi, who turned out to be the strongest marshmallow I'd ever met. Not Brooks. I definitely didn't want to see him ever again.

Yeah, Tabs didn't believe me, either.

But it didn't matter what I wanted; there was no reason to stay at Lowry. I'd only been there for Claire, and without her, everything was a reminder of how I'd failed to do anything I set out to accomplish, and how I had almost made things worse than Dex could have dreamed.

Ironic, isn't it? That first day, I'd sat in the cafeteria thinking about the final destination on that road of good intentions. And I'd certainly meant well—as well as one can mean when the goal is to make someone's life so miserable they'd rather not live it, anyway—so it shouldn't have been such a shock when my life took a detour through the hot zone.

My first impulse was to go back to Oregon in shame. Join a convent, or a commune, or a circus—one of those things people join that always seem to start with a "c." My mother practically insisted on it, saying that the humiliation was unbearable (mainly hers, of course), but Dad was getting better at standing his ground on things he thought were important, and he told me to stay put.

Technically, what he said was if I showed up in Oregon, he'd have me on the next flight back to Aunt Helen's if he had to drive me the whole way himself. Sure, it didn't make much sense, but he was trying not to pass out at the time, while avoiding the sort of "face your mistake" character-building clichés dads are so famous for.

His only concessions were sending me my cat and letting me transfer back to Ninth Street. That one was a no-brainer. Even if I hadn't turned myself into the local pariah, I was on track to fail out of Lowry by the end of term, and I couldn't see too many tutoring sessions in my near future to pull my grades out of the gutter. I decided to go back to being regular smart and leave the advanced stuff to the people suited for it.

I also discovered that my natural hair color was not, in fact, dirty blond. It turned out that the "dirty" quality had been the result of my repeated dye jobs hanging on to my hair, because it began to grow out strawberry blond at the roots.

I ditched all of my piercings except two: the one in my nose and the dragonfly belly button ring. When I actually considered each piercing on its own, it was a shock to realize those were the *only* two I liked. I didn't even miss the barbell through my tongue—or the lisp, which eventually stopped. I was done playing parts that didn't involve a stage and makeup. I needed to figure out who I was, and there was less "back-off black" involved than I expected. (Though I still wasn't in a rush to fill my closet with pastel pink. I seriously hate that color.)

My "avoid all Lowry references" plan worked brilliantly for about a month; it failed at 3:17 in the afternoon on a Tuesday, the exact time I walked out of Ninth Street with Tabs and saw a familiar face standing next to her car.

"I expect details," Tabs said. She headed for her assigned spot in the junior year parking lot and left me to decide whether I should walk over to Brooks or let him make the next move.

We started walking at the same time and met in the middle. Tabs gunned her engine and took off, clearing the immediate area of nosy pedestrians.

"New ink?" he asked. No introduction, no time to be awkward or to let me blurt out another apology. He just picked a subject and started talking. Not quite as smooth as Dex, but I envied him for being able to start a conversation like that.

I glanced at the small script "Cuckoo" on my right wrist, where it intersected the first "o" on "Dodo," and traced it lightly with my fingers. The ridge had faded, but it was still red.

"For Claire," I said. "Cuckoo was her nickname."

"It suits you."

Now it was my turn to pick the topic.

"Navy blue," I said, nodding to his blazer. "I assume you're still at Lowry?"

"Your mea culpa worked on Dad, and the letters to Kuykendall, and the school paper, and the board of regents, and all my friends . . ."

"Brucey," I said. "He still had your contact list from synching the phones, and he's really good with computers."

"Tell him thanks for me. You saved my future."

"I almost ruined it."

Small-talk time was over.

"Yeah, you did."

I flinched.

He didn't scream or curse or do any of those things that I would have understood as a reaction to what I'd done to him. Violence or venom would have made sense, but he chose to agree with me, and do it in the same tone of voice he'd have used if we were discussing answers in trig.

"But I think I understand why you did it." He cut his eyes toward my wrist, and I stashed my hands behind my back. I'd spent so much time trying to figure out the person I thought Brooks was, and forcing his actions to mean things based on my assumptions, that I'd completely missed the person he turned out to be. And that was a really great guy. "I'm not sure I would have gone to the same lengths you did, but it's still rather awesome and terrifying."

Yep, that's me in a nutshell. Minus the awesome, of course.

"We could be a movie of the week," he said.

It was a weak joke, too close to the truth, so neither of us laughed.

"Thanks for talking your dad out of pressing charges."

"Are you kidding? Even if you hadn't gotten me off the blacklist, he hasn't stopped babbling about your 'spirit' and 'initiative' at random intervals. Apparently you 'exemplify the sort of tenacious determination required for success in business.'"

I couldn't tell if he was joking or not. (Considering his dad's personality, I was leaning toward "not.")

"Well, tell him thanks for the lawyer, at least."

Without the Waldens pressing charges, most of the things my friends and I had done got me a lot of stern warnings but not much else. The vodka and pills in the back of Brooks' car were a different matter. They'd meant an actual police report, so they'd also meant actual charges against me. But when Brooks' dad supplied the lawyer and asked the judge for "leniency due to extreme circumstances," all I got was a year's worth of weekends cleaning up trash on the highway.

Dex had been right about one thing: Brooks' old man was Teflon.

"He doesn't expect a thank-you," Brooks said. "As far as he's concerned, he never wants to hear about it again. That way people can forget. Plus, I think he may be considering an adoption offer, if you're interested."

That one I was fairly sure he meant as a joke, but still, I said, "I'll pass."

"Good. I really don't want to put you into sibling territory."

That made two of us, though it might have been worth it to see Mom's face when I told her adoption meant I suddenly qualified for a title of some kind, even if it was only honorary.

Our conversation, or whatever it was, stuttered in bursts. We'd say a lot of nothing, then lapse back into a soundless void as awkward as the way we stood together on the asphalt while the rest of Ninth Street swerved around us. Brooks and I must have looked strange out there. Me in my jeans and silver, him in his jacket and tie, hovering near the muddy flagpole plot.

"Did school let out early today?" I asked. He shouldn't have been there if they'd had class. Our day was usually shorter, but Lowry had a few holidays that we didn't—one of the perks of getting to make their own schedule.

"Technically, I'm in the bathroom," he said, "but I'm fairly certain Mr. Cavanaugh knew I wasn't coming back by the time

I got to the back doors. I didn't want to come to your uncle's house unannounced. I figured your friend's purple car would be easy enough to spot anywhere."

"Yeah, Grimace is pretty hard to miss."

"It has a name?"

I nodded again, hugging myself.

"Do you . . . um . . . like it here?"

"I *fit* here," I said. "No quantum physics pretending to be plain old chemistry and all that."

No one whispering about what I'd done to Brooks as I walked down the halls, or reminding me that I'd been so friendly with Dex. No uniforms where every plaid stitch made me lose my appetite . . . Brucey and I had compromised on that one. I'd given him Claire's skirt for his (shockingly not-porn) film, and he'd made sure it died a fiery death in the final scene. Her name made the dedication crawl at the end, after the credits.

Brooks nodded again and glanced back at the emptying parking lot for about the seventh time. This was getting unbearable.

"Would you please just yell at me or something?" I said. "The polite conversation thing is weirding me out."

I think it was having the same effect on him, but he didn't know how to move past it.

"Look. I'm not going to pretend everything's okay. You nearly destroyed me, and no matter what you did to fix it, that's hard to forget."

"You don't have to forget anything. I'm staying here in cinder block land while you go back behind the ivy and gated walls. And I promise not to climb any more of your trees. Peaceful coexistence and mutual avoidance."

"If I wanted to avoid you, I wouldn't have come all the way down here, but not climbing my tree is probably a good idea. Next time my room might be empty. Stick to the front door."

"Will anybody answer?"

"Maybe," he said. "Or maybe I'll just watch you squirm and set the dogs on you."

"You don't have any dogs."

"I'll ask Dad to buy some. Rottweilers. With really big teeth. Of course, you'd probably have your friends make poison hamburgers, so it wouldn't do me much good."

He bumped my shoulder with his, giving me a weak grin and a weaker laugh, but it was a start. By that point, the only cars left were his and mine, but they were close enough to each other that we could walk the same direction and keep talking. Brooks put his hands in his pockets and shuffled off with me beside him.

"Did you hear about Dex?" he asked.

"The police called Uncle Paul about adding Claire to the list of charges against him and getting copies of her letters, but that's all. He says Dex could get some serious time, so I figure there was more to it than I know."

"A lot more. Enough that I was sick for two days thinking of how many times I ignored things he did or said because I didn't want to believe anything could be as wrong as it was. Jordan talked Abigail into giving a statement, and after that three others came forward."

He sounded like he was apologizing.

"I don't suppose your dad's going to be offering *him* any lawyers?"

"Not likely."

"We're at my car," I said. I wasn't stating the obvious so much as giving him an easy out if he wanted an excuse to leave.

"Walk me to mine?" he asked.

I dumped my books in my seat and put my hands in my pockets the same way he had his.

"Chandi made me come over here, you know," he said.

"Oh . . ." My stomach dropped, a feeling I was far too acquainted with. "She shouldn't have done that."

"She claimed I was moping and that you were the reason, and then told me that if I couldn't get off my butt on my own, I had to bring you something for her. I have a feeling it was an excuse, but I promised her I'd give it to you."

He reached into his pocket and pulled out a very familiar straight pin topped with an enamel butterfly. I held out my hand so he could drop it.

"She gave this up?" I asked, now smiling for real. Whether this was Chandi's reaction to the removal of Dex from her life or her way of removing temptation, I had to believe things had improved.

"She said she didn't need it anymore. Why? Does it mean something?"

"More than you can imagine. Just don't ask me to explain."

No more diving into other people's business for me. From what I'd seen at the fairgrounds, it seemed that Brooks knew Chandi was a cutter but didn't know the details to go along with it. If she wanted to explain, she would. If she didn't, she had her reasons.

"She gave a statement, too. A very long, very detailed statement . . . How could she not tell me what was going on? How could I not see it?"

Why is a raven like a writing desk? Some questions don't have answers that make sense.

"Dex is a sociopath—they're chameleons." Or so said Dr. Useless. "They're also very convincing."

"I still can't believe Chandi thought I'd take Dex's side over hers. She must have been terrified. . . . I'm surprised Jordan didn't rip him to shreds."

She probably would have if she'd known things had gone farther than name-calling and mutual loathing.

We'd reached the Beemer, but he didn't get in. He stood by the door while I leaned against the side, soaking up the warmth from the engine where it bled through the panel.

"If Chandi came forward, does that mean she and Jordan are officially out?" I asked.

"Jordan's never really hidden anything, but yeah—Chandi's folks know. Only her mom was surprised. Honestly, Dex is lucky he's locked up. Max has raised Chandi since she was a year old; he'd kill him."

I stopped myself from saying "I know the feeling."

Brooks opened the door and climbed behind the wheel, but he didn't start the engine. He sat there and waited.

"I have no idea what happens next," he said. "I don't know what I should do, or say, or anything. I don't know if I should keep my mouth shut and go home like today never happened."

I knew exactly what he meant. Brooks' appearance had dredged up too many things I'd hoped to keep buried, but at the same time, I was afraid he'd drive off and I'd never see him again. And if that happened, I'd never know if the version of him I'd settled on was the real one. He was still that puzzle I hadn't figured out how to solve.

"What do we do?" he asked. "How do we fix this?"

There was no way to fix it, but maybe there was a way around it; whether it worked or not would depend on his reaction. I stuck my hand out the same way I had in the Lowry theater to give myself a do-over. We needed a new start, or at least a real first one.

"Hi, I'm Dinah Powell," I said. "I have a habit of jumping to conclusions and disengaging my brain when it doesn't agree with my temper. My mom's nuts, but the rest of my family is relatively sane. We've spoken, but I don't think we've ever actually met."

My hand hung in midair until the chill made my fingers tingle. I started to pull them back when Brooks raised his own hand and wrapped it around mine.

"Brooks Walden," he said. "I'm a terrible judge of character and a lousy actor. I have a dad who's finally coming to grips with the fact that he's a widower and that my mother's memory isn't going to strike him down if I don't turn out perfect. It's nice to finally meet you."

ABOUT THE AUTHOR

Josin L. McQuein was born and raised in Texas, where she used novel writing as a way to escape when she needed a break from caring for ailing relatives. Now she and her three crazy dogs live in a town so small that the buffalo outnumber the people and things like subways and consistent Internet access are fictional creations of the faraway fantasy land known as civilization.

5/14, 11/14, 9/15, 4/17, 12/17